BOOK 3 OF THE MOURNING DOVE MYSTERIES

A LIGHT
TO
KILL BY

MIKEL J. WILSON

MOURNING DOVE MYSTERIES: A LIGHT TO KILL BY

Cover design by Damonza.com.

Author portrait by Dave Meyer at DaveMeyerDesign.com.

Mikel J. Wilson
555 W. Country Club Lane, C-222
Escondido, CA 92026

MIKELJWILSON.com

Paperback ISBN: 978-1-952112-52-2
Hardcover ISBN: 978-1-952112-53-9

First Edition, June 2021

Printed in the United States of America through Acorn Publishing at AcornPublishingLLC.com.

Dedicated to my BSM.

CHAPTER 1

I KNOW WHO the killer is.

Juniper Crane's yawn morphed into a gasp as she watched the masked ripper slash the throat of a young girl, silencing her screams.

Great, I'm never going to be able to sleep now.

The fiftyish woman with flowing brown hair reached for the joint in the Dollywood souvenir ashtray on her nightstand. She relit it and sucked the flame down to her coral-painted nails before returning it to the ashtray. Her exhaled smoke drifted up to the light smog lurking beneath the ceiling of her bedroom – one of the smallest at the Geisterhaus estate.

I need to turn this off. Grabbing the remote next to the ashtray, she instead set the sleep timer for the TV mounted on the wall. As the masked villain chased down another victim, Juniper sunk deeper into the gray flannel sheets of her bed and closed her hazel eyes. The movie's staccato score tensed her grip on the downy quilt clutched at her neck until the violin flourishes distorted into static.

"What happened?" Juniper unclenched her eyes and saw the screen go blank. "Is the cable out?" The middle of the screen bulged out. "Oh my lord!" She jerked up in bed. "What is that?"

A volleyball-sized sphere of white light bubbled out from the screen and separated from the TV. Dozens of tiny tendrils reached out from the orb at random points along its surface, giving it the appearance of a miniature sun.

Juniper screamed and kicked out of the sheets, backing herself into the headboard.

Her bedroom door burst open, and a dark-haired man in flannel pajamas bolted inside. "Ms. Crane, what's…" Tommy Addison's voice trailed off when he saw the reason for her fear. "What the hell is that?"

The orb floated across the room toward the door, and Tommy approached it, extending his hand.

"Tommy, what are you doing?" Juniper jumped off the opposite side of the bed. "Don't touch it!" Her warning came too late.

Two tendrils reached out to Tommy's fingertips, and an enormous *POP!* followed a flash of light.

The force of the explosion shoved Juniper's back against the wall before dropping her to the floor. Ears ringing, she pushed herself up enough to peek over the bed. *It's gone.*

"Tommy?" She rose to her feet and shuffled over the hardwood floors, looking around the room. "Tommy, where are you?"

Once on the other side of the bed, she spotted a body in the hallway just beyond her open bedroom door. "Tommy!"

The man's body settled into stillness, and his vacant eyes locked onto the ceiling – although Juniper felt them watching her as she rushed to his side.

"No, no, no, no." Juniper cupped her mouth as tears dripped from her cheeks. She retrieved her phone and called 9-1-1. While imploring the operator for help, she hurried up two flights of stairs to her employer's closed bedroom door. "Ms. Geister!" Her knuckles thumped against the solid oak. "Ms. Geister, it's an emergency!" Hearing no response, she turned the copper knob and rushed inside.

"Ms. Geister!" Juniper shook the shoulder of the unresponsive woman lying on her side within the gold bedframe, and yet she didn't respond. She clicked on the nightstand lamp and pulled the sleeping woman's shoulder to roll her onto her back.

As Blair Geister's head turned on the overstuffed pillow, a final breath whistled through her gritted teeth.

Emory Rome parked his white crossover on a street in Knoxville's trendy Old City – an area formerly called The Bowery, which served as the red-light district during the first half of the last century. The pale, handsome man with brown eyes and matching hair looped a wool satchel over his shoulder before pulling his lean and muscular six-foot-two frame from the vehicle. He retrieved a twenty-dollar bill from his wallet, folded it twice and slipped it inside the sleeve of one of the paper coffee cups resting in the center console. Grabbing both cups, he closed the door with his foot and headed down the sidewalk toward the two-story, brown-brick building with a painted window sign that read, "Mourning Dove Investigations."

Emory smiled at a young Bohemian sitting on the sidewalk playing guitar as he handed him the coffee with the twenty-dollar bill. "Good morning, Phineas." The twenty-three-year-old PI had never asked the homeless man his age, but he assumed him to be two or three years younger than himself.

The attractive man with Prussian blue eyes stopped strumming. "Hey, thanks man. I was just about to move. It's too noisy. What's going on in there?" Phineas pointed over his shoulder with his thumb to a brick building with a connecting wall to Mourning Dove.

Emory heard the sound of hammering coming from inside. "Oh, they finally started. They're adding this old comic book store to the firm. It's going to be my new office."

Phineas took a sip of the coffee. "Sweet."

Jeff Woodard stepped onto a small debris field of drywall crumbles and aimed an exasperated hand toward the wall with the body-sized hole in it. "Is there no quieter way to take that down?!"

The coveralled man rested the sledgehammer on his shoulder. "Sure. I could pare through the wall with the spoon I used to dig my way out of prison, but I have other jobs lined up this year."

Jeff clenched the left side of his face, depressing the natural smirk from his full lips. "You know, nobody likes a smartass." Leaving the construction worker to his task, he walked through the lobby of Mourning Dove Investigations, eyeing the clear plastic tarp covering the desk and bookshelves as he returned to his office. When he started closing the bookshelf door between his office and the lobby, a voice chided him from behind.

Virginia Kennon, a beautiful young woman with flawless ebony skin and curly black hair, looked up from her laptop at the side of Jeff's desk. "Keep that door open."

With each punch of the sledgehammer against the wall, Jeff's muscles popped into unintentional flexes, further stressing the Italian fabric of his stylish green shirt. "I'm trying to buffer the noise so we can work."

"We have a nine o'clock appointment. She won't know we're in here if you close that door."

Jeff asked his other partner, Emory, who had just entered the office. "You see the trouble we're going through for you?"

"How is that my fault?" Emory asked.

Jeff plopped into his desk chair. "We bought that building next door so you could have your own office."

Virginia spoke up for Emory. "Stop trying to make him feel guilty. We needed the space."

Emory proceeded to a tiny desk in the corner of Jeff's office and hung his satchel on the back of the adjacent chair. "How long will the construction take?"

Virginia replied, "They told me a week. The full crew should be here at 10."

A woman with a tensed but pleasant face and wearing a camel pashmina draped over a navy pullover wandered through the office door. "Excuse me. I have an appointment."

Virginia jumped up to greet her. "Mrs. Crane?"

The woman's latte-shaded lips eked into a half-smile. "It's Ms., but please call me Juniper."

Jeff stood for a second to wave her toward one of the two chairs in front of his desk. "Please have a seat. I'm Jeff Woodard, and these are my associates, Virginia Kennon and Emory Rome."

Emory shut the door to the lobby before rounding the larger desk to stand at Jeff's side.

Jeff let loose a sigh of relief at the noise reduction. "That helps." A second later he tensed once more when the sledgehammer again hit the wall in the lobby. Though muffled, the sound of the impact still thumped through his bones. "A little."

Virginia reclaimed her chair and faced their potential new client. "How can we help you, Juniper?"

The woman clutched the faux snakeskin grocery-bag of a purse resting on her lap, and she touched three fingers of her shaky right hand to her upper lip. "My boss is trying to kill me."

All three PIs gasped, but Jeff was the first to speak. "Whoa. Seriously?"

Emory crossed his arms. "Ms. Crane, what makes you think that?"

Fingers still on her lip, Juniper shook her head. "She blames me."

"Blames you for what?" asked Virginia.

Juniper struggled with her next words. "Something... A... A

few months ago something happened... An overnight guest of Ms. Geister's... His face..."

Never one for patience, Jeff asked, "Well? What happened?"

Juniper snatched a tissue from her purse and pressed it to her mouth. "His face... disappeared, and he sued her."

Virginia and Jeff jerked back in their chairs, while Emory whispered, "Disappeared?"

Jeff patted his desk twice. "How does a face disappear?"

Juniper waved her tissue. "I can't go into detail. Ms. Geister made all her employees sign a non-disclosure agreement."

"You're seriously going to leave us hanging?" asked Jeff.

"I'm sorry. Like I said, I can't talk about it."

Emory stepped forward to rest his palms on the desk, his brown eyes locked on Juniper's blues. "Ms. Crane, I have to say that doesn't sound like much of a motive for murder to me. If you're responsible for a lawsuit against your boss, why wouldn't she just fire you?"

Virginia forced a reassuring yet skeptical smile. "Murder does seem extreme."

"Ms. Geister had her good and bad qualities, like all of us. She was brilliant and passionate about her work. She was also ruthless and vindictive. Ms. Geister *hated* to be embarrassed. She was phobic about it." Juniper took a moment to catch her breath. "Some information was brought up in the deposition. She was mortified. I can't say anything more."

Jeff tensed his body at the thump of another sledgehammer impact. "You keep leading us onto these dead-end narratives. How about getting us onto the straight and unimpeded explanation of why you're here and what you'd like us to do?"

Emory backhanded Jeff's shoulder.

"Well, I'm sorry," said Juniper. "This is a new situation for me. It's difficult to explain it to strangers, knowing how you're probably going to react."

Emory asked, "Ms. Crane, has your boss threatened or otherwise menaced you?"

Jeff snickered at Emory. "*Menaced* her?"

Juniper pinched her lips. "Two nights ago, I was in bed watching TV. It had been such a long day. I was exhausted, but I couldn't sleep." Her trembling hand returned to her lips. "Ms. Geister came for me."

Virginia asked, "She showed up at your home?"

"No, I live on her estate, a few miles from Calhoun. But I've been staying up here with my daughter since that night."

"Calhoun?" asked Emory.

"It's in McMinn County, about ninety minutes southeast of here."

"Hold up." Jeff leaned in on his elbows. "Estate? You're not talking about Blair Geister, the construction tycoon, are you?"

Juniper almost whispered her response. "Yes."

Jeff threw up his hands. "Problem solved. Maybe you haven't heard, but your boss died a couple of nights ago."

"I know she's dead!" Juniper shook her tiny fists as tears cascaded into the mouth of her giant purse. "That didn't stop her from killing Tommy!"

"I read about Blair Geister's death," said Emory. "No cause given yet, but they said an employee died in an accident at the same time. That was Tommy?"

"Yes. He was the facilities manager for Geisterhaus. His room was down the hall from mine. But it wasn't an accident. Ms. Geister was coming for me when Tommy got in the way."

Virginia asked, "Did they kill each other?"

Juniper hesitated as her eyes seemed to search her purse for a response. "Ms. Geister died first."

"How did Tommy..." Jeff began. "What's his last name?"

"Addison."

"How did Tommy Addison die?"

"Ms. Geister killed him."

Jeff shook his head. "I'm not following."

Virginia placed a comforting hand on Juniper's wrist. "Do you think your boss killed Tommy after... she had already died?"

"You mean like a zombie?" Jeff asked with a grin. "Is the apocalypse here already?"

Juniper jumped out of her chair. "I didn't want to come here. My daughter insisted. She likes your ads. I told her a private investigator isn't what I need." She headed for the hidden door but saw only a painting on the wall. "How do I get out of here?"

Virginia intercepted her. "Please, don't go. We want to help you. Just tell us how we can."

Juniper turned around and frowned at Jeff. "It wasn't a zombie. It was her spirit."

"Ms. Crane, can you describe for us very specifically what you saw?" asked Emory.

Juniper took a deep breath. "When I was watching TV, Ms. Geister's spirit... emerged from the screen."

"Like *Poltergeist*?" asked Jeff, excited while derisive.

Emory squinted at Jeff. "Did any ghosts actually come out of a TV in that movie?"

Jeff stretched out his arm in an overhand grasp. "I remember a ghostly hand reaching out of a TV."

"Guys, what does it matter?" asked Virginia. "Juniper, you actually saw her ghost?"

"I didn't know it at first. It looked more like a ball of light. I screamed, and that's when Tommy showed up. His room is next to mine." Juniper broke down and let the tears flow. "Ms. Geister's rage filled the room. It knocked me against the wall. If Tommy hadn't gotten in the way... It must've weakened Ms. Geister because she disappeared after that."

"What makes you certain the light was Ms. Geister's spirit?" Emory asked.

"I ran upstairs to tell Ms. Geister about Tommy, and I found she was dead too. That's when I realized it. She had to have died first." Juniper shivered. "I just ran from the house."

"Geister died first," said Jeff. "What does that prove?"

"You don't understand." Juniper stared at the space between Jeff and Emory. "There's a knowing that comes with dying. Unimpaired clarity. You remember everything that happened, but more than that. You see your life, your *whole* life from every point of view. Parts of it you didn't know before. Things people did for you that you never saw. Things people did against you. When Ms. Geister died, she must've become aware of what I'd done. That's why her spirit came for me. For what I'd done." Juniper looked at the PIs one-by-one. "I know you must think I'm crazy. So does my daughter. She wants you to prove there's something else behind it, but I know what I saw. I just want to be able to sleep without worrying that she's going to appear again. I don't think her spirit can leave the house, but I'm not certain."

Emory asked, "Ms. Crane, would you mind waiting in the lobby while we discuss your case? We'll just be a minute."

"Sure."

Virginia pulled on the painting, opening the hidden door to the lobby just as the construction worker's sledgehammer hit again. She closed the door behind Juniper and turned to her partners to say, "I'm torn about this one. I want to help her, but I don't know how."

"What's to be torn about?" asked Jeff. "The woman needs a shrink, not us."

"I think we should help her," said Emory.

Jeff smirked at his partner as if waiting for a punchline that never came. "Were you listening to the same campfire story I just heard?"

Emory shook his head. "You're just hearing what she thinks she saw, but there's a difference between explanation and understanding."

Jeff tapped Emory's chest. "You know, that is *so* annoying."

"What is?"

"You always have to play devil's advocate."

"I do not."

Jeff threw up his hands. "There you go again."

Virginia stepped between them. "Guys, could we please focus on the business at hand?"

Emory held up two fingers. "The fact is two people are dead under mysterious circumstances, so this case falls smack dab in the middle of our wheelhouse."

"Smack dab?" mocked Jeff. "She wants us to protect her from a ghost."

"Regardless of her version of events, finding the truth behind the deaths should deliver the result she's seeking."

Virginia placed a hand on Jeff's forearm. "You know he's right."

"Now you're with him?" Jeff rolled his eyes. "All right. Let's take the case, but we're charging her our premium rate. And I'm picking the next case without any objections from the two of you."

Virginia shrugged. "Fine with me."

While she opened the door to the lobby to let their new client know their decision, Emory squeezed Jeff's shoulder. "Are you okay? You seem really on edge today."

Jeff pointed at the noise coming from the lobby. "That! That's why I'm irritable. How are we supposed to work in this office with all that racket? I can't concentrate."

"You could stay at Geisterhaus," replied Juniper. "The estate. The sheriff has already gone over it and released it."

Her offer drained the smile from Virginia's face. "You want us to stay in the house where two people just died?"

"You wouldn't be in any danger. She's not after you."

"We appreciate the offer—" Emory began.

"I think it's a great idea!" Jeff grinned at his partners. "What a perfect way to immerse ourselves in the case, and it'll save us three hours of driving every day."

"I'm actually okay driving," said Emory.

Virginia added, "And someone needs to stay here at the office for any potential clients who come by."

Jeff told her, "Don't be ridiculous. How many walk-ins do we get, and how many will we get with this damn construction going on? We'll just forward the office phone to your cell."

Virginia shook her head. "I can't work in a bedroom. I need an office."

Juniper told her, "You can set up in Ms. Geister's office."

"Well, I think that settles it then." Jeff shook Juniper's hand. "We accept."

CHAPTER 2

EMORY FOLLOWED THE powder blue Mercedes as it wended along a narrow road with illogical curves. On either side, a dense spring-leaf forest embanked the pavement and filtered out all but the most stubborn specks of sunlight.

"I'm not staying in that house," Virginia said from the backseat.

Jeff tilted his head to see her in the rearview mirror, holding up fingers as he counted. "One, you've been saying for months how you wanted to do more field work. Two, you sided with Emory about taking this case. Three, if we're staying, you're staying. Fair's fair."

"Why do any of us have to stay?" asked Emory. "That motel we passed would be great if you're concerned about the driving time."

"Your fiscal carelessness astounds me. Not only are we investing heavily in an office space just for you, but now you actually want us to put you up in a hotel—"

"It was a *motel.*"

"Whatever. You want us to put you up in a hotel instead of taking accommodations we're being offered at no cost to us. Virginia, what were you able to find out about Blair Geister?"

"Nothing."

Jeff frowned into the mirror. "What do you mean, *nothing?*"

Virginia poked his shoulder. "I told you I needed to sit in the front seat. You know I can't read while I'm sitting in the back. I get carsick."

"It's all right. I'll do it." He pulled out his phone and searched the internet for information about Blair Geister. "I found a wiki page on her. She was born in Calhoun, nineteen blah, blah, blah. Father was a teacher. Mother worked in a paper factory. Never married. No kids. She was an architect before she began constructing her own buildings in Nashville, Atlanta and Knoxville."

"Offices or residential?" asked Emory.

"Both."

Virginia scooted up and rested her forearms on the front seats. "Any buildings we might know?"

"Let's see." Jeff scrolled down. "The Somerset—"

"Ooh, I like that place," said Emory. "I wouldn't mind living there."

Jeff gave him a look of mild but impressed surprise before returning his attention to the phone. "She had focused more on environmental issues in the past few years, although she owned a coal mine."

"A coal mine?" asked Virginia.

"That's what it says."

Emory said, "That's a bit incongruous."

Jeff continued reading. "She formed a foundation. Her crown jewel is The Monolith, a new forty-four story, eco-friendly commercial complex opening next week. It's now the tallest building in Knoxville, surpassing previous record-holder Godfrey Tower… Whoa! She was worth $625 million when she died!"

Virginia looked at Jeff's face in the rearview mirror. "You can almost see the dollar signs in his eyes."

Emory laughed. "His eyes are green for a reason."

"Very funny. It's just such a waste we didn't reach out to Blair before she died. Someone this rich I'm sure could've used our services for something. Kept us on retainer." Jeff gasped as he swatted Emory's arm and gleamed at Virginia through the rearview mirror. "That's what we need! We need some rich people keeping us on retainer. Virginia, you should work on a business model focused on that."

"I'll get right on that. You know, it couldn't have been easy for her. A woman entering a man's world of construction. Anything else on her death?"

"Not much. She was found dead at her twelve-acre estate near Calhoun, Tennessee. The cause is currently under investigation."

Emory's eyes landed on a marker ahead on the right. The only patch of color on the grey sign with black letters came from a red-encircled blue field of three white stars – symbolic of the Tennessee state flag. Underneath it was a header and text too small to read in passing. "What does that sign say?"

"The Trail of Tears," answered Jeff. "I can't make out the rest."

"I'll slow down."

"Don't do that. We'll lose Juniper."

"Just long enough to take a pic."

Jeff stuck his phone out the window to snap a picture, and he read from the image as Emory regained speed.

THE TRAIL OF TEARS

In the valley to the south, that part of the Cherokee Nation which took part in the enforced overland migration to Indian Territory rested for three weeks in 1839. About 15,000 persons of various ages took part in the march. Several who died while here were buried in this area.

"Seriously?" Jeff pocketed his phone. "Not only did people die in the house we're going to, but it's also near an old burial ground."

Emory scolded him. "Hey, don't joke about that. Almost six thousand Cherokee died on the Trail of Tears."

"I'm sorry. I didn't mean to make light of that. It's just all that's missing now is a shady real estate developer and a little blonde girl."

Emory slowed down when he saw Juniper's Mercedes coming to a stop at the gate of a wrought-iron fence that extended on either side at least two hundred feet before disappearing into the surrounding flora. The vertical posts in the fence rose ten feet from the ground into spikes, but the gaps between were large enough for a coyote to slip through. The word *Geisterhaus* fanned across the top of the gate in twisted metal letters. Juniper reached a hand from her window to punch a code into the keypad, and the gate crept open.

"That's the house?" Jeff tilted his chin toward the windshield. On a hill a few hundred yards inside the fence stood a sprawling stone house with a grey roof.

Virginia craned her neck between the front seats. "It's huge."

The driveway emptied into a large parking area built from brown and tan pavers and big enough for two dozen cars. The parking area connected to an eight-car garage and the steps to the raven-hued front door. Juniper parked and hurried out of her car to confront two men leaving the house with a plastic-wrapped king-size mattress.

Emory pulled in behind Juniper's car, and the PIs exited the vehicle in time to hear her tell the mattress movers, "Drop that this instant!" The men complied, lowering the mattress onto the driveway as Juniper turned her attention toward the open front door.

A fortyish woman with straight black hair brushing the shoulders of her cranberry knee-length dress appeared in the doorway. She squinted her stringent face at the movers and waved at them to keep moving. "Get that out of here."

Juniper met her at the front step. "Eden, what do you think you're doing?!"

"Replacing the bed."

"You can't do that! It's Ms. Geister's bed."

"I'm keeping the frame. It's real gold. They just delivered a new mattress, and now they're taking away the old one."

Juniper pointed to the mattress. "That's not yours to replace."

Eden crossed her arms. "You don't expect me to sleep on the same one my cousin died on."

"I don't expect you to sleep here at all!"

As the movers again picked up the mattress, Emory stopped them. "Guys, we need to have a look at that." He faced his partners. "It's where she died."

Once the movers again dropped the mattress, Jeff asked them, "Can you take this plastic off?" One of the movers pulled a boxcutter from his pocket and slit the plastic up the middle, slicing part of the black, satin sheet fitted over the mattress along the way.

"This estate is not yours to alter in the least," said Juniper.

"Of course, it is!" countered Eden. "Who else would it belong to?"

"We'll find out once the will is read tomorrow."

"I'm the only family Blair had. I have more right to be here now than you do. As a matter of fact, you're fired."

With the plastic peeled away, the three PIs gathered to inspect the mattress.

"Who has black sheets?" Virginia pointed to the small slash the movers had cut into the sheet. "Is the mattress black too?"

Jeff pulled a corner of the fitted sheet and removed it to expose the bare mattress. The PIs gasped at their first glance of its quilted top. Like an old photograph negative, a shadow had been transferred to the fabric. The captured image appeared to be a freeze-frame of a running woman, with one hand above her head, one behind her and legs in a running stance. A small crimson stain was visible in front of the shadow's face as though she had sneezed blood.

Virginia asked, "How on Earth did this happen?"

"I don't have a guess," replied Jeff. "Emory?"

Emory snapped pictures with his phone before kneeling for a closer look.

A few feet away, Juniper told Eden, "You can't fire me. I oversee this property for Ms. Geister's estate."

"Not after tomorrow, you don't." Eden huffed past her, toward the PIs.

"I hate to break it to you, Eden, but the estate attorney called me this morning to let me know Ms. Geister appointed me executor of her will. It's going to be up to me to carry out her wishes – at any pace I deem necessary."

"Why would she make you the executor? And who are these people?"

"Because I'm organized!" Juniper joined the others at the mattress. "They're private investigators, and they're here to figure out what happened that night."

Eden smirked at her. "We know what happened. Blair had a heart attack, and that handyman… Well only you know for sure what really happened to him. But the sheriff will find out soon enough."

Emory asked, "Is a heart attack the official cause of death for Ms. Geister?"

Juniper answered, "The coroner hasn't released an official one yet, but the sheriff told me the doctor who pronounced her thought that was what killed her."

Eden gave Emory's car a side-glance. "Why do they have suitcases?"

"They're staying here." Juniper's eyes fixed on the figure in the mattress. "What's that?"

Jeff replied, "We don't know."

Eden told Juniper, "I'm not sleeping in a house with strangers."

"Then don't stay here!"

Virginia waved toward the mattress. "It could just be an old stain, built up over time from natural body oils and sweat." She extended a hand to Eden and introduced herself. "I'm Virginia."

Eden didn't reciprocate. "I don't care who you are."

Emory shook his head. "No. Maybe if she slept in exactly the same position every night for months on end. Regardless, we shouldn't get rid of the spot where she died until we know more about her death."

"We'll store the mattress in the supply closet in the basement." Juniper asked the movers, "Would you mind taking it back inside and down the back stairs at the end of the hallway? It's next to the theatre. Thank you."

Jeff grinned at his partners. "There's a theatre."

"This is ridiculous!" Eden jumped ahead of the movers and retreated inside the house.

Juniper turned a forced smile toward the PIs. "Welcome to Geisterhaus. I apologize for the scene. That woman showed up the day after Ms. Geister died and started barking orders like she already owned the place."

Virginia glanced at the front door. "We'll be staying here with her?"

"Unfortunately, it looks that way." Juniper pulled a key and an envelope from her purse and handed it to Virginia. "Here's a key to the house, and the code to the gate is 0422. I've also sketched a layout of the floors to map out where everything is and where you can sleep."

Emory frowned at their client. "Aren't you going to show us around?"

"I'm not stepping foot in that house again. I'm heading back to Knoxville."

"But we really need you to take us through exactly what happened that night."

"I've told you—"

Jeff widened his bright green eyes. "We're visual people."

Virginia touched their client's arm. "Nothing is going to happen to you with all of us here."

Juniper hesitated, but Virginia's reassuring face seemed to

convince her. "All right, but I'm running for the door at the first sign of trouble." With Virginia at her side, Juniper led the PIs into the house. "I'll just show you where Tommy…" She cut herself off, gaze growing distant, before she continued. "Explore the rest of the house on your own."

As they approached the door, Jeff touched the rough exterior wall. "Wow, blue stone."

Juniper nodded. "Brought in from the Shenandoah Valley."

"Will we be able to see Ms. Geister's bedroom?" asked Emory.

Juniper opened the front door and shuffled inside, followed by the PIs. "I guess Eden is squatting there, but feel free to go in as you need. I should call the sheriff and have her removed, but I don't want the headache." After a few steps through a glorious atrium of marble, they entered a majestic, bright rotunda. "This is the locutorium, Ms. Geister's primary room for indoor entertaining."

"I can see why." Jeff gawked at the crystal chandelier hanging from the ceiling, centered above a brown circle of flourishes in an otherwise white-tile floor. Furnishings included four gold-silk sofas, two Chippendale end tables, a white grand piano and five pedestals supporting bronze sculptures depicting pre-Columbian life in America. Three Western paintings hung from the gilded white walls. "Did she have a lot of parties?"

"Ms. Geister didn't have any family she was close to, so she loved having company."

Emory followed Jeff and Virginia into the locutorium. "I had the impression she was more of a private person."

Juniper kept one foot in the atrium. "She was, in the sense that she didn't openly share aspects of her personal life, but that didn't keep her from being a generous host. Her usual guests fell into one of two categories – business associates, out of necessity, and those who shared her passion for the environment and science."

Virginia clinked a far-right key on the piano, causing Juniper to jump. "Sorry."

Juniper exhaled a shaky breath. "It's okay. I'm just a bit skittish being back here."

Virginia wiped her hand on her pant leg, as if to remove the piano *faux pas*. "This is really a beautiful home."

Juniper smiled as if the compliment were meant for herself. "Ms. Geister renovated most of what you see."

Jeff stood before a white stone fireplace, admiring the grazing buffalo painting mounted above the mantle. "Judging from the craftsmanship and the furnishings in here alone, that must've set her back a pretty penny."

"Four times the purchase price of the house. This place used to be a convalescent home, if you can believe that. Ms. Geister rehabbed the hell out of it. If you walk around the property, you'll notice, in spite of how much land surrounds three-quarters of the house, the neighbor's house is actually really close to this one."

"Seriously?" asked Virginia. "Why wasn't it built closer to the center of the property?"

"This all used to be one huge property, owned by a surgeon. He lived in the house next door, and then he built the convalescent home here to treat his patients so he didn't have to drive. Apparently, he had a horrible car accident when he was younger and vowed never to drive again. After he died, they had a hard time selling the property with two houses on it, and they ended up dividing it into two lots. The Strands bought the one next door, and then Ms. Geister bought this one and erected the fence." Juniper raised her fingers to her lips. "I forgot where I was going with this. Oh yes. This place was more of a standard four-walled structure when Ms. Geister bought it about five years ago. She built out the locutorium shortly afterwards to add some character. Then after moving in, she would renovate a different room just about every quarter. Up until a few months ago, she oversaw all the construction herself. For some of the renovations, she would even relieve the crew before they were done so she could put the finishing touches on each room by herself."

Jeff scoffed. "Sounds like she was a bit of a control freak."

"You could say that. She did have to relinquish some control when construction of The Monolith began consuming all of her time. That's why she brought Tommy down here from her company in Knoxville." Juniper smiled and nodded toward the locutorium. "This was always my favorite part of the house. Ms. Geister's too. It has standing room for one hundred guests and offers the best views on the estate."

Emory walked to one of seven sets of French doors spaced at equidistant points around the circular room and looked at the narrow balcony wrapped around the exterior. Above each double door rose multi-paned windows that reached almost to the twenty-foot-high ceiling, drenching the room in late-morning sunlight. The room did indeed offer quite a scenic view of the backyard, where three distinct levels descended from the adjacent pool to the muddy bank of the river, on which a large boathouse protruded halfway to the other side.

Jeff approached the French doors to Emory's left. "Is that the Tennessee River?"

"It's actually the Hiwassee River," replied Juniper.

Emory noticed the poolside furniture, including two cast-iron tables – one with a tied-down indigo umbrella. He saw the other umbrella open and upside-down halfway down the lawn. "One of the pool umbrellas has come loose."

"What?!" Juniper's tone jumped to panic. "Someone must've forgotten to close it, and the wind took it. Ms. Geister always insisted the outdoor umbrellas be closed and tied when not in use. I can't believe one was left open. She would've run out there to close it herself if she'd seen it."

Emory glanced at his partners to see both grimacing at Juniper's overreaction at such a minor infraction.

"I'll ask the gardener to retrieve it." Juniper took a step back. "Please, I really don't want to be here longer than I must."

The PIs joined their host in the atrium, near a grand ascending staircase and an adjacent set of steps going down. "We could go down this way, but I'll take you to the back stairs because it's closer to my room."

With Jeff at his side, Emory followed Juniper and Virginia into the wide hallway past the front stairs. "Who all had access to the house?"

"Tommy and I were the only staff members who lived here. Ms. Geister also retained a chef, a maid and a groundskeeper."

Jeff asked, "Tommy's job again?"

"Live-in facilities manager. He led one of Ms. Geister's construction teams in Knoxville before she brought him down here to take care of the estate."

Jeff shot a curious glance Emory's way. "That seems like a step down. What exactly did he do here?"

"In addition to overseeing the room renovations, he was in charge of maintaining the house and all components. The original structure is almost fifty years old, so it needs constant attention. If something broke, Ms. Geister insisted it be fixed right away. As the head of a construction empire, she felt it reflected badly on her business if anyone spotted something amiss with the property." Juniper paused as she looked at the dining room on the right, where the overhead light flickered. Her fists clenched, releasing when the light regained its composure two seconds later.

Emory distracted her with a question. "Why did you live here?"

"Convenience. As Ms. Geister's assistant, she needed me to be available."

Virginia said, "It must've been tough being constantly on call."

"It took some getting used to when I first started, about ten years ago, but it got easier. She was such a dynamic person and a generous teacher. I learned so much from her about business, it got to where I knew her decisions before she did. She was always encouraging me to start off on my own, but I never had any interest in that. She depended on me, and it was nice to be needed. A couple of years ago, after my daughter moved out, Ms. Geister offered me the room downstairs, and I didn't hesitate. It meant a lot less driving back and forth from Knoxville, and I had total access to the estate's amenities, as long as she didn't have guests."

Jeff asked, "Wasn't it difficult, always being around your boss?"

"Actually, it brought us closer. We became really good friends."

"Yet, you still call her Ms. Geister."

"Just a habit."

Jeff gasped with a horrified look toward the kitchen they approach on the left. "What's that?"

Juniper jumped and clutched Virginia's arm with both hands. "What? What is it? A ghost?"

"Oh no." Jeff relaxed. "My mistake. It's just the way the sun's shining off the tile."

Steadying her breath, Juniper released Virginia's arm and continued toward the back stairs.

Walking behind the two women, Emory elbowed a grinning Jeff and mouthed, "Cut that out!"

Virginia pivoted the conversation to a stairwell ahead, with its walls of white brick and metal beams running the entire length from top to bottom. "How unusual."

Juniper smiled. "Ms. Geister had such a great eye for beauty in utility. This used to be an elevator. She had the car removed, but she liked the walls so she kept them intact. It's the only noticeable remnant of the home's previous purpose."

Jeff touched the wall. "I really like her style."

Juniper led them down the stairs. "The rooms on the lower level were mainly administrative offices for the convalescent home, which is why you'll see that our bedrooms are rather small. There was also a pharmacy down here, but it's now a wine cellar."

Jeff said, "I definitely want to check that out."

"Help yourself to anything you want while you're here. I do apologize if anything's a bit messy. The maid took the week off."

Emory asked, "You're not convinced it was a ghost?"

"Ms. Geister wasn't killed by a ghost. I know the sheriff thinks it might've been a heart attack, but he's still looking into it."

"We can help with that," said Jeff.

"If you want, but your primary reason for being here is to prove that I didn't see what I believe I saw when Tommy died."

"Question for you," said Virginia. "We read that Blair was an environmentalist. Why did she own a coal mine?"

"She bought that to turn it into a nature preserve."

Jeff grunted. "I imagine the employees weren't too happy about it."

Juniper stopped when she reached the lower level. "They don't know. Well, some of them practically rioted when they found out who was buying it. I guess they assumed, knowing who she was. Ms. Geister had to give them assurances that she wasn't going to shut the mine down."

"She lied?" asked Emory.

"Not technically. This isn't public knowledge, but as soon as she purchased the mine, she signed it over to her foundation. The foundation is going to shut it down. Right now, the employees think the mine is temporarily closed to map out new tunnels, but it's actually in the process of being restored to its natural state. Miners are still being paid, but that's going to stop once the preserve is officially announced."

Juniper waved to the first door on the right. "That's Tommy's room. One of you can stay in there. There's also a guest room on the top level." She opened the second door on the right. "And this is my room. Virginia, I thought you could stay in here."

Emory held his palms over the floor just outside the room. "Is this where you said Mr. Addison died?"

Juniper's eyes welled as she clutched herself. She walked across the room and touched the TV mounted on the wall. "This is where I first saw it. The spirit. It came out of the screen toward me. I was in bed. Tommy came in and got between us. That's when it attacked him. Killed him."

As Jeff inspected the TV, Virginia found the remote on the bed and hit the power button. From the screen erupted a loud *POP!*, flourished with sparks and smoke.

Juniper shrieked and ran from the room.

"Damn!" Jeff yelped and jumped out of the way, patting his head to make sure no sparks ignited his hair.

Emory watched Juniper run up the back stairs. "I guess that's the last we'll see of her today."

Virginia dropped the remote. "Sorry."

"If Virginia's done trying to kill me, I need to show you guys something." Jeff beckoned them to the TV. "Look at the power cord."

Emory placed the side of his face on the wall so he could see behind the monitor. "The wire's exposed. It looks like someone took a cigarette lighter to the sheathing."

Jeff knelt to inspect the floor. "There are drops of melted rubber or whatever it's made of."

"PVC," said Virginia. "Couldn't that have happened when the TV blew just now?"

"I noticed it right before you tried to kill me." Jeff unplugged the cord from the outlet and the back of the TV, and he held it so Virginia could see the exposed wire. "Someone has tampered with this TV, and it's not a ghost. I bet Tommy touched it and electrocuted himself."

Virginia walked to the spot where Tommy had died. "How could he possibly have reached the cord from here?"

Emory knelt in front of Jeff and rubbed his fingers across the small black blobs on the floor. "Witnesses get details wrong all the time. She said something was going on with the TV, and it scared her. Maybe she looked away, and he was actually standing closer to here. He reached up to fix the TV."

Jeff continued Emory's train of thought, "And the electricity threw him across the room, like that kid climbing the electric fence in *Jurassic Park*."

Virginia said, "But that's not at all how she described it."

Jeff crossed his arms. "What's more believable: that an angry ghost came out of the TV and attacked Tommy Addison, or he was electrocuted when he touched a deliberately exposed wire?"

CHAPTER 3

SHERIFF ROME PARKED his truck in the driveway of his yellow-brick house in the Smoky Mountains town of Barter Ridge. Through the windshield he spotted a brown package on the front porch. "There it is."

He grabbed his hat from the passenger seat and slid his rugged five-foot-ten body from behind the wheel before placing the hat on his thinning black hair. He swept the door closed and hurried up the walkway to the ten-inch-squared box with the familiar smiling arrow logo. Tucking the box under his arm, the sheriff pulled a ring of keys from his pocket and flipped through until he found the one with a white thumbprint from when he painted the split-rail fence around the property.

As soon as he opened the door, Sophie squeezed through the crack to greet him. The white French bulldog stood on her hind legs and clawed at his pants for attention. "Sophie, I love you, but I have to hurry before your mama gets home." Sheriff Rome gave the dog a quick pat on the head before stepping inside. "Go pee. I'll leave the door open for you." While Sophie bolted for the overgrown grass on the other side of the walkway, the sheriff hightailed it to the kitchen.

Sheriff Rome placed the box on the kitchen table and sliced it open with his housekey. He removed from it a smaller box labeled *Ingtec Bug and Hidden Camera Detector.* "I hope you work like in the video." He reached two fingers inside and pulled out a device about the size of a garage door opener with a silver antenna. "Are you charged?" He pressed the power button and jerked his head back when the device squelched. "Now you're supposed to only go off when you detect something giving off electromagnetic signals... Oh." The sheriff removed the radio from his belt and placed it on the table, along with his hat before stepping back a few feet. The squelching diminished. "Well, I guess you work then. Let's take you for a spin."

Sheriff Rome took the device to Emory's old room, where an intruder had entered their house the previous month. He'd assumed the blame for the open window, not telling his wife he found the telltale signs it was pried open from the outside. Nothing had seemed to be missing, though, so he had no idea why anyone would've gone through the trouble. Later, when his son told him he had found a bug in his apartment, the sheriff wondered if that might've been the reason for the break-in.

Sheriff Rome scanned the entire room with the bug detector, but it never squelched above normal levels. "Of course. Why would anyone bug this room? It's a museum."

He retreated back to the hallway and scanned the walls on the way to the living room. He scanned the furniture and the lamps before his eyes fixed on the fireplace. "We haven't used it since February."

He knelt on the brown-brick hearth and stuck his head inside the fireplace. The sheriff raised the device toward the flue. The low squelching grew louder, and he was certain it wasn't just from the sound echoing within the metal firebox. "Who would put a bug—"

"What are you doing?" a voice asked from behind.

Sheriff Rome jerked up his head, hitting it on the lintel. He spun himself around to sit on the hearth. "You startled me."

Lula Mae Rome stood before him in full uniform. "I didn't

mean to." She reached to the back of his head to rub it. "Are you okay?"

The sheriff looked up at his wife, who was a ranger for the Great Smoky Mountains National Park, and he spotted the radio in her belt. He moved the bug detector closer to it. "That's what it was."

Lula Mae backed up and raised her fingertips to her ears. "What on Earth is that, and why's it making that awful noise."

Sheriff Rome hit the power button on the device. "It's something for work. I was just testing it."

"And you had it delivered here? I saw the box on the kitchen table."

The sheriff chuckled. "Sometimes I think we should've switched jobs." He scooted over and patted the space next to him. "Have a seat. I need to talk to you."

Lula Mae joined him on the hearth. "What is it?"

"You remember Emory showing us that bug he found in his apartment?"

"How could I forget. The TBI planted it to get some sort of information on him and force him to drop his lawsuit against them. But that's past now. He's not suing them anymore."

"Well, that bug's the same type of device the TBI uses, but he didn't know for certain they were the ones listening to him."

"Who else would it be?"

"I don't know, but it got me thinking that whoever it was might've bugged our house too." The sheriff held up the device. "That's why I got this bug detector."

"Why on Earth would anyone want to bug our house?"

"I don't know."

"Then why do you think it?"

Sheriff Rome exhaled a sentence devoid of words.

"What?" asked Lula Mae. "What is it?"

"You found the window to Emory's room open a few weeks back."

"You said that was you!"

The sheriff shook his head. "It wasn't."

"Then why would you say that?"

"I was just trying to protect you."

Lula Mae stood and threw her hands up. "I don't need your protection. I need your honesty."

"You're right. I'm sorry." Sheriff Rome pushed himself up and placed an arm around her. "We're a team."

Lula Mae nodded toward the detector. "You think that thing can find the bug?"

"If there even is one."

"You think there's another reason someone would break in? Nothing was taken."

The sheriff waved toward the sofa. "Sit. I need to show you something."

"What is it?"

"I'll be right back." Sheriff Rome exited the house to retrieve two plastic baggies from his truck's glove compartment. When he returned to the living room, he found his wife standing with her arms crossed, eyes fixed on him.

"What's that?"

He handed one of the baggies to her. "It's a picture of Emory when he was a boy. You can see Crescent Lake behind him."

"Ooh, that is old." Lula Mae scrutinized the bag's contents. "I don't think I've ever seen this picture. What does this writing on the back mean? *Who bears the iniquity of the son?*"

"I'm not sure. That picture was in his granny's house before it burned."

"It survived the fire?"

"Emory didn't have it on him, and that house completely burned down. I remember walking through it for clues, and there was nothing. The only other person who made it out of the house, besides Emory, was Carl."

"But he's dead."

"I know. I'm figuring either the TBI found it among Carl's possessions and took custody of it, along with everything else after… the incident on the mountain, or he gave it to one of the people with him at the time. Whoever's hands it ended up in, someone is now using it to try and rattle Emory. Now take a look at the envelope."

Lula Mae inspected the other baggie, and saw a blank envelope bearing a thin red border and a small tornado icon on the flap. "This looks familiar."

"It should. Remember when we went to Sedona for our twenty-fifth anniversary?"

"Of course." Lula Mae gasped. "This is my stationery!"

"If not, it's a big coincidence. It was slipped under Emory's apartment door the night he was let go from the TBI. It was a month before the open window here."

"What are you saying?"

"I think someone's broken into the house twice."

"Twice?!"

"The first time, they took the stationery—"

"But why take stationery, and how would they even know I had any?"

"I imagine they were just looking for something that would've let Emory know they could get to us. The second time – when they left the window open – was either to plant a bug or for some reason we haven't thought of yet."

"You shouldn't have kept this from me."

"You're right. I'm sorry."

"We need to get busy." Lula Mae headed for the living room door. "While you're scanning for bugs, I'm going to scour the house, looking for anything that's gone missing, no matter how small."

Almost an hour later, Sheriff Rome found his wife sitting at the kitchen table, staring at the cell phone in her hand. "Lula Mae?"

She jumped at the sound of his voice. "Nick. Did you find anything?"

"This house is clean. Did you?"

"I noticed an empty space on the shelf in the armoire, where I keep my books."

"They stole a book?"

"It was Emory's journal – the one the psychiatrist had him keep when he first came to live with us."

"I remember that book. It was as big as the Bible."

"He wrote in it for three years. He was going to throw it away when he went to college, and I told him he'd regret it and to just let me hold onto it. I had to promise not to read it."

"And you're sure it's gone."

"Positive."

"Well maybe he took it with him the last time he was here."

"That's what I was thinking. I'm certain it was there when we did our big cleaning for the church sale, right before he came down last. I would've noticed it missing, but I haven't looked on that shelf since. Something else I was thinking. Why break in twice? Why not take the journal when they were here the first time taking the envelope?"

"I don't know. Maybe they didn't know about the journal the first time but somehow found out about it and came back for it. The only way to know for sure it was actually taken is to ask Emory."

"I was going to text him to ask, but what if he didn't take it? What would that mean? I don't want him to panic."

"We can't keep it from him."

"You're right." She held up her phone. "Here goes."

CHAPTER 4

AS THE THREE investigators retrieved their luggage from the car, Jeff surveyed the surroundings. "We should check out the grounds."

Virginia slammed the trunk shut. "No one died outside."

"That we know of. Maybe Blair Geister's ghost killed the gardener, too."

"Still alive." Emory tilted his head to the side, toward a fifty-ish man sporting a safari hat and canvas gloves, standing amidst several plastic pots of blooming daffodils. He appeared to be ready to plant them in the patch of dirt between two anemic hemlock bushes at the side of the house, but at the moment, he was engaged in a coughing fit.

"All right. I'm just curious then." Jeff dropped his bags beside the car.

Virginia pulled up the handle of her white suitcase with brown trim. "You two go ahead. I'm going to find the office and set up shop."

Emory pulled his wool satchel and two gray, wheeled duffle bags from the backseat. "I want to unpack and then pay a visit to the local sheriff."

Jeff smirked at him. "You really think he's going to tell us anything?"

"I'm hoping he'll at least tell us where he sent the bodies. Autopsies in Tennessee are performed at one of five regional forensics centers – Knoxville, Nashville, Memphis, Chattanooga and Johnson City."

"Probably Chattanooga," said Jeff. "It's the closest."

Emory agreed. "That'd be my guess too. Assuming the sheriff won't give us details about the deaths, we'll have another chance with the medical examiner."

"Before we start spinning our wheels, I'm going to take a few minutes just to relax and take in the scenery."

Emory raised his luggage-laden hands. "At least wait until I get these inside."

"Good lord, no one's going to steal your bags. If they did, they'd bring them right back once they saw the clothes inside."

As Virginia snickered, Emory clinched his lips and lowered his luggage to the pavers. "What's the big rush?"

"I just want to do it before it gets dark. You can join me or not. Whatever." Jeff headed toward the wooded area that cloaked the western edge of the estate. Before Emory even caught up with him, Jeff spoke as if they were side-by-side. "Six hundred and twenty-five million, and she buys this."

"I know." Emory brushed aside the bristly branches of a cedar tree. "Why live here instead of a penthouse in one of her buildings?"

"No, I mean why just twelve acres? Why not a thousand acres? She could've had her own Balmoral, owned everything as far as the eye could see."

"Mine's a better question. Why here at all?"

"She grew up around here." Jeff took a breath of a dogwood bestrewn with white blossoms. "I guess it's home."

"You don't think it's something more than that?"

Jeff turned his head to flash a smirk back at Emory. "Not everyone runs from home the first opportunity they get."

Emory jerked his head back. "You did!"

Jeff motioned ahead. "I was running *toward* something. Can you honestly say the same? Ooh, locust." He pulled an insect husk from the bark of a maple tree and held it up to Emory. "I used to collect them and have them fight my army men. *Attack of the Giant Locusts!*"

Emory laughed at the thought. "That's actually a cicada husk."

"Really? We always called them locusts. *Attack of the Giant Cicadas* doesn't instill quite the same air of terror." Jeff dropped the husk and continued forward.

"How much further do you want to walk?"

"To the end."

"But we don't know where the property lines are."

Jeff nodded ahead. "I see a fence up there."

Emory peered over his partner's shoulder and glimpsed through the foliage the same vertical iron posts he saw extending from the driveway gate. He felt his phone vibrating in his pocket and retrieved it to see a text message from his mother. Emory stopped talking to respond.

Lula Mae: *Did you take your journal with you the last time you were here?*

Emory: *No. Why?*

Lula Mae: *I must have put it somewhere else when I was cleaning. I'll find it. Don't worry.*

Emory: *Let me know if you don't.*

Emory pocketed his phone, along with the uneasiness memories of his journal brought. He turned his attention back to his partner, and the first thought to come to mind was of the file on Jeff that TBI Director Anderson Alexander had given him after their last case. Ever since, he had wanted to talk to Jeff about its contents, but he kept putting it off, afraid of where the confrontation might lead. Was now the right time?

"Look at that tree!" Jeff, several yards ahead, hurried toward a huge cedar within the fence line.

Emory quickened his pace to catch up with his partner. When he did, he saw a twelve-foot gap in the property fence, in the middle of which stood the giant cedar tree. A chain draped from knee-high stakes created a five-foot perimeter around the base of the trunk. "That's a big break in the fence. Anyone could just walk right onto the property from the woods on the other side."

"Kind of defeats the purpose. I wonder why they didn't continue the fence all the way up to the tree, or cut down the tree."

"It's protected." Emory read an engraved marker embedded in a large stone block just outside the circle of the chain. "It's an eastern red cedar tree, estimated to be 250 years old."

"Cool."

"No, it's officially designated a Historic Tree by the state of Tennessee. The Cherokee considered cedar trees sacred, believing they housed the souls of the dead. They gathered around this one to honor those who died on this stretch of the Trail of Tears. The fallen were buried in unmarked graves in the area..." Emory stopped reading when he saw Jeff about to step over the chain. "What are you doing?!"

"I've never touched a 250-year-old tree before."

"You can't do that. The perimeter around the tree is protected by the state. It can't be touched."

Jeff put a toe on the muddy ground within the chained perimeter. "I think I just did." He brought his other foot over.

"I wish you wouldn't do that. It's probably bad for the roots."

"Relax. The roots are fine." Jeff touched the trunk and looked up at the nearest branch, ten feet above their heads. "How tall do you think it is?"

Emory shrugged. "Eighty, ninety feet."

Jeff looked past Emory. "I can see the house from here."

"Fascinating. Now would you please come back on this side of the chain?"

Jeff shook his head and complied. "You know, you worry too much."

"And you don't worry nearly enough. Let's get back to the house."

"We're not done with our tour. I can hear the river down this way."

As Emory followed Jeff along the fence, the sacred tree brought a story to mind. "Did I ever tell you about Hugo Hickory?"

"It sounds familiar, but—"

"It's the ghost story my granny used to tell me."

"If it's a ghost story, save it for bedtime." Jeff motioned ahead. "There's the river."

They emerged from the woods at the muddy bank of the Hiwassee River, where the wake of a passing motorboat slapped against the final post in the bordering fence.

"Nice!" Jeff leaned his back against the trunk of a sycamore tree, entwined in cerulean morning glories, and took in his surroundings. The afternoon sunlight skipped across the ripples in the river and strobed the erratic flightpath of a green dragonfly skimming its golden surface. The bank on the other side abutted tree-covered hills and held no edifices as far as could be seen in either direction. Eastward on their side, a pier stretched from Blair Geister's property to a large boathouse about halfway across the river. Jeff smirked at Emory. "Let's take a dip in the altogether."

"In the al—"

"You know. Nude."

"I know what it means. I don't swim." Emory's eyes fixed on the flowers behind Jeff. "Could you move?"

"Why?" Jeff pushed away from the tree. "Am I on something?"

"No. Let's just walk."

Jeff laughed. "What, are you afraid I'm hurting the morning glories? They're fine."

"That's not it." Emory shifted the subject as they continued along the water. "I wonder if Geisterhaus is off the grid."

"Why do you say that?"

Emory eyed the boathouse, coming up on their left. "Solar panels on the roof and a waterwheel." He looked to his right and saw Geisterhaus on the hilltop. A lawn about one thousand feet wide ascended from the riverbank to the house and the pool. Dotted with occasional trees and islands of flowering plants, the grass separated the woods they had just left from the less-wooded area on the opposite side of the property.

"Maybe." Jeff followed Emory's gaze up the hill before spotting a long silver pole protruding up from the roof. "Huh, you don't see big antennas on house rooftops much anymore. I wonder why she didn't have it removed."

Emory stopped to pick up a flat rock. "I didn't think much of it at first, but this really is a beautiful property." He threw the rock at the river, and it skipped three times before sinking beneath the surface.

Jeff threw a rock of his own, skipping it five times. "I was thinking the same thing. Makes me think about an old friend from college. He would've loved this place. We used to canoe down the Tennessee River on the weekends."

"What's his name?"

"Trevor."

Emory perked up at the name. "Do you stay in touch?"

"Not since he died."

"Trevor Park?" Emory pinched his lips together.

Jeff tilted his head. "How'd you know his last name?"

"You've mentioned him before."

"I'm pretty sure I haven't."

"It must've been Virginia then." Emory's eyes darted about before finding a point of focus. "Is that a woodcock?"

"What?" Jeff looked down.

Emory nodded downriver. "The big-beaked bird over there."

"I have no idea. How do you?"

"I used to be into birds when I was a kid." Emory took a step up on the grass. "It's getting late. Let's get back to the house."

"We're not done with the tour." Jeff grabbed his partner's hand and pulled him back to the bank. "The fence for the other side of the property is right up ahead. We'll follow it up and cut over to the house."

Emory complied but made sure to keep the topic of discussion innocuous as they approached the property's western boundary and ascended the hill. "I wonder how the construction's going at the office."

"I'm fine staying here until it's done." Jeff called his attention to the house on the other side of the fence. "Look how small the neighbor's house is compared to Geister's." He stopped in his tracks. "What the hell is that?"

Emory followed his partner's line of sight to a huge black statue by the fence. Atop its body of roughly six feet rested a much larger head with a snarl of a grin focused on the neighbor's house. "Is that art? I don't get it."

"I wonder how the neighbors feel about looking out their window every morning and seeing this guy sneering at him."

"Not just this one." Emory pointed up the hill toward at least three similar statues, all facing the neighbor's house. "It's like Easter Island."

Jeff gawked at the hideous figures. "Something tells me Blair Geister and her neighbor didn't get along."

CHAPTER 5

EMORY WALKED THROUGH the parking lot of the local sher-iff's station with Jeff at his side. "How are we going to play this?"

"Are you seriously asking me how we're going to lie our way into getting information?" Jeff grinned and threw an arm over Emory's shoulders. "Welcome to the Dark Side."

"I'm serious. You know they're not going to tell us anything. What's your plan?"

"We're clerks at the law firm Blair Geister had on retainer, Geralt and McCree."

"Video game characters?"

Jeff opened the door for Emory. "If it ain't broke."

Inside, they approached a woman in uniform at the desk closest to the front door. Jeff smiled at the deputy and flashed his bright green eyes as he glanced at her name tag. "Good afternoon, Deputy Nunley. We need to speak to whoever is in charge of the investiga-tion into Blair Geister's death."

The twentyish woman with dark blonde hair wrapped in a loose bun asked, "And who can I say needs this conversation?"

"Jeff and Emory from Geralt and McCree, Ms. Geister's retained legal counsel. We're here to get all the details on her death to file with the estate."

Deputy Nunley half-rolled her blue eyes. "No, you're not."

Her assertion smacked the smile from Jeff's face. Emory wanted to intervene, but deception was his partner's purview and a sport at which he excelled.

Jeff said, "I can assure you—"

The deputy cut him off. "Sheriff Flynn is handling that case personally, but I happen to know he's already been contacted – this morning, in fact – by Neal and Reinhardt, Blair Geister's actual legal counsel. I answered the call myself. Care to try again?"

Perhaps drawn by the deputy's escalating tone, a sturdy man in uniform sidled up to her desk. "Deputy, what's happening here?"

"These reporters are trying to get information on Geister."

"We're not reporters," said Jeff. "As I was trying—"

Emory interrupted, stepping in front of him. "The truth is we're private investigators. We've been retained by Ms. Geister's estate – Ms. Juniper Crane, specifically – to find out what happened to her boss and her colleague, Mr. Tommy Addison."

The sheriff snorted. "Why didn't you just say so?"

"We figured you wouldn't talk to us."

The sheriff shook his head. "I don't much care how we get to the bottom of what happened, as long as it's gotten to. Besides, if Juniper hired you, she must have good reason."

"Sheriff, how do you know they're telling the truth?"

The sheriff eyed the PIs up and down before responding to the deputy. "I trust my gut, but go ahead and call Juniper Crane to double-check it." He cocked his head to the left. "This way, gentlemen."

Emory and Jeff followed the grey-haired man in the too-small campaign hat to a tiny but tidy office with glass walls. The sheriff waved them to a wooden bench in front of an old metal desk. "Have a seat."

Emory complied. "Thank you for seeing us."

Jeff scooted next to his partner. "What can you tell us about the deaths?"

"We thoroughly catalogued the scene around both bodies and found no apparent sign of foul play or…" Sheriff Flynn chuckled. "Haunting. I'm assuming you don't buy Juniper's version of events."

Emory responded, "We think her interpretation of what she saw is inaccurate."

"Funny you should say that." The sheriff creaked back in his chair. "Did she tell you she'd been smoking marijuana?"

Emory and Jeff looked at each other, and both answered, "No."

"Her room reeked of it that night, and we found a bit left in an ashtray on her nightstand. That aside, I do want to believe her, but I'm in the business of facts."

"And what are the facts?" asked Emory.

The sheriff held up counting fingers as he relayed his facts. "Blair Geister died in her bed sometime between ten p.m. and midnight. Tommy Addison died just after midnight based on the one sure fact from Juniper's recounting. Doc Riley – he's the one I called to make the death pronouncement – thinks they both died of a heart attack, but the mere fact that two heart attacks occurred in such proximity – both in time and physical distance – leads me to believe the deaths were not natural. I suppose that's more of a gut feeling than a fact on my end."

"I agree, Sheriff," said Jeff. "That would be too much of a coincidence."

"Agreed." Emory scooted forward on the bench so he could tap on the desk. "Assuming their deaths were not natural, did you find any evidence to suggest murder in either case?"

"Well, I don't see how Tommy's death could've been murder, if you believe even an ounce of Juniper's eyewitness account. Unless, of course, you think Juniper murdered him and then made up this wild story in hopes of throwing off suspicion. But if true, why would she hire you gentlemen?"

Jeff asked, "What about Blair Geister?"

"She had a look of pain frozen on her face, but the room appeared to be undisturbed."

Deputy Nunley knocked on the door but didn't wait for an invitation to open it and pop her head into the office. "Sheriff, you were right," she muttered, as if the words, "Ms. Crane vouched for them," would sear her tongue.

"Thank you, Deputy." As the door closed, the sheriff returned his attention to the PIs. "Why don't we give the medical examiner a ring?"

Emory noticed the rotary phone on the desk. "Does it have speaker function?"

Sheriff Flynn laughed. "Not on that. That's just something I picked up at auction. My brother collects them. Old phones and old glass insulators. No, I'm going to video-call her." The sheriff turned his computer monitor around to allow all three to see, and he contacted the medical examiner.

As soon as the face appeared on the screen, Emory smiled. "You sent the bodies to Knoxville."

Jeff waved. "Hi Cathy."

"Emory and Jeff!" Cathy Shaw pulled the surgical mask from her face to reveal a broad grin. "Good to see you guys. What can I help you with?"

Sheriff Flynn tapped his desk. "You all know each other?"

Emory nodded. "Cathy's an old friend from my days at the TBI."

"I didn't know you were with the TBI."

The sheriff leaned over his desk to push more of his face into view of the camera. "Hi Dr. Shaw."

"Perfect timing, Sheriff Flynn. I was just finishing up with your cases. Um, did you want to speak in private?"

"That won't be necessary. These gentlemen are helping me figure things out."

Emory leaned forward. "Cathy, I'm relieved to know you're on the case. You can get to the truth. We know they couldn't both have died from—"

"Myocardial infarction. I'm sorry, but it's true."

"Doc Riley was right," said the sheriff. "They died of natural causes."

Cathy waved her hands in front of her. "I didn't say that."

"Please tell me the heart attacks were induced." Emory's words drew a strange look from the sheriff. "Not that I want them to be murders, but I can't believe in such a big coincidence."

"I can give you a definite maybe in at least one of the deaths. Now Blair Geister did suffer from hypertension, according to her medical records, so a heart attack in her case is not terribly suspicious. But there was an anomaly."

"What kind of anomaly?" asked Jeff.

"I almost didn't notice it. There was just a drop of blood in the right ear that led me to it. Blair Geister had a ruptured eardrum."

"Could the heart attack have caused it?" asked the sheriff.

"No."

Emory asked, "Could a heart attack have been induced through the ear somehow?"

"No way I can think of, unless something like potassium chloride were injected through the ear into the auricular artery in the hopes the injection site wouldn't be found during the autopsy."

"Did you find elevated potassium in the blood work?" asked Emory.

"Yes, but her physician had her on a low-sodium diet for the hypertension, and the primary ingredient in many salt substitutes is potassium chloride. Again, I didn't say the rupture was related to her death. Just that it was odd. She might've had an ear infection at the time of her heart attack. The 'definite maybe' I was referring to was actually in the case of Tommy Addison, where I discovered another anomaly. I found petechia in his eyes."

"Petechia?" asked the sheriff.

"Burst blood vessels."

Jeff asked, "Could a heart attack cause that?"

"Not that I've seen. It's commonly a sign of asphyxiation or electrocution."

"Like touching an exposed TV wire?" Jeff pulled from his pocket a clear bag containing the cord to Juniper's TV and held it up to the monitor so Cathy could see the exposed wire.

"I didn't find any burn wounds on his hands, or anywhere for that matter. If not for the witness account and the fact that there are no indications the body was wet at the time of death, I would think he was maybe electrocuted in a bathtub, causing the heart attack."

The sheriff took the cord from Jeff as Emory returned his attention to Cathy. "You said it could also be caused by asphyxia."

"If that were the case, I'd expect to see signs of bruising around the nose and mouth, or a blockage in the airway or a chemically induced causative, but I found no evidence of any of that."

"Still, something had to cause it."

"I agree, but I can only report on the evidence in hand. If you uncover anything new, let me know. I'd prefer to move the anomalies into the explained column."

"Thank you, Dr. Shaw." The sheriff disconnected the call. "Well gentlemen, we have a problem. I can't believe it, but it appears Juniper Crane lied to us."

Emory frowned at the sheriff. "I agree that she didn't see an actual ghost, but I don't think she intentionally misled us."

"Were you listening to Dr. Shaw? Signs point to Tommy Addison being electrocuted or asphyxiated. If that's true, Juniper flat-out lied about how he died and might even be the one responsible."

"How do you figure that?" asked Jeff.

"Say she electrocuted Tommy while he was taking a bath, dried him off and then dragged him to the hallway. Then she made up that cockamamie story to cover it up."

Emory asked, "Why?"

"Don't know yet, but it's up to us to find out."

"What about Blair?" asked Jeff. "You think she killed her too?"

"Maybe. Or maybe she died of a heart attack like Cathy said, and then Juniper seized the opportunity. Face it, gentlemen. Unless she can come up with an explanation of what happened that's based in reality, your client is our number one suspect."

CHAPTER 6

SEATED ON THE bed in Juniper Crane's room, Virginia typed away on her laptop. As her fingers stilled, she thought for a moment before lying back to rest her head on the pillow. She crinkled her nose and turned it toward the fabric. "Smells like pot. I'm going to need fresh bedding." She exited the room and returned moments later with folded sheets, pillowcases and blankets she found in the large supply room on the lower level.

Virginia reached for the nearest pillow to strip it until a curious noise summoned her attention. She heard a low creaking, like a rocking chair in extra slow motion. She tilted her head. "Where's that coming from?"

The sound continued as Virginia tried honing in on the source. Her eyes scanned the room before fixing on the TV mounted on the wall just beyond the foot of the bed. "It can't be that. Jeff took the plug."

Virginia crept in her socked feet past the open bedroom door. She placed her ear an inch from the nearest lavender-tinted wall and listened. She shuffled forward, following the wall and the intensifying sound. "Is it... scratching?"

She felt the hair on her arms starting to stand at attention. "Stop it! You're not scared! Don't be an idiot." She moved forward and returned her attention to the TV. "It's definitely coming from th—"

Before she could finish her whispered words, the TV emitted a final and stronger creak. It fell from the wall mount and crashed to the floor.

Virginia jumped back into the bed's footboard and muffled a yelp with her hand. She shook her head and scolded herself for her atypical reaction. "That doesn't count as a scream. I'm sure there's a very logical reason for a TV spontaneously falling from a wall. Can't think of it now, but that's what tomorrows are for."

A few minutes later, Virginia was rolling her suitcase down the sconce-lighted hallway on the top floor, clutching the fresh bedding against her torso. The first door on the right led to a dusky room, lit only by the setting sun's exhausted rays crawling through one massive window. She pushed up the dimmer switch to illuminate an extra-long blue linen sofa, dozens of framed photos on the white narrow-slatted walls and a modern wooden desk the size of a dining room table. "Blair Geister's office."

She parked the suitcase beside the sofa and dropped the bedding onto one of its cushions. The pictures on the wall caught her eye, so she strolled by each to learn more about the former mistress of the house. Every picture but one featured Geister either in front of one her buildings or hobnobbing with the famous, including Al Gore, Tim McGraw, Elon Musk and the governor of Tennessee. The one outlier was an older photo of a couple with two children in Gatlinburg. Virginia tapped the girl in the photo with her fingernail. "That looks like Blair Geister." She moved her finger to the boy. "Does she have a brother?"

When her picture tour ended, she found herself in front of the window, witnessing the day's twilight. Her new perch overlooked the sloping grounds, the oversized boathouse and the rippling river. "Great view."

The overhead lights flickered. She turned around to see a hand reaching for her.

Virginia screamed.

While Emory drove back to Geisterhaus, Jeff wondered aloud about the merits of Sheriff Flynn's fingering of their client as his prime suspect in the two deaths at the property. "I don't see her killing them and then making up that ridiculous story to cover it up. Although I don't believe she's telling us everything."

"Of course, she isn't." Emory lowered his window. "Even if she truly believes what she told us, she hasn't told us why she thinks Blair Geister would want to kill her."

"And she teased us about a guy with a disappearing face but didn't elaborate. What the hell does that even mean?"

Emory pulled up to the gate and punched in the code. "Either she's a purposeful liar or she has an imaginative way of looking at things."

"Agreed. We should also face the possibility that we don't have a case here at all. Blair and Tommy could've actually died of heart attacks, and Juniper could be delusional."

"I know you don't buy that." Parking the car, Emory could see glints of light even after his headlights dimmed. Lightning bugs were now emerging from the woods to embrace the gloaming. "Even if you completely negate Ms. Crane's eyewitness account, we still have evidence of something unusual in their deaths."

"The anomalies Cathy mentioned."

"That and the unexplained silhouette on Ms. Geister's mattress."

Jeff squinted toward the house. "He's working late."

Emory followed Jeff's gaze to see the gardener exiting the house and covering a cough as he shut the front door. They hurried from the car and intercepted the gardener before he could reach his truck. Emory glanced inside the truck's bed, which held a scattering of at least a dozen plastic pots filled with dirt and plants that had been cut down to the bulb, having no more than an inch of green remaining. *That's odd.*

The burly, black-bearded man with a pronounced widow's peak looked for a way past Jeff, but the PI mirrored him lockstep.

"Working kind of late, aren't you, Mr…"

The gardener frowned under confused eyes. "Who are you?"

"Uh-uh. I asked you first."

Coughing again, the gardener extended his hand. "George Henry."

Jeff kept his hands at his side. "That's quite a cough you have there."

"Hay fever."

Jeff snickered. "Then you're in the wrong line of work. Getting in a little night gardening? Is that such a thing?"

"Who are you?" the impatient gardener asked again.

"Jeff Woodard."

Emory said, "We're private investigators working to explain the death of your employer."

"I don't bother you at your job. Don't bother me at mine." George plowed between them and entered his vehicle.

As the truck pulled away, Emory asked, "Why were you giving him such a hard time?"

Jeff headed for the house. "Has your gardener ever come into your house?"

Emory followed his partner. "I've never had a gardener."

"Me neither, technically. He was my parents. As nice as he was, I don't remember him ever stepping foot inside the house." Jeff opened the front door. "What was he doing?"

"Good que—"

A scream from inside the house interrupted Emory's response.

Jeff froze for a split-second. "Virginia!"

Emory and Jeff ran up the front stairs and down the hallway on the top floor, each checking a different room.

"Jeff, here!" Emory signaled his partner before entering Blair Geister's office, where he saw someone unexpected with Virginia.

Short-statured in spite of her high hair, the woman in the purple polyester pantsuit took a silent step toward Virginia. "I didn't mean to frighten you. I'm Miss—"

Emory interrupted her as Jeff stepped into the room. "Miss Luann?"

"Emory." Miss Luann came to him with open arms and hugged his torso. "Good to see you're doing well."

"You too." Emory avoided eye contact with his partners as he returned her embrace, if lacking reciprocal intensity. He had never told them about his visit to the clairvoyant after the Crick Witch placed a supposed curse on him, and he had no plans to ever do so.

Jeff rushed to Virginia. "Are you okay?"

"Just startled. Miss Luann? Why does that name sound familiar?"

The older woman broke from Emory and smiled at Virginia. "I'm a clairvoyant. Best in Knoxville."

"That's it. I pass by your shop every day on the way to work."

Jeff wagged a finger between Miss Luann and Emory. "And how do you two know each other?"

As his face reddened, Emory ignored the question and posed one of his own. "Miss Luann, what are you doing here?"

"Juniper Crane hired me to escort the restless spirits from this house. She told me she'd hired some private investigators to appease her daughter, but she didn't tell me it was you and your team."

Jeff asked, "Shouldn't you have known?"

The clairvoyant shot him a scolding glance. "I'm not the Lord. I see more than most, but I don't see all. Emory, you should not be here. Did you forget my warning? There are woods all around this house."

Jeff scoffed. "What's this about the woods?"

Emory brushed off the question, much like he had Miss Luann's so-called vision of an unseen danger awaiting him in some unnamed woods. "It's nothing. Miss Luann, are you staying here too?"

The older woman laughed. "Oh no, I'd never get any sleep. I have a cousin who lives in town, so I'll be staying with her until I've done what I came here to do."

Virginia crossed her arms. "And what is that exactly?"

"Convincing spirits to cross over can be an arduous undertaking. They need to get to know me first and trust me before they'll listen to me. I just came to introduce myself tonight and get a feel for where they're at."

Jeff smirked at her. "Can't they move around, or are they chained in placed?"

"I meant where they are in their spiritual journey. They're in three different places."

Emory corrected her. "Only two people died here."

Miss Luann grimaced. "Two spirits are here at the moment, but another will come."

"Wait a minute," said Virginia. "Are you saying someone else is going to die in this house?"

Miss Luann waved a finger at the question. "I follow a very strict code of ethics. If I can't influence what I see, I keep it to myself. It's better that way." She headed for the door. "Now I'm going to mosey around a little longer, and then I'll be out of your hair. It was nice meeting y'all." The clairvoyant left the PIs alone in the office.

"Okay, I'm not staying here." Virginia grabbed the handle of her suitcase.

Jeff placed a hand on top of hers. "Why? Because of that fortune teller?"

Emory said, "She doesn't like to be called that."

"And how do you know?"

"She's a friend of my mother's."

Jeff tapped his own head a couple of times. "Is her zodiac missing a couple of fire signs?"

"I don't know."

"That's a yes." Jeff put his foot in the path of Virginia's rolling suitcase. "You're not going to let the Oracle of Knox County dictate your actions."

Virginia looked down at Jeff's foot. "No, because that's *your* job."

"Right… No, of course not." Jeff stopped blocking the suitcase.

She took a step before stopping. "And it's not just her."

"Whatever it is, I know you. You were a Marine. You'd never abandon your post."

Virginia released the handle. "If I see even the slightest haze that could be construed as ghostlike, consider me AWOL."

"Great!" Jeff gave her a pat on the back.

Emory asked, "Did you find anything interesting in the house?"

Virginia steered her suitcase back to the sofa. "I haven't had a chance to really look around yet."

Jeff greeted the news with frowning eyes. "Haven't had a chance? What have you been doing while we were gone?"

"I've been working. Among other things, I spent an hour on the phone with the contractor. He had some questions about the basement."

"The basement?" asked Jeff. "What about it?"

"If we wanted a door between the basements in our old office and the new space or if we wanted the whole wall torn down. He also asked about buying some of the antique fixtures down there. Don't worry, I told him we want to keep them."

Emory noticed the bedding on the sofa. "I thought you were staying in Juniper's room."

"I was until the TV came crashing down. And before you ask, I don't know why."

"Seriously?" Emory headed for the door. "I need to check that out." He left the room and descended the back stairs to the lower level. There he found Miss Luann standing in the spot Juniper had identified as Tommy Addison's place of death.

Rocking with her eyes closed, she appeared to be in a trance. Rather than disturb her, he sidled around her to enter Juniper's bedroom. There he saw the busted TV face-down and scattered parts on the floor. He tried not to step on anything, but he heard crunching under the thick rubber soles of his size fourteen zip boots as his eyes focused on the wall mount. He didn't see any plastic from the back of the TV on the mount. Instead, the metal itself had broken. He touched the jagged edges that used to hold the TV, and bits of the heavy-duty aluminum crumbled between his fingers.

What on Earth could have caused that? He turned around to leave and was surprised to find Miss Luann no longer outside the doorway. *I didn't even hear her move.* He stepped into the hallway and glanced at the closed door to Tommy Addison's bedroom. *Probably in there.*

He turned the doorknob with great purpose to minimize any sound and eased the door open. The room was devoid of clairvoyants. Emory flipped the light switch, which did little to brighten the bleak, windowless space. Identical to Juniper's room in square footage, about the size of a college dorm room, it held a full-size bed with a brown blanket, a simple oak dresser and a closet door. He frowned at the footboard, realizing he would not be able to stretch out. *I'd have to sleep diagonally.* He closed the door and headed back to the stairs.

In Blair Geister's office, Virginia pushed down on the sofa cushion. *Good thing I prefer a firm mattress.* She moved the stack of bedding to a small wooden file cabinet on casters and grabbed the fitted sheet. As she unfurled it over the sofa, Emory came into the room.

"Where's Jeff?"

Virginia tucked a sheet over the sofa cushions. "He went to check out the guest room."

"I'd like to see that too. I want to see what kind of bed it has."

His comment elicited a grin from her. "I'm sure it's of sturdy build."

Emory half-frowned at her. "Not that. The beds downstairs are too short."

She fluffed the pillow and placed it by the sofa arm near the file cabinet. "From Juniper's description of Blair, I'd imagine she'd have an impressive room for guests, including a good-sized bed."

"You're right. Hopefully, no footboard. I'll go check." Before he could take a step toward the door, Jeff entered.

The green-eyed PI smiled at Emory. "Dibs on the guest room."

Virginia threw the blanket over the sheet. "I figured it'd be impressive."

Emory tsked. "Small bed?"

"California king."

"You're going to keep it for yourself?"

Jeff tilted his head and hardened his face. "I did call dibs."

"Okay, I'll go set up in Tommy Addison's room."

Virginia ran her hands over the blanket, smoothing any bumps or wrinkles. "Anyone hungry?"

Jeff answered as if he had been waiting for someone to bring it up. "Yes! Starving."

Emory shrugged. "Sure."

Virginia took a second to admire her work before facing her partners. "Great. Let's meet in the kitchen in ten minutes. See what we can scrounge up."

Emory stepped into the hallway. "You want me to bring your bag up from the atrium?"

"I'll get it. Thanks though." Jeff shut the door with Emory on the other side.

Virginia turned her attention to Jeff. "Okay, what's going on here?"

"What do you mean?"

"You and Emory. You look for any excuse to get with him, and here you have a golden opportunity."

"Seriously? He's the one who's had every opportunity to get with me. I've been completely open with him, and he's surrounded that openness with a wall of indifference, pierced by sporadic windows of passion. I'm weary of it." Jeff plopped down on the makeshift bed. "I've moved on."

Virginia crossed her arms and squinted at him. "Have you?"

"Look, I'm a catch, and he has too many issues. I've moved on."

She aimed an accusing finger at her partner. "You're playing hard-to-get, aren't you?"

"Well, don't tell him that."

Emory rolled his suitcase into Tommy Addison's former room, and his shoulders slumped. *Why couldn't we stay in a hotel?* He noticed the pace of his breathing increasing. *Something about this room unnerves me. Tommy's ghost? That's ridiculous!* Emory gasped. *I know what it is!*

His breaths turned to pants. He sat on the bed, hands on his knees, and tried to relax. Unsuccessful, he pulled a pill box from his pocket and popped an oval, peach-colored pill into his mouth. With his eyes closed, he moved his hands to the edge of the mattress so they could grip something easier to squeeze.

Pull yourself together. It's not that much like my old room. His mind's eye strobed between Tommy's room and the bedroom he had as a kid, before he'd met Sheriff Rome. *Both in the basement. Same walls. But that's it! My room was bigger. More furniture. And it had a window, or I wouldn't be here.*

Emory took a deep breath and exhaled. He opened his eyes. *Okay. Step by step. First step, hang up my clothes.* He pushed off the bed and rolled his suitcase toward the closet. *I hope there's room.*

He opened the closet door and perused the blue-collar shirts and lone buckskin jacket hanging from the wooden pole. The shelf above held a camouflage-patterned suitcase. On the floor he saw four pairs of work boots, a tool box, a rifle leaning against one of the back corners and a stack of bedding. *That'll be step two.*

Emory opened his suitcase on the bed, pulled out a twist-tied set of hangers and hung his clothes. He zipped up his suitcase and placed it beside the bed. *Step two.* He stripped the bed, leaving the dirty sheets and brown blanket in a neat pile under the wall-mounted TV. He took the fitted sheet from the closet and threw it over the mattress, but it drooped over all sides. *Huh. It's too big. Maybe he had a bigger bed before he moved in here. I wonder if he was married.*

Emory tucked the fitted sheet under each side of the mattress and finished making the bed. *Step three... Oh, it's been more than ten minutes. I better get up to the kitchen.* Emory left the room and headed upstairs.

After dinner, Emory ambled into the locutorium, clinging to a dwindling glass of red wine. Lowering himself onto the gold sofa by the fireplace, he stared at the dimming twilight beyond the French doors, glimpsing the flickers of lightning bugs emerging from the trees. His eyes drifted to the fireplace and the logs within the hearth. *Are those real?* He placed his wine glass on the tile floor beside the couch and went to check. *Fake. How do you turn it on?* He dropped to his hands and knees to search for a switch.

Jeff came in with a full glass of wine in one hand and a bottle in the other. "What are you doing?"

"I'm trying to figure out how to turn on the fireplace." Emory felt a hot whoosh on the side of his face as flames erupted from beneath the logs. He jumped back, falling on his ass.

Jeff laughed. "You found the magic words."

"I didn't realize it was voice-activated."

"There's a little wine left in this bottle. We should finish it."

Emory picked himself up. "I think I've had enough. Give it to Virginia."

"She's gone to bed." Jeff spotted Emory's glass on the floor, and he emptied the bottle into it before Emory could stop him.

Emory reclaimed his seat on the sofa. "Aren't you going to bed?"

"I'm not quite tired enough yet." Jeff laid down on the sofa, plopping his socked feet onto Emory's lap. "Tell me a bedtime story."

"I don't know any bedtime stories."

Jeff locked his fingers behind his head and fixed his eyes on the ceiling. "Make something up. Ooh, tell me that ghost story you were talking about. The one about Mapleleaf."

"Mapleleaf? Do you mean Hugo Hickory?"

"I knew it had something to do with a tree."

"All right." Emory began massaging Jeff's feet. "Well, you know that in the 1830s, the U.S. government began rounding up Indigenous Peoples in the South and forcing them to walk to territories in the West."

"The Trail of Tears."

"Yes. Well, in a small Cherokee village in the Smoky Mountains, a mother was weaving in her tiny house when her son ran in with terrible news. 'Watch your step,' she said, pointing at the young man's muddy feet. 'I don't want you to dirty this blanket I'm making for you. As I weave it in the four sacred colors I cry on every thread, binding my love within, so the blanket will not only protect you from the cold, but shield you in my strength and that of our ancestors.'

"Her son, whose name was Waya'ha, told her, 'Soldiers are coming to take us from our home. You have to run and hide. I will stay and fight with the others.'

"His mother continued weaving, saying, 'This is our home,' and she refused to leave. Waya'ha tried to convince her, but he was too late. The soldiers arrived, led by the merciless Captain Hugo Hickory.

"The Cherokee fought, but there were just too many soldiers. Hugo Hickory forced all the fighting men, including Waya'ha into the center of the village. He then went to each dwelling to force everyone else outside. When Waya'ha saw Hugo Hickory heading for his house, he escaped from the captured and ran inside to find the captain aiming a pistol at his mother, who was still weaving the blanket. Waya'ha ran between them just as Hugo fired. He died on the dirt floor in his mother's arms.

"Hugo Hickory started to drag the mother outside when she pleaded with him to let her bury her son. Hugo agreed to allow her and some of the elderly to dig a grave, saying, 'We don't want him stinking up the woods after you're gone, so go ahead.' He told one of his soldiers, 'Watch them. I have more stubborn savages to round up.'

"Now the Cherokee had a tradition of burying their dead in the spot where they died, so that's just what she did. Once he was buried, she could still see her son's blood on the dirt floor, and she couldn't bear it, so she took the blanket she had been working on and covered the spot before leaving her house forevermore.

"The soldiers marched the Cherokee from the village, but a few, including Hugo Hickory, remained behind to round up those who had fled into the surrounding woods. That evening, the soldiers who stayed took shelter in the abandoned homes, and Hugo Hickory chose a house with a beautiful rug on the floor, thinking it would make a more comfortable bed than the dirt floor in the other houses. That night, as Hugo slept, a hand thrust up from the ground and into his back. Waya'ha's ghostly hand clutched Hugo's heart and pulled it from his body.

"As Hugo lay dying, he heard a voice say, 'I now hold the heart of your body, the heart of your spirit, and I will hide it along the path you've cursed my people to walk. As your spirit leaves your body, I curse you to forever wander this Trail of Tears, for you will never know peace until you find your dark heart. Until then you will bear witness to the suffering you have created, and every pain my people endure will in kind inflict your spirit.'

"Today Hugo Hickory still wanders the Trail, searching for his heart. However, his pain has so blinded him that he can no longer tell which heart is his, so he takes any dark heart he can find."

"He kills people?"

"He can kill anyone with a dark heart who steps foot on the Trail. And he has."

Jeff laughed. "Yes, there's been a rash of people with their hearts ripped out of their bodies all over Tennessee."

"He doesn't take their physical heart. He takes their spirit heart."

"Are you saying they die from unexplained heart attacks – like our two victims?"

"That's what made me think of the story."

"Hugo Hickory certainly deserved his fate. Cool story."

"Ah, but there's a twist. Waya'ha's spirit still walks the Trail too, in the form of a red coyote."

"Why red?"

"The color of the innocent blood that was shed when he was murdered. Now whenever Hugo Hickory gets close to finding his actual heart, Waya'ha takes it and hides it somewhere new, dragging his mother's blanket behind him to cover his tracks.

"Waya'ha has also become known as a trickster spirit. To keep living people from finding Hugo Hickory's heart and returning it to him, he scares them off when they get too close."

"Scares them off how?"

"He rustles the bushes, moves things as campers sleep, growls behind people and disappears before they turn around. Things like that."

"What constitutes a dark heart?"

"I'm not sure. That's what made the story scary to me as a kid. One of the Trail's starting points is right near where I grew up, and I didn't know if I had a dark heart."

Jeff whispered, "Me either. And here we are a few feet away from it." He dropped his arms to his side. "Did you lock up?"

Asleep on the sofa in Blair Geister's office, Virginia awoke from a dream immersed in the sensation of being watched. She sat upright and felt for her phone, charging on the nearby file cabinet. She turned on the phone's flashlight, and shuffled around the room, shining it behind every piece of furniture. After searching behind the desk, she relaxed and turned off the light. She was about to return to the couch, when she noticed the lightning bugs outside the window. She watched with a nostalgic smile, remembering how she danced among them when she was a child. One light in particular caught her eye, but it wasn't flying. It came from the part of the river by the boathouse, beneath the water's surface. "What is that?" The light continued to shimmer under the water for several minutes before she decided to investigate. After throwing on pants, a jacket and shoes, she opened the office door.

She was about to head down the stairs when she heard a clink behind her. She turned toward the source of the noise and crept down the hall to Blair Geister's bedroom, where Eden Geister had taken up residence. Virginia walked past the open door with just a glimpse inside in case Eden sat watching from the other side. The lamp from the end table was on, but it was lying on the floor beside the bed. *What happened?*

Virginia saw a pair of hands emerge from under the bed and grab the side frame. She gasped and covered her mouth, eyes as wide as they could go.

Eden pulled herself from under the bed, her back scooting against the floor.

Virginia hurried down the hall to avoid being seen. *What the hell was Eden doing?*

Descending the stairs, she made her way to the locutorium. She reached for the knob to one of the French doors, but stopped short of opening it. The light in the river had disappeared. "Huh. I wonder what it was."

CHAPTER 7

IN FULL UNIFORM, Sheriff Rome entered his kitchen with a mug in hand and found his wife pouring the last of the coffee into her own. Still in her robe, she stopped mid-pour. "Do you want any more coffee?"

"No, I need to get going." The sheriff placed his mug in the sink. "I'm driving to Knoxville this morning."

"What for?"

"I need answers, and the best place to start is the TBI." He grabbed his hat from the kitchen table.

Lula Mae took a quick sip of her coffee before emptying the mug into the sink. "Give me ten minutes to change."

"Why?"

"I'm off today. I can help."

"Lula Mae, I'm going to have enough trouble getting them to talk to me."

"And why wouldn't they talk to me?"

"You're not law enforcement."

"I'm a national park ranger, which means I'm technically a federal peace officer. I also carry a firearm, same as you."

"That doesn't give you any jurisdiction over the matter. It happened in my county."

"And within the boundaries of the Great Smoky Mountains National Park." Lula Mae patted the lapel of her robe. "My turf."

Sheriff Rome grinned. "You know, you should've been a lawyer."

Sheriff and Lula Mae Rome walked through the parking lot of the Tennessee Bureau of Investigation Knoxville Consolidated Facility. The sheriff opened the front door of the large brick building for his wife. "Hopefully, he's here and he'll agree to see us since we drove all this way."

"Who?"

"Emory's old partner." In the narrow lobby, he introduced himself to the man behind the counter. "Hello. I'm Sheriff Nick Rome, and this is Lula Mae… Park Ranger Lula Mae Rome, that is. We're here to see Wayne Buckwald."

"Do you have an appointment?" the clean-cut young man asked.

"No, but it's about a case I need his help on."

The man frowned but made a call. A moment later, a balding man in his forties entered the lobby. Wayne greeted the sheriff with a warm handshake. "Good to see you again, Sir."

"Good to see you, too. This is my wife, Lula Mae."

She shook his hand. "Nice to meet you."

"You too, ma'am. Sheriff, how's Deputy Harris doing?"

"Doing good. Engaged now. To someone he arrested a couple of months ago."

Wayne laughed. "Serious?"

"As a copperhead bite."

"What can I do for you?"

Lula Mae replied, "We need your help."

Wayne motioned them to the door. "Come on then. Let's talk at my desk."

They entered an auditorium-sized room rowed with desks of TBI special agents busy on phones or computers or talking to one another. Wayne led them to an empty desk in one of the last rows, next to a desk where a blond bear of a man was seated. "This is my new partner, Steve Linders. Steve, this is Sheriff Rome of Barter Ridge and his wife... Lily?"

"Lula Mae."

Wayne apologized and asked his partner to round up a couple of chairs. Once everyone was seated, he waited for someone to speak.

Hesitant to begin with an unexpected set of ears listening, Sheriff Rome tried to signal with his eyes that he'd rather talk in private, but Wayne seemed incapable of receiving or translating the message. After an uncomfortable pause and a glance of encouragement from his wife, he explained the reason for their visit. "I don't know if you're aware of what happened to Emory when he was a teenager."

Wayne snorted. "He never shared it with me, but I've since found out."

"What happened?" asked Steve.

"I'll tell you later. Not to be rude, Sheriff, but why exactly are you here?"

Sheriff Rome pulled two items from his shirt pocket and placed them on Wayne's desk. He placed his fingertips on the first item. "This bug—"

"I recognize this." Wayne picked up the listening device. "We use these. Did Emory take one when he was working here?"

Lula Mae jumped back in her chair. "Of course not!"

The sheriff glared at Wayne. "My son has never stolen anything in his life. As I was trying to tell you, he found that thing in his apartment."

Lula Mae clarified, "Placed there by someone else, in case that wasn't clear."

Steve chimed in with a question. "Who would want to spy on your son?"

"We're not sure." The sheriff moved to the other item he had placed on the desk. "But it might have something to do with this picture. That's Emory when he was a kid, before we adopted him. The last time he remembers seeing this picture is in his granny's house before it burned down. That was until someone slid it under his apartment door with that note scribbled on the back."

Steve said, "Someone could've just found it online and printed it."

The sheriff shook his head. "They were pretty poor. Emory never had a phone or computer until he came to live with us, and he's never had a social media account to post a picture on."

Wayne picked up the picture, turned it around and read it aloud. "'Who bears the iniquity of the son?' What's that supposed to mean?"

Steve took the picture from his partner. "It's likely a biblical reference. There are several verses about the son bearing the iniquity, or sins, of his father. The Bible actually goes back and forth, saying they do bear it and they don't, even within the Old Testament. I'm not aware of any verse that states the father bears the iniquity of his son, but that seems to be what the message on the back of the picture is implying."

The sheriff cleared his throat. "After the incident eight years ago, the TBI took possession of the evidence left behind, and I turned over all I had, which didn't include this picture. We figured Emory's biological father took it from the house before starting the fire and that it eventually ended up in the TBI's custody. The question is how did it find its way from TBI evidence to Emory's apartment and why was a bug commonly used by the TBI also planted there?"

Wayne took the photo and dropped it onto his desk. "And you

assume that there's some nefarious plot by the TBI, the agency that fired Emory, to set him up for some reason?"

"We never said it was a plot by the TBI, but we need you to tell us if that picture was ever here in evidence. If it was, then yes, I think someone here is out to get my son. If it wasn't, the only explanation I can think of is that one of Carl Grant's followers kept it all these years and has hatched some kind of revenge plot that involves taunting Emory and spying on him. Either way, we need your help to find whoever it is before he does anything more serious."

Wayne leaned back in his chair. "You know, on our last case together, your son lectured me about something called Acme's Razor."

Steve corrected him. "I think you mean Occam's Razor."

Wayne clenched a fist at his partner. "Don't you start!" He turned his attention back to the Romes. "The gist of it is the simplest explanation is almost always right. Now I'm thinking Emory took the bug and had the picture all along, and he's just making all this up to help in his lawsuit. You heard he's suing the TBI, right?"

"He dropped that!" said Lula Mae. "And Emory would never do something like that. He's a good man."

"Yeah, well maybe you don't know him as well as you think. No offense."

"I have to tell you, I do take offense to that," said Sheriff Rome. "And who are you to tell us we don't know our own son?"

Wayne smirked. "Do you know he's gay?"

Sheriff Rome took a second before replying. "Excuse me?"

Wayne tapped his desk with each word he repeated. "Emory. Is. Gay."

Her face frozen, Lula Mae made only a slight movement with her lips as she asked, "Why would you say that?"

"Because it's true. I caught him sucking face with that PI. The one he's working with now. I'm sorry. I thought you knew."

Sheriff Rome frowned at Wayne's smug expression. "No, I don't think you did."

From the back of the room, a woman with stern demeanor and bright red hair approached. "Hello." Her eyes dripped contempt over the sheriff and Lula Mae.

Wayne introduced her to them. "This is Eve Bachman, Special Agent in Charge."

Eve fixed her eyes on her subordinate. "Special Agent Buckwald, I assume this interview is related to the Curson case."

"Actually, no. This is Sheriff Rome and his wife, Lula Mae. We worked together on the Algarotti case a few months ago."

"Rome?" Eve glanced at the picture and listening device on Wayne's desk. "As in Emory Rome?"

"We're Emory's parents," said Lula Mae.

"My apologies," replied Eve, although unclear for what she was apologizing. "Special Agent Buckwald and Special Agent Linders, I'm certain I stressed the importance of the Curson case in our briefing this morning. Please schedule personal visits for hours past five."

"It's not a personal visit," said Sheriff Rome. "We came to ask for Agent Buckwald's help with a case."

"Special Agent Buckwald receives his case load directly from me. If you have a formal request for TBI assistance in a legal matter within your county—"

Sheriff Rome grabbed the picture and bug from Wayne's desk. "It was an informal request for help. Consider it withdrawn. Lula Mae, let's go."

CHAPTER 8

EMORY AWOKE IN Tommy Addison's bed, his eyes on Jesus. He wondered if the facilities manager had hung the framed print on the wall beside the bed to watch over him while he slept, although the subject's eyes were fixed upward as if nothing else mattered. Along with Jesus, the bone-colored walls held a foot-long wooden cross above the bed and a mounted TV on the opposite side but nothing more.

Emory slipped from under the sheets, sitting on the edge of the bed. He looked down at his white V-neck T-shirt and gray cotton pajama bottoms. *I'll shower after breakfast.* He picked up his phone, charging on the floor, and tapped it for the time. *I better go wake up Jeff so we can get an early start.* He made the bed, threw on clothes from the previous day and left for the guest room.

Once upstairs, he noticed an open door that had been closed when he passed it the night before. It led to a beautiful room with more artwork of Indigenous Peoples, as well as tapestries, and exquisite furnishings, including a large gold bed. He spotted fresh daffodils in an ornate blue vase on the nightstand. *The gardener's flowers?*

From somewhere in the room behind the open door, Eden

Geister appeared. She seemed as startled to see Emory as he was to see her.

"The peep show starts at noon! Come back then." Eden slammed the door in his face.

He shook his head and continued to the guest room to wake up Jeff, if the slamming door hadn't already accomplished that task. He knocked on the closed door to the guest room. No response. He opened the door, which clicked several times as he pushed it ajar. "Are you kidding me?!"

The guest room was everything Tommy Addison's room was not – spacious, cheerful and luxurious. The rich indigo walls with elegant fixtures rose to a coffered ceiling segregated into indigo panels by a wide lattice of oversized white-wood beams – like an elaborate board for tic-tac-toe with a few too many squares. The widest, most ornate end tables he had ever seen bookended a huge four-poster bed with disheveled satin blue sheets and a white duvet. *That son of a bitch. This is spectacular!*

Emory sauntered from the sleeping level to a sunken seating area with a small writing table, couch, coffee table and TV. The extra space and furnishings gave the room the feel of a five-star hotel suite. He noticed two doors on his left. He approached the open one and saw it was a huge walk-in closet with Jeff's unopened suitcase perched in the center. After kicking the suitcase, he continued to the closed door and knocked. Again, no response. He turned the handle and pushed it open, noticing that it also clicked, and he beheld an unoccupied bathroom the size of his living room – double-headed shower, two sinks and a privacy room for the commode.

He's already awake?

Emory descended the front stairs, and before he even reached the main floor, he smelled fresh pastry and heard muffled conversation coming from the kitchen. Approaching the kitchen doorway, he found Jeff in nothing more than boxer shorts, leaning against the island as he was hand-fed a piece of crusted pancake topped with blueberries.

The apron-shielded feeder asked, "What do you think?"

Jeff chewed a couple of times. "Delicious."

Emory stepped into the kitchen, brandishing a new scowl. "Don't mind me. I'm just getting coffee."

"Emory!" Jeff pushed off from the island. "This is Kenn Marty, Blair Geister's chef."

The short-statured strawberry blond with blue eyes sucked his own fingers clean. "Hello."

Emory gave him the slightest glance. "Morning."

"I'll show you where the coffee is." Jeff grabbed a pitcher of orange juice and put an arm around Emory to escort him from the kitchen. "Kenn is making breakfast. Wait 'til you try this… What's it called again?"

"Dutch baby," answered Kenn.

Jeff led Emory across the hall, to the dining room. "Let's go in here. Kenn said he'd serve us." He placed the pitcher of orange juice on a buffet, next to a stainless-steel carafe. "Here's the coffee."

Emory poured himself a cup of coffee. "Why are you in your boxers?"

Jeff withdrew three place settings from the buffet. "I came down to put on some coffee. I didn't know there was going to be anyone here. Well, I thought there was a chance Eden might be, and I figured I could get more information out of her with a little honey." He bounced his pecs a couple of times to demonstrate.

Emory pulled out a chair at a black locust table with seating for twenty-six. "I'm surprised there's a chef even working here now. He didn't come in just to cook for us, did he?"

"No, he's here for the reading of Blair Geister's will." Jeff placed a glass, a plate and silverware on the opposite side of the table.

"To cater it or because he's in it?"

He paused for a moment. "Huh. I don't know."

"Hadn't flirted your way around to that question yet?"

Jeff ignored the question. He put a plate and silverware in front of Emory and another set beside him. "Anyway, Kenn offered to cook breakfast for me... us."

Emory thought again of the TBI file on Jeff and decided to wade into a conversation on the matter. "How did you sleep last night?"

"Out like a light." Jeff sat across the table from Emory. "You?"

"Same. Although I did have a strange dream. I was back in my organic chemistry class at Vanderbilt."

"What's strange about that?"

Emory struggled to think up something. "I, uh... was naked."

Jeff leaned in. "I'm listening."

"That's all I remember."

Jeff backed into his chair. "Not much of a story there."

"Sorry. It seemed more interesting in my head." Emory offered a clumsy segue. "Did you take chemistry at UT?"

"Only what was required. I was always good at science, but it just didn't interest me. Kind of like you with math. Why are you asking?"

"I want to get to know you better. The best way to know someone is to learn more about their past."

Jeff let out a roar of a laugh. "Oh, that's hilarious coming from you. Indiana Jones couldn't uncover the secrets you've buried. You fill me in on your past, and I'll tell you mine."

Virginia strode into the dining room with a sigh of relief. "There you are."

Jeff waved his arms over the table. "Just in time for breakfast."

She took a seat next to Emory. "Did you guys see anything strange last night?"

Emory shook his head. "I don't think I stirred all night."

"Me neither," replied Jeff. "Not much of a haunted house, is it? Not so much as a *boo*."

"I saw something weird. Jeff, are you naked?"

"I have boxers on."

Kenn Marty entered, arms laden with three platters. "Breakfast is served." He placed the platters on the table, naming each as he did. "Here we have chard and Gruyère eggs in the hole. These are breakfast tacos." He smiled at Jeff. "And you've already sampled my Dutch baby."

Jeff returned his smile. "Everything looks wonderful."

"It does," said Virginia. "Thank you so much."

Sans smile or any other semblance of gratitude, Emory asked, "Mr. Marty, before you go, could we ask you some questions?"

"What about?"

"Blair Geister."

Kenn pinched his puffy lips into a downward arc. "I'm not sure what insight I can provide. I've been her chef for little over a year now, but I honestly didn't know her terribly well. She was usually on her phone or laptop during meals. When she did talk to me, it was just to plan menus for her parties."

Emory asked, "During these parties you worked, did you ever see her get into a disagreement with anyone?"

"At a party? Only one that I can think of – Myles Godfrey."

"The one who built the Godfrey Tower in Knoxville?" asked Virginia.

"That's the one."

Jeff told Kenn, "We had a case there not too long ago. What was the argument about?"

The chef sat next to Jeff. "You see, they're competitors, or they were. You all need to try the Gruyère before they get cold." He scooped one from the platter onto Jeff's plate.

Virginia held up her plate. "Did he crash the party?"

Kenn dropped the serving spoon without dishing any out for the others. "Oh no, he was invited. One thing about Blair – she was fearless. She invited friends to her parties, but she also invited people she despised and those who despised her. She felt the most stimulating social gatherings included voices from every ideology, and she could eloquently debate anyone."

Virginia placed her plate back on the table. "What was the argument about?"

"I didn't hear everything, but from what I gathered, she was accusing him of sabotaging her new building."

"The Monolith?" asked Emory.

"I thought they were going to actually come to blows, but then a couple of guests intervened and encouraged him to leave. That's really all I know." With that, Kenn stood and left the room.

Emory turned to Virginia. "Before he came in, you were saying you saw something weird."

"Right. Two things actually." Virginia looked over her shoulder and at the doorway before whispering, "Is Eden down here?"

"Haven't seen her." Jeff took a bite of the Gruyère. "Man, that's a good egg."

Emory glanced at the doorway before whispering to his partners, "I think she's sleeping with the gardener."

As Virginia gasped, Jeff laughed. "Seriously? How funny is that? He's tending the garden of Eden. Why do you think that?"

"I saw the flowers he cut yesterday now in a vase on her nightstand."

"That doesn't mean anything. Maybe she asked him to cut them for her."

"They weren't cut from the yard. They hadn't even been planted yet."

Virginia slapped the table. "Guys, could we get back to my news?"

Emory tsked. "Sorry."

"Last night I saw Eden crawling out from under the bed."

Jeff's head jerked back. "Your bed?"

"Blair Geister's bed."

Emory poked at his food with his fork. "What's unusual about that? Maybe something of hers rolled under there."

"She wasn't looking at the floor. She was on her back. It was weird."

Emory took a bite of the egg. "What's the second thing?"

"There was a strange light in the river last night." Virginia waited for a response. "For real."

"What kind of light?" Jeff shoved half a taco into his mouth. "Damn, this is *good*!"

"I couldn't make it out. It was near the boathouse."

Emory hummed. "It was almost a full moon last night. Could it have been a reflection on the water?"

Virginia stabbed the Dutch baby with her fork. "No, this was under the water."

Jeff gulped his orange juice. "Hey, how about we watch a movie in the theatre tonight?"

Virginia released her fork so it clinked against her plate. "Okay, change the subject. I'm coming to get you two the next time I see anything. I don't care if you're sleeping or… or whatever."

"Good plan," said Jeff, finishing his taco. "Do you know the time for the will reading?"

"It's at noon in the locutorium," replied Virginia. "Juniper texted me she's coming early to oversee preparations. She wants me to meet her outside and stay with her while she's in the house."

"Kenn told me they're going to have a little event with the beneficiaries before the will reading."

Virginia asked, "A wake?"

"I don't think anyone's going to be speaking. Kenn called it a commemoratory cocktail party – just one last party for her. Well, her ashes."

Emory was about to sip coffee when he heard Jeff's last remark. "She's been cremated already? Cathy just finished her autopsy yesterday afternoon."

"I guess so."

Emory placed his hands on the table to call for his partners' undivided attention. "We all need to be on high alert. Anyone in the will is an obvious suspect if Blair Geister's death proves to be murder, although that could be more difficult to prove now without the body."

"Are we even invited to the will reading?" Jeff asked. "Isn't that a private affair for the beneficiaries?"

Emory replied, "Our client is the estate executor, so I assume she can get us in."

"All right. We have that on our plate for today. Virginia, can you also find out why Blair hated her neighbor?"

"How do you know she did?"

Emory pulled out his phone to show her pictures he taken the day before. "She placed these along the fence, facing the neighbor's property."

Virginia winced at the pictures. "Ooh. They look like those Easter Island statues. I'll see what I can find. I also want to check out Blair's..." She stopped talking.

Dressed in a blue silk bathrobe with her hair wrapped in a golden scarf, Eden Geister entered the dining room. "Check out Blair's what?"

"Her client list," Virginia answered without hesitation. "Looking for anyone who might not have been happy with her work."

"Don't waste your time." Eden took a seat at the head of the table. "My cousin died of a heart attack. That's non-debatable." She took a slice of the Dutch baby. "Now the handyman. There's your mystery." She sneered at Jeff. "Would you go put some clothes on? You're a distraction."

"Fine," Jeff groaned. He scooted away from the table and left the room.

"I'm well aware of what Juniper said happened, but I think all of us here at this table know that's the babbling of an idiot. She's obviously trying to cover up some affair between her and the handyman."

Virginia asked, "What makes you think they were having an affair?"

"Are you kidding? She admitted he was in her bedroom at midnight." Eden pointed with her fork. "You two have seen her room, right? He was either watching TV, which makes no sense because he has the same TV in his own room, or he was burning down her she-shed. Excuse the euphemism. The hazards of teaching college students. Some of their vernacular inevitably seeps into your own."

Emory wiped the corners of his mouth with his napkin. "You seem to be awfully familiar with their rooms."

"I looked around. This house is mine now."

"You know the contents of the will?" Jeff asked as he returned fully clothed.

Eden watched him reclaim his seat. "Let's just say if her estate goes to anyone but her sole blood relation, someone's going to have a legal battle on their hands to right the wrong." She nodded at Jeff's shirt. "That's better."

CHAPTER 9

LOOKING INTO A full-length mirror in the guest room, Jeff fidgeted with the fit of a white dress shirt. "Don't get me wrong. There are rare occasions when I'm glad you're a boring dresser, so I can borrow from you for unexpected funerals. But for a little variety, maybe get some shirts that aren't fitted." Jeff turned around to show Emory the distorted placket of the shirt in the chest area. "I'm going to pop some buttons if I inhale too deeply."

Emory knotted a tie around his neck. "Then it's a good thing you're borrowing my tie too. It'll keep the buttons from flying across the room when you Hulk out."

Jeff tapped Emory on the chest. "You joke, but you won't be laughing if a button shoots the urn and spills Blair Geister's ashes all over the gathered. We're lucky I put off my workout to make coffee, or I'd have a crazy pump right now. Hey, have you seen the gym?"

Emory pulled the knotted tie over his head and slipped it over Jeff's. "Just a glance."

"It's the best home gym I've ever seen. Let's hit it after the will reading."

"Maybe a quick workout. We do need to figure out what happened with Tommy Addison and whether Blair Geister really did die of natural causes."

"And we will, but what's the hurry? We have no office right now, and this place is amazing. It's like a work vacation."

"For you maybe. You're in the luxury suite, while I'm in steerage."

"Speaking of work, we should get downstairs." Jeff opened the door for him. "After you."

The PIs descended the front stairs and stepped onto the main floor, in view of the locutorium. Emory followed Jeff into the magnificent room, where party staff were making final preparations for a commemoratory cocktail party and the will reading. The four golden sofas that had been positioned around the room were now lined in two rows of two sofas like church pews, facing a small table with a chair behind it. To the side of the table stood an easel with a framed photograph of Blair Geister and a marble pedestal displaying a glistening golden urn. In front of the set of French doors at the far end of the room, a table draped in black cloth supported an elegant spread of hors d'oeuvres, a bottle of French champagne on ice and half-filled flutes. Under the crystal chandelier in the middle of the room, a young woman in a formal black dress sat at the white grand piano, playing Dolly Parton's *Tennessee Homesick Blues*.

"Nice final resting place," said Jeff. "You think it's real gold?"

Emory glanced at the urn. "Probably."

Virginia and Juniper walked into the room behind them. Wearing a black dress with long sleeves, Juniper half-smiled at Emory and Jeff. "Virginia tells me you all would like to attend the will reading."

Emory responded, "If that's okay."

"I think it's fine. Just stay in back."

"Will do." Jeff set his eyes on the poster-sized picture next to the urn. "That's a great shot of her."

Juniper smiled at the upward perspective image of her former boss standing in front of a sparkling black skyscraper. "This was going to be the cover of next month's *Architectural Digest*. I don't know if that's happening now."

"Is that The Monolith?" asked Emory.

"It is. The building doesn't officially open for business until Monday, but we have the grand opening tomorrow evening. Actually, because of everything that's happened, it's been downgraded to an open house. You all are welcome to attend."

Jeff responded, "We'd love to."

Emory nodded and asked her, "How are you feeling?"

"I'm okay." Juniper fussed with her dress. "I don't like being here, and I have mixed feelings about Ms. Geister now, but I recognize that I have a job to do."

Jeff gestured toward the atrium. "I noticed the alarm panel by the front door. Was the alarm on the night they died?"

"Yes. I'm always the last to bed, and I always arm the system. I set off the alarm when I ran from the house that night."

Emory asked, "How many people have a key to the house and the code to the alarm?"

Juniper counted on her hand as she answered. "Besides Ms. Geister, Tommy and myself, there's Kenn Marty and Rebecca Gibbs, the maid. I can give you the code if you want to turn on the alarm while you're here."

Virginia shook her head. "That's okay."

"What about Miss Luann," asked Emory.

"Oh yes. I gave her a key. Not the alarm code, though."

Jeff smirked. "She's psychic. Let her guess it."

From the atrium appeared a man in a navy-blue suit. "Hello."

Juniper jumped but relaxed when she saw who it was. "Dr. Sharp. I didn't hear you come in."

"I apologize. The door was unlocked, so I let myself in." The six-foot man, whose thick silver hair belied his thirty-odd years of age, gave her a quick hug. "My condolences."

"Thank you." Juniper introduced him to the PIs. "This is Dr. Barry Sharp. He's a recipient of a research grant from Ms. Geister's EARTH Foundation."

The doctor cleared his throat. "Not yet. I'm still waiting for the funds to clear." His face flushed, as if he were embarrassed at voicing the clarification.

"Just a few more days." Juniper explained the holdup to the PIs. "EARTH grants are put into an escrow account for sixty days before the funds are released."

"What sort of research?" asked Jeff.

"I'm an environmental climatologist, and the grant is primarily to study the relationship between lightning and climate change."

"Oh." Emory's ears perked up. "Is there a link?"

"Absolutely. Models have shown that one-degree Celsius increase in global temperature can result in as much as twelve percent more lightning activity worldwide."

Emory noticed more people entering through the front door. "I know this isn't a good time, but I'd love to talk more about it."

"Why don't you come by my lab tomorrow, and I'll show you my research?" Dr. Sharp handed him a business card.

"I'd love that, but I don't know if I can tomorrow."

"I'm there from eight to five every day but Sunday, whenever you can make it."

Jeff took the business card from his partner. "We'll be there tomorrow."

"Great! Text me your full names today, so I can get you on the list of visitors. Security's tight at Oak Ridge."

Once the doctor walked away, Jeff sneered at Emory, "I thought you were going to have a nerd-gasm."

Emory snatched the card from Jeff's hand. "What are you talking about?"

"All anyone has to do is start spouting science, and you get all gaga. It doesn't even seem to matter which field of science."

Emory retorted with an unconvincing laugh. "That's not true." He noticed a distant look on their client's face and saw an opportunity to change the subject. "Ms. Crane, what is it?"

Juniper snapped back to the moment. "It's nothing. I was just reminded of the last phone conversation I had with Ms. Geister. She called me from Knoxville Friday evening, the night before she died, to tell me to schedule time on Monday with the escrow company. She wanted to extend Dr. Sharp's grant escrow by another thirty days."

"Why?"

"I don't know, but Dr. Sharp came by the house the next morning and waited around a couple of hours for her to arrive so he could talk to her."

Jeff asked, "Did you hear what they talked about?"

"They didn't. He got tired of waiting, and she didn't show up until nightfall." The doorbell chimed. "I need to get that." Juniper excused herself to answer the door, with Virginia at her side.

Jeff grinned at Emory. "Your silver fox has a secret."

Emory replied, "Will you stop with that. He's not *my* silver fox."

"Oh, but you do agree he's a silver fox."

Emory scoffed as they walked into the atrium. Juniper had finished greeting a couple of women, so he took the opportunity to ask her, "What is the EARTH Foundation?"

"EARTH stands for Environmental Advocacy, Research, Teaching & Healing. It's an endowment Ms. Geister established to oversee all her environmental initiatives, like research, rehabilitation of damaged property into wildlife preserves. Things of that nature. She put half her fortune into it."

Jeff's eyes popped wide open. "Half her fortune?!"

"You can tell from the house, she used to spend money on extravagances. The solid gold bed, the paintings. But she had an epiphany about ten years ago. I had only been her assistant for a couple of months, but I could tell she had lost her groove. She achieved all her goals, had no kids and just seemed... uninspired. I suggested she take a vacation to get away from it all and clear her head, and she thought it was a great idea. Actually, I thought she'd take me with her, but she decided she needed to be by herself. She spent two weeks hiking alone in Sedona. When she came back, she had this renewed focus to do whatever she could to heal the environment. The EARTH Foundation's grants are now the most coveted in the field. She's had scientists from all over the world apply for them – including some whose research is not remotely eligible, but they sure twist themselves into pretzels trying to offer even a tenuous link to environmental applications."

"How much are we talking about with these grants?" asked Jeff.

"The amounts vary."

"And how much is Dr. Sharp getting?"

"His grant is just shy of six million dollars, paid out in annual installments of about $500,000. Escrow is used for the first but not subsequent installments to avoid interruptions in research."

"Whoa!" Jeff elbowed Emory. "That could be a lot of motive."

Juniper looked puzzled. "Motive for what?"

"If it turns out your boss was murdered."

"But she died of a heart attack."

Emory replied, "Yes, but the medical examiner found an anomaly that's nagging at us. She had a busted eardrum, so someone could've injected something to induce the heart attack through the ear, thinking it wouldn't be noticed."

Juniper looked like she was about to respond, but another guest came through the front door and took her attention.

"Hey guys." Virginia waved her partners over to a corner. "I found out why Blair Geister had it out for her neighbor. Juniper told me earlier he's filed three lawsuits against her since she bought the place."

"Three?" asked Emory.

Virginia counted on her fingers. "One was about the boathouse. Another was about the big giant heads. The third was over gargoyles."

Jeff squinted at the last one. "Gargoyles? I haven't seen any gargoyles."

"Me neither," said Emory. "We need to talk to the neighbor."

Jeff waved a finger at him. "Remember, we have a date with the gym after this."

"I think interviewing a potential suspect takes precedence."

Virginia waved for silence. "Guys, you go to the gym, and I'll interview the neighbor."

"There's the plan!" Jeff wrapped an arm around them both and steered them toward the hors d'oeuvres and champagne flutes. "You know, I heard expensive champagne has smaller bubbles than the so-called champagne we're used to. Let's investigate."

Within half an hour, the locutorium was buzzing with the somber conversation of two dozen guests. The attorney had arrived and was unloading her briefcase on the makeshift desk positioned in front of the sofas.

Sipping from the champagne flute he had been nursing, Emory noticed the absence of one presumptive beneficiary. "Where's Eden?"

Jeff looked around the room. "Don't know. Haven't seen her."

Juniper announced to the crowd, "Ladies and gentlemen, we're going to get started with the reading of the will, if you'd care to take a seat."

"Look." Jeff hit Emory on the shoulder and pointed to Eden descending the front stairs. "As soon as the money bell rang."

The pianist stopped playing and left the room, while the guests either sat on one of the sofas or opted to stand nearby. At the back of the room, Juniper huddled with the PIs.

The thirty-something lawyer with blonde hair and a pinstripe pantsuit told the attendees, "Good afternoon everyone. I'm Jennifer Boone, and I'm the estate attorney for the decedent, Ms. Blair Louella Geister. This afternoon, we'll be going over her last will and testament, filed two months ago today. Ms. Geister appointed Ms. Juniper Crane as the executor of—"

The attorney stopped speaking and gasped when she saw someone new enter the room. One by one, the attendees turned around to see a six-foot-six man walking toward the desk. As he tramped up the aisle between the sofas, each guest elicited a reaction similar to the lawyer.

The man wore construction boots, white pants and a red long-sleeve shirt, but his face could not be seen. An olive vinyl mask with cotton lining shrouded everything from his curly black hairline down to the front half of his neck. It had holes for his eyes, but the openings for the nose and mouth were covered by flaps attached with snap buttons. The mask was held in place by straps that stretched around the back of the head from the jawline, temples and middle of his forehead.

Emory asked, "Who is that?"

While her wide eyes watched the man find a seat, Juniper whispered, "It's Zyus Drake!"

CHAPTER 10

"WHAT ON EARTH is he wearing?" asked Emory in reference to Zyus Drake's bizarre face-covering.

Virginia answered, "It's a military cold weather mask. I used one when I was stationed in Finland."

"Is he at war?" Jeff replied before snapping his fingers. "He's the man with the disappearing face!"

Juniper nodded, while Emory shushed Jeff out of the side of his mouth.

Zyus found a small opening on one of the front sofas, but he waited for the bookending people to scoot over before he plopped down.

Attorney Jennifer Boone regained her composure. "Ms. Geister left very specific instructions for the reading of her last will and testament."

"Of course, she did," Juniper said under her breath. "Ever the control freak."

The attorney produced from her briefcase a stack of gold sealed envelopes. "She wrote letters for each beneficiary to read aloud."

Jeff whispered, "They look like the envelopes used to announce the Oscar winners."

"Each beneficiary must read precisely what's written or forfeit their inheritance." Esq. Boone held up a folder. "I have a copy of all the text and will be following along as you read to ensure compliance to this stipulation. Any forfeiture will return to the estate." She pulled the first envelope. "We'll go alphabetically, beginning with Tommy Addison. Now, since he is deceased and unable to read his letter—"

"He has a son," blurted out Juniper. "Since Ms. Geister couldn't possibly have foreseen his death, his inheritance should go to his family."

Eden stood to object. "If he can't read the letter, he can't inherit! Whatever she bequeathed him should revert back to the estate."

Juniper waved off her suggestion. "As executor, it's within my purview—"

"How many times are you going to play the same card?" asked Eden.

Juniper asked the attorney, "Could we please continue?"

"Very well. Ms. Geister did afford the executor wide latitude in fulfilling the spirit of her wishes. Mr. Addison's bequeathal will go to his son. For the benefit of all here, I will let you know that it's $250,000 in cash." She picked up the next envelope. "Juniper Crane."

Juniper walked up the aisle between the sofas to the desk and took the envelope from the attorney. "Do I just read it from here?"

"I think that's fine."

Juniper broke the seal on the letter and began reading in a voice just above a whisper. "I, Juniper Crane, have worked for Blair Geister—"

"Louder," said Eden, although she was seated not ten feet from her. "We can't hear you."

Juniper frowned at Eden before starting over in an elevated voice. "I, Juniper Crane, have worked for Blair Geister for more than a decade. In that time, I have shown myself to be an invaluable assistant and a..." She paused to wipe her eyes. "...and a trusted friend. In recognition of my service and aptitude, I will receive one million dollars in cash—" An audible gasp from Eden interrupted her. "I will also take over as the president and CEO of the nonprofit EARTH Foundation."

"Unbelievable!" Eden said in obvious disgust.

"I understand that I'm being entrusted with implementing the vision and maintaining the mission of the foundation and its founder. I will devote myself to this role until such time I am ready to step down and a worthy successor is found." Juniper looked up from the letter and stared at the back of the room as if she didn't want to make eye contact with anyone.

"I wonder if she knew," Jeff whispered to his partners.

"No way," replied Virginia. "She's clearly stunned."

Juniper continued reading. "Finally, I will take Ms. Geister's ashes to Sedona to spread them in Boynton Canyon, so she can be at peace in the place that renewed her spirit." She glanced at the urn and muttered as if no one else were in the room, "So she can be at peace." Juniper attempted to hand the envelope back to the attorney, but Esq. Boone told her it was hers to keep.

Juniper clutched it at her side and returned to the PIs. "This is insane," she whispered. "Why would she give me control of her foundation."

Emory answered, "She trusted you."

"I didn't deserve her trust. At least now I know what I have to do to put her spirit to rest."

"You're going to Sedona?" Virginia asked.

"On the first plane I can get."

The attorney called out the next name. "Zyus Drake."

Accompanied by muffled chatter, Zyus pushed off the sofa and approached the attorney. He wasted no time in opening the envelope and reading the text in a baritone voice. "I, Zyus Drake, was never a friend to Blair. I just liked to play games with her because I knew what she wanted, and I took full advantage of it."

Jeff whispered to Emory, "I wish he'd take that mask off," prompting an elbow in the ribs from his partner. "What? Like you're not curious?"

"After the..." Zyus took a breath. "...*incident*, I blamed her. I sought retribution by suing her, and I dictated embarrassing details into court records. My actions put her on the defensive. I didn't take into account her feelings and that maybe she felt overwhelming guilt for what had happened to me – whether it was her fault or an act of cruelty by Fate. Now my future is once again left to Fate. Since I so enjoy games, Blair has created one especially for me. She bequeaths to me the Pangram Box and all its contents if I can find it within 114 hours of right now."

Esq. Boone looked at her watch and announced, "The time is 1:20 p.m."

Zyus continued reading. "The Pangram Box is to be turned over to Esq. Jennifer Boone with the seal intact so that she may open it to reveal its contents. Furthermore, if I do find it in time, Blair accepts some fault for the incident, and this inheritance is to be considered her penance. If Blair had no fault, I won't find it in time, and the Pangram Box and all its contents will revert to the estate. I am to be given a key to the house and free reign to search, but I must under no circumstances damage the house or property in my search, or I forfeit any claims."

"You have until 7:20 a.m. next Monday to find the Pangram Box." The attorney handed him a tiny manila envelope. "Here's a key to the house."

After pocketing the key, Zyus crumpled the letter and dropped it as he marched from the room and out of the house.

Jeff whispered a question to his partners and Juniper. "What the hell is a Pangram Box, and why 114 hours?"

Juniper shook her head. "I don't have a clue."

Emory told them, "A pangram is a sentence that uses all the letters of the alphabet like *Jackdaws love my big sphinx of quartz.*"

Jeff shot him a confused look. "What did you just say?"

"It's one of the shortest English sentences that uses all the letters."

Virginia asked, "How do you even know that?"

"I like puzzles. And word trivia."

Jeff chuckled. "You really are a nerd."

The attorney pulled the next envelope. "Eden Geister."

Eden sauntered to the desk, took her envelope and slit the seal with her pink thumbnail. She scanned the text before reading it aloud.

Juniper grinned and pulled out her phone. "This should be good. I have to record it."

Eden took a breath to begin reading but stopped when she saw Juniper. "Seriously?" She turned to the attorney. "I'm not going to read this until she puts that camera away."

Juniper told her, "You don't read, you don't inherit."

Eden shook her head and read like an auctioneer who was about to pee her pants. "I, Eden Geister, am the last living relative of my *beloved* cousin Blair Geister. In spite of having demonstrated a clear propensity to fluid morality in financial matters, my generous cousin is bequeathing me the sum of one million dollars in cash. Hopefully, I will use this money to better myself and one day pay it forward to someone far more deserving, who shouldn't be difficult to find. Until then, I hope I have enough sense to reflect on my life and my more dubious choices, so that I may repair the damage I have inflicted on my family name."

As soon as she finished reading, Eden ripped the letter to shreds. She grabbed the urn and lifted it above her head. "Record this!" She hurled it at Juniper.

Jeff intercepted the flying urn but couldn't lock his fingers onto the slippery gold surface. The urn clanged to floor, knocking off the top.

The attendees gasped, either at Eden's startling act or in

dreaded anticipation of Blair Geister's ashes dispersing throughout the room, but not a single ash left the urn.

Jeff picked it up and looked inside. "It's empty."

Juniper took possession of the urn and returned it to its perch. "Her ashes haven't been delivered yet. Thankfully."

On the verge of hyperventilating, Eden smoothed out her dress and reclaimed her spot on the sofa.

As if in reprieve to the unexpected excitement, the next few beneficiaries offered little drama, since they were mostly representatives of various charitable organizations – except for the chef and maid, who each received $250,000.

Jeff said to Juniper, "Looks like everyone who worked here at the house is getting a quarter of a million. Everyone but you."

Emory nodded to one of the locutorium's windows, through which a man in a safari hat could be seen working on the flower bed by the pool. "Not the gardener."

Juniper told them, "George Henry has only been here about a month."

Jeff clicked his tongue. "Sucks for him."

The attorney reached for the last envelope. "Finally, Dr. Barry Sharp."

Dr. Sharp approached the desk and read his letter. "I, Dr. Barry Sharp, an environmental studies professor at the University of Tennessee, have already been awarded a grant for my research from the EARTH Foundation. In addition to this, Blair Geister asks me to announce and oversee the establishment of the Geister University Environmental Studies Scholarship Fund at the University of Tennessee, Knoxville. The GUESS Fund will pay the complete tuition of every student currently enrolled in environmental studies who goes on to graduate in that major. It will also pay for the tuition of up to fifty students in that field of study every year." Dr. Sharp finished reading. "That is most generous, and I can't wait to announce it." He looked at the urn. "Thank you, Blair."

As the professor took his seat, Esq. Boone said, "That's it for the envelopes—"

"Wait a minute!" Eden popped off the sofa. "Wait a minute! What about the house? What about the mine? What about all the buildings she owned?!"

The attorney flipped a page in her folder. "I was getting to the house. She left this part for me to announce." The attorney read from the will. "My house and all items within it – apart from the contents of the Pangram Box – shall remain in trust for one year while the property is converted to the Tennessee Museum of Indigenous Peoples Art. The trust is endowed with enough money for the conversion and to run the museum for fifty years. In addition to the art pieces already on display, I have a large collection in storage that shall be moved to the house. I have left architectural plans for the conversion with my attorney, and I entrust Juniper Crane to oversee it. Once converted, the house and property will be donated to McMinn County with all proceeds going to public schools in the county." The attorney looked up at the attendees to say, "And that's it for now."

"That's it?" asked Eden. "What about the mine and all her buildings?"

"Any asset not specifically mentioned in the will or contained within the Pangram Box would fall under the residuary clause, wherein everything remaining would go to a specified beneficiary or beneficiaries."

"Then read it to us," insisted Eden.

"I can't do that for another 114 hours. There are items in the Pangram Box that would impact it, based on whether or not Mr. Drake finds it in time. If he finds it before the deadline, he is to present it to me before the reading of the residuary clause, which will occur here immediately following the deadline. Whatever is in the Box will be signed over to Mr. Drake, should he succeed."

Eden threw up her hands. "What's in the Box?"

Esq. Boone replied, "She didn't tell me."

"Who are the residuary beneficiaries?" Eden asked.

The attorney closed her folder. "I can't divulge that until the appropriate time has elapsed."

"What you're telling us is Blair's entire fortune – deeds and all – is in this hidden Box, and she gave it all to that freak!" Eden punctuated the last word with an angry point to the front door.

"That's not what I'm saying. Again, I don't know what's in the Pangram Box. It could contain absolutely nothing. She did say it was a game. On the other hand, it could contain ownership rights to part or all of Blair Geister's assets that were not specifically bequeathed to someone in her will today. What is certain is that if Mr. Drake finds the Box in time, everything in it is his, and then all remaining assets would go to the beneficiary or beneficiaries listed in the residuary clause."

Juniper asked, "And if he doesn't find it?"

"Anything not specifically mentioned today, including the unclaimed items in the Pangram Box, would be covered by the residuary clause and therefore go to the beneficiary or beneficiaries listed within."

As Eden stormed from the room, Jeff turned to Juniper and asked, "Who is Zyus Drake?"

CHAPTER 11

WEARING A WHITE rolled-up ski mask as a beanie, Phineas stared at the Mourning Dove Investigations office from across the street. He glanced down at the phone in his hand to see the time of 11:30 a.m. He watched as construction workers piled out of the building and into two utility trucks. Once the trucks left, the athletic young man with a guitar case strapped to his back brushed aside drooping tousles of black hair and crossed the street.

A sign posted on the front door of the office stated, "Accepting appointments offsite during construction. Please call…"

He tried the doorknob and found it unlocked. He stepped inside, closing the door behind him, and he scanned the reception area to ensure the place was empty. All the furnishings were covered in clear plastic. On his right, he saw the bookshelf door to Jeff's office was open, as was the hidden door to the spiral staircases that led to the upstairs apartment and the basement. To his left he saw a new doorway cut into the wall, leading to what would be Emory's office, and he walked through it.

At the moment, the new office was nothing more than a large rectangular room with what looked to be a bathroom in back. Most of the wall space was open, exposing brick, two-by-fours and wiring, but a few panels of drywall had been screwed into place.

Wood, sawhorses, copper pipes and tools were littered about, and a stack of drywall leaned against one wall.

Phineas placed his guitar case on the unfinished hardwood floor and opened it to reveal no musical instrument. Instead, the case held a thirty-inch bronze cross on a stand. He grunted as he pulled it out and stood it up.

"It's hot in here." Phineas pulled the beanie from his head and flicked it into the guitar case. "Let's get this done."

Phineas picked up the cross and shuffled over to an exposed area of the brick wall, placing the cross in the open space. He retrieved a sheet of drywall from the stack and covered the open area with the cross now inside. He drove a couple of nails through the drywall into the studs to keep it in place before grabbing the drill to finish the job with screws. At five-foot-ten, he couldn't reach the top of the panel, so he slid a toolbox over to stand on.

He had no sooner put the drill down than he heard a voice from behind. "I thought you all went to lunch. I just finished in the basement."

Without turning to face him, Phineas reached for the beanie in his guitar case. "I'm not with the crew."

"Then you can't be in here. This office is closed."

Phineas put the beanie on and unrolled it over his head. "I was just checking it out."

"You're here for the copper, aren't you?"

Phineas glanced at the copper pipes on the floor to his left. He could hear the man place something on the floor that sounded like a toolbox.

"You should just turn around now and go on home," said the man.

Phineas did turn around, revealing the face of his ski mask with its red-circled eyes and hideous, jagged grin that zigzagged from ear to ear.

A thick pipe wrench in his hand, the robust man jerked back

with a muffled gasp when he saw the mask. His soiled blue-striped shirt read, "Knoxville Plumbing."

The plumber was almost twice his size, but Phineas approached him with the confidence of a serpent cornering a hobbled mouse.

The plumber raised the wrench and warned, "Don't do it."

Phineas skipped the final two steps to pounce forward. He swiped the wrench before the plumber could react, swooped down and swung it to the back of his knees.

As the plumber's legs buckled, Phineas tossed the wrench. He drop-kicked the back of the plumber's head, sending him bowing forward until his forehead bounced off the floor.

Phineas walked on the panting man's back to retrieve his guitar case. He snapped the case shut and headed to the door.

The plumber pushed himself back to his knees and lunged his body at the intruder in an apparent move to tackle his legs.

Phineas sidestepped his vascular hands, held the guitar case like a thick bat and swung at the man's head. Still conscious, the plumber stayed on the floor until Phineas left the room.

Once outside, Phineas zoomed around a couple of corners before looking behind him to ensure he hadn't been followed. Satisfied, he removed the mask and made a call on his cell phone as he slowed to a normal pace. "It's me," he said on the phone. "Calvary is prepared."

CHAPTER 12

FROM A FRENCH door in the locutorium, Emory stared at the boathouse. He could see the top of the waterwheel on its far side as it rotated with the river's rapid current. He lowered his eyes to the pool by the house and noticed the table umbrellas were now all in place. Reflected in one of the French door panes, he watched Juniper usher Esq. Jennifer Boone – the only remaining guest – to the front door. Emory turned from the door and saw his partners stepping away from the hors d'oeuvres table.

Jeff waved to the piano. "Hey, why don't you play something?"

Virginia scooted onto the piano bench. "What do you want me to play?"

"The *Halloween* theme."

She scoffed. "You always ask for that." As she began to play, Emory came to the piano to listen alongside Jeff. When Juniper followed a moment later, Virginia stopped playing. "Sorry."

Juniper brushed aside her concern. "Please. I told you to make yourself at home. I'm heading back to Knoxville."

Emory asked, "Will you be back tomorrow?"

"Not here, but I'll see you at The Monolith. The ashes should be ready now, so I'll take them to Arizona tonight and fly back in the morning. Will you all be okay until I return?"

"Of course," replied Virginia. "And we have your number in case anything comes up."

Jeff scanned the room. "Is Eden around?"

Juniper grabbed the golden urn. "She went to sulk, but not before telling me that if she isn't listed as a beneficiary in the residuary clause to receive at least one building, she plans to contest the will. And she's not moving out until the matter is settled."

Jeff pointed at their host. "Now that everyone is gone, you need to answer my question. Who is Zyus Drake?"

Juniper scrunched her face into an angry frown. "I told you I'm not at liberty to discuss the matter."

As Jeff sighed in frustration, Emory asked, "Did you know what was in the will?"

Juniper threw a hand to her chest. "I had no idea."

"But you seemed to know what was going to happen with Eden."

"Oh, that. I know how Ms. Geister felt about her cousin, and I figured she was going to take the opportunity to zing her."

"What's with the bad blood?" asked Virginia.

"From the moment I met her, Eden has treated me like a servant. At first, I took it because she was Ms. Geister's relative, but Ms. Geister's the one who told me to speak up for myself and not to let Eden get away with it. I did, and we've been fighting ever since."

Virginia said, "Actually, I meant what's with the bad blood between the cousins."

"I don't know where that began. As long as I'd known Ms. Geister, I think she'd seen Eden maybe two dozen times. They always treated each other like family – bickering at times and chummy at others. It did get really bad a few months ago, when Eden was turned down for an EARTH Foundation grant. She did not take it well."

Emory asked, "She's a researcher?"

"A microbiology professor."

"Why was it turned down?"

"Ms. Geister never told me, but my guess was she didn't want any semblance of nepotism within her foundation. She saw it as her legacy and wouldn't risk tarnishing its name."

"What else can you tell us about Eden?" Emory pulled out his phone to type notes.

"Let's see." Juniper set the urn on the piano. "Her father was the brother of Blair's mother. They grew up together here in Calhoun. She married some rodeo bull-rider when she was in her twenties, but it didn't last long, and she retook her maiden name. By that time, Ms. Geister was already making a name for herself in the construction industry."

Emory asked, "What do you know of the Pangram Box?"

"Nothing. That was the first I'd heard of it." Juniper shuddered. "Honestly, I hope Zyus Drake doesn't find it, whatever it is. I'd rather everything go to the beneficiaries of that residuary clause."

"Hold up," said Jeff. "Do you know who the beneficiaries are?"

"No, but it has to be better than Zyus. I'd be happier if I never hear that name again."

Emory asked, "What if the residuary clause awards everything to Eden?"

Juniper thought for a moment. "I don't believe Ms. Geister would do that. Perhaps she was right that it's better for us to leave it to Fate. I should get on the road. Call or text me if you need anything." Urn in hand, she walked out the front door.

Jeff smirked at Emory. "But we're not going to leave it to Fate, are we?"

Emory replied, "No, we're not."

With four plates loaded on each side, Jeff positioned his traps under the middle of the barbell and lifted it from the squat rack.

Spotting him, Emory kept his forearms beneath Jeff's lats and mimicked his motion while they discussed the case. "Why 114? That's such an odd choice. It's not quite a week. It works out to just over six-and-a-half days. There must be some significance to it. Maybe it's a clue to the location of the Pangram Box."

Jeff put the bar back on the rack after a few reps. "You know, it's a little difficult to concentrate on squatting when you're whispering case notes in my ear."

Emory stepped to the right to take off a couple of plates. "I'm sorry. It's just—"

"You can't encounter a puzzle without trying to solve it." Jeff removed two plates from the left side of the bar. "Leave this one alone. It's not meant for you. It's for Zyus Drake. We have enough on our plate trying to figure out if and how two people were murdered in this house." He tapped the barbell. "You're up."

Emory began his squats with Jeff spotting him, but he paused after a single rep. "You're right. We shouldn't interfere with a potential beneficiary and the contingency placed on his inheritance. What would we do if we found it? Put it back so he could find it on his own?"

"Exactly. Keep squatting. Remember, our client is Juniper Crane, and she told us she'd rather everything in that Pangram Box go to the residuary beneficiaries."

"That's another thing." Emory put the bar back on the rack, and looked at Jeff in the mirror mounted on the wall. "The attorney must know the location of the Box, right? Surely Blair Geister wouldn't take a chance on it never being found."

"Maybe." Jeff cupped Emory's shoulders, both men looking in the mirror. "We still haven't toured the whole house. How about we look for the Pangram Box as we do, keep it where it is—"

Emory turned around and faced Jeff. "How is it you get me so well?"

Jeff kept himself from smiling, even as he could see Emory's brown eyes trying to lock on his. "Leg press."

"What?"

"Next is leg press." Jeff led him to the machine. "You sure don't make it easy."

"Working out?" Emory added plates to the leg press.

Jeff sat in the machine. "Figuring you out."

"What do you mean? I'm an open book."

Jeff laughed. "Sure, you are. One that snaps shut on your nose as soon as you start reading it."

"I don't think I'm that bad."

Jeff started his set. "What are we doing?"

"Legs."

"No, I mean you and me. There are times I feel like we're getting close, but most of the time, I sense you blocking me."

"I'm sorry." Emory turned his focus to the floor. "I don't mean to."

Jeff stepped out of the machine and lifted Emory's chin, forcing eye contact. "Then why do it? We work together. We have fun together."

"I put myself out there for someone once, and it didn't go well."

"In college?"

Emory took Jeff's place in the leg press. "Before that."

"What happened?"

"I almost died, but I don't want to go into it." Emory started his set.

"Of course, because that would be telling me something about you."

"You're one to talk."

"Are you kidding?!" Jeff scowled and opened his arms. "I actually am an open book. Thumb through at will."

"Are you though?" Emory jumped up after three reps.

"What do you mean by that?"

"Just that I don't know everything about you I'd need to before—"

Jeff tapped on Emory's chest with his index finger. "No, you meant something specific. What is it?"

"Seriously, nothing."

Jeff sighed. "It's like seeking warmth from a snow blanket."

"I'm not cold. I'm just cautious."

"You're too damn cautious!"

"You're not cautious enough!"

"Just tell me what you meant."

Emory blurted out, "I don't trust you!"

Jeff caught his breath, shook his head and side-eyed him. "And there it is."

"I'm sorry."

"It's okay." Jeff headed for the door. "I'm done. And you can trust me on that."

Virginia knocked on the rustic mahogany door and waited for Edgar Strand to respond. She glanced at Blair Geister's property to look for the Easter Island heads, but when she couldn't spot them, she figured they must be further down the wrought iron fence line, toward the river. She noticed one side of Geisterhaus was just a few feet from the fence, and she was about to check the roof for gargoyles when she heard a sound coming from the door. She muffled a gasp but couldn't keep her shoulders from jumping when the unpleasant face of a middle-aged man with thinning black hair and brown eyes popped into the peephole window. "Edgar Strand?"

"That's right," he rasped in the voice of a heavy smoker. "Who are you?"

"I'm Virginia Kennon, private investigator. May I talk to you about your neighbor, Blair Geister?"

Edgar shut the peephole and opened the door. "I don't know how much help I'll be, but come in."

Virginia scanned the interior as he led her to a large living room with picture windows overlooking an immaculate and extensive lawn stretching to the riverbank. The house's décor could not have been more different from the neighboring house – framed pictures in place of artwork, mismatched furnishings representing every decade from the past half-century and beige carpeting instead of tile or hardwood floors.

Virginia plastered on a smile. "You have a lovely home. Do you live here alone?"

"My wife and I are separated for the moment, and the kids are in college."

"What do you do for a living, if you don't mind my asking?"

"I own a business that builds, inspects and repairs water towers." Edgar waved her to the off-white couch as he sat in a black recliner. "Have a seat."

"Thank you." Virginia sat and continued looking around as if admiring her surroundings when she was in fact searching for any clues about her host. She saw pictures on a lace-covered table shoved against one wall for no apparent reason, and one in particular caught her attention – a photo of Edgar with two other men standing in the foreground of a water tower with the city of Calhoun's name painted on it. "Your house reminds me of Blair Geister's."

"Mine's a few years older."

"Do your lights sometimes flicker too?"

"Of course not. Are they LED lights on a dimmer?"

"I'm not sure."

"Check to see. It could be that the dimmer switch isn't compatible with the bulb."

"I'll check." Virginia laughed. "Good to know it's not a ghost. Speaking of which—"

Edgar cut her off. "Before you go asking me questions, you need to know my view of the dearly departed is tainted by the fact that I couldn't stand her."

"Why is that?"

"She was the *worst* neighbor you could possibly imagine. We tried to be neighborly when she first moved in. We introduced ourselves, took over a nice casserole and even gave her a beautiful white-leather family Bible as a house-warming gift. You think she appreciated it?"

"I'm guessing no."

"She could not get us out of her house fast enough, like we were unwelcome. Then she started building that monstrosity out there on the water."

"The boathouse. I understand you were suing her over that."

Edgar shook his head. "Your information is outdated. The rigged courts decided against me. No justice in this world."

"I wasn't aware. What was the boathouse suit about specifically?"

Edgar pointed in the direction of the water. "There was a normal-sized dock when she bought the place, and then she built it out all the way to the middle of the river and put all that machinery in it."

"I actually know a little something about riparian rights from another case I worked on. Doesn't a property's rights to an adjacent river extend to the middle of the water."

"Not if it impedes other people's use of it!" Edgar's face burst from pasty to red. "I'm telling you, she must've bribed the Army Corps of Engineers to approve the permit."

"I apologize. I didn't mean to upset you."

Edgar didn't acknowledge her apology, instead continuing with his rant. "After that, she was at it again, putting up those giant pagan idols all along my fence. Can't even enjoy the river anymore

CHAPTER 13

EMORY AND JEFF stood in the lower-level hallway before a door that was different from the others they'd encountered at Geisterhaus. The warm chestnut surface held a speakeasy window with an iron grill. Emory turned the bronze lever doorknob and pushed it open. He felt a slight change in pressure and drop in temperature as he stepped inside the wine cellar. He flipped on the light switch. "I feel like we just walked into one of your dreams."

"Uh-huh," Jeff replied.

Emory's eyes wandered the room, starting at the iron chandelier hanging from the white batten ceiling above the thick chestnut table with six chairs and moving to the more than one hundred wine racks attached to walls of white stone tile that continued across the floor. "Hey, I have an idea. We could convert the new basement space at the office into a wine cellar. You'd love that."

"Would I?" asked Jeff.

"I know how much you love wine."

"Do I?" Jeff ran his hand over some of the bottles. "Or is that just something I said?"

Emory was about to respond when a painting at the far end of the room caught his attention. "Holy crap!" As he approached it, he saw an emaciated man in a nineteenth-century American military uniform on a dirt trail surrounded by cedar trees. He had a long, bleak face with vacant eyes and a red-dripping hole where his heart should have been. Hiding in the shadows was a red coyote with a heart in his mouth. "It's Hugo Hickory." Emory pointed to an object beside the coyote that was painted red, blue, white and black. "There's Waya'ha's blanket in the four sacred colors. I never knew there was a painting of the story."

Jeff hummed with disinterest and a passing glance at the painting.

"Okay. Well, I think it's cool." Emory had hoped for more than a tepid response at his discovery, but he shrugged it off and snapped a few pictures with his phone. "Do you see anything else of interest here or any sign of the Pangram Box?"

Jeff crouched to look under the table. "No, but you can't take my word for it."

Emory sighed and shook his head. "Can't we put our feelings aside and be professional about this?"

Jeff gave the room a final scan. "I'm sorry, Mr. Spock, but that's an area in which I don't excel. That and trustworthiness."

"Let's move on." Emory left the cellar with Jeff and continued down the hall to the next door, which stood ajar. "Bathroom. I didn't see bathrooms in Juniper's or Tommy's rooms. They must've shared this one."

"How communal." Jeff headed to the next door. "Ah, here we have your basic little supply closet."

Emory walked into the room past his partner. "I can't believe this."

"Right? She has her own 7-Eleven right here."

Emory walked along seven aisles between shelves stocked with food and other supplies. "This is bigger than my apartment."

"Apparently, Blair Geister did not like to run out of things." Jeff grabbed a bag from one of the shelves. "Veggie chips. I'll try them." He ripped open the bag and ate a chip. "Not bad."

Emory patted a stack of sheets on a shelf devoted to bedding. "I could've used these last night." Something leaned against the wall caught his attention. "Blair's mattress." Not seeing the silhouette stain, he tilted it away from the wall to check the other side. "There's the stain."

"Did you think it disappeared?"

"Just making sure it's the right mattress." Emory reached for the bag of veggie chips. "Can I try one?"

Jeff blocked the bag with his body. "After touching that mattress? No, you need to wash your hands first."

"I barely touched it."

"You know where the bathroom is."

"Fine." Emory left the supply closet and washed his hands in the bathroom. He met his partner outside the only other room on the lower level they had yet to explore. Jeff extended the bag of chips, but Emory didn't take one. "I changed my mind." Instead, Emory reached for the knob, opening the door to darkness. He ran his hand along the wall until he felt the dimmer switch to turn on the overhead lights. "Oh, you're going to like this."

Jeff stepped in front of him onto a narrow walkway above a set of stairs, and his mouth gaped open as he took in the massive room.

Black quilted padding covered the ceiling and walls of the large rectangular space, except for the far wall, which held a screen at least nine-feet high and sixteen-feet wide. The room had four rows of seats with five reclining chairs in the front, with each subsequent row having an additional chair from the row before it.

Jeff's demeanor seemed to tick up a degree at the sight. He said, almost to himself, "*This* is what we should do with the office basement. A movie theatre."

"I don't think the ceiling in our basement is high enough."

"We could lower the floor like Blair Geister did with this room."

Emory pointed to a black door at the other end of the walkway. "Where does that door lead?"

"Probably the projection room."

Emory opened the door and found a digital projector, sound equipment and a computer monitor for selecting movies. "You're right."

Jeff descended the eight steps to the inclined, red-carpeted floor and stepped into the aisle at the left of the chairs. "We have to watch a movie here." He tilted his chin toward a muted red *Exit* sign above a door to the right of the screen. "Look, it even has an emergency exit. What row are you?"

Emory followed him down the stairs. "What do you mean?"

"When you go to a movie, where do you sit? I like to sit as close to the front as possible." He hurried to the front row and plopped down in the middle chair.

"I'm more of middle-row guy." Emory took the seat next to his partner. "This is too close for me. I don't want to have to look up to see a movie."

"You have to recline the chair." Jeff pressed a button on his chair and it almost flattened. "See. Now I just look straight ahead to see what's playing on the screen."

"This is incredible!" Emory heard from behind. He turned around to see Virginia descending the stairs. "It must be great to have all the money in the world."

Jeff waved to the chair on his right. "Sit with us. Did you talk to the neighbor? What's his name again?"

Virginia joined them in the front row and reclined her chair. "Edgar Strand. Yes, and now I know why Juniper is so worried that her former boss' ghost is out to get her. For all the good Blair Geister did, she was also *very* vindictive."

Emory kept his chair upright so he could face his partners. "How so?"

"Edgar Strand initially sued her about the boathouse, claiming it impeded common use of the river. Even though Blair won the suit, she got back at him by putting those big head statues along the fence and some really grotesque gargoyles on the roof, facing right into his office windows."

Jeff cupped his hands behind his head. "Do you think Edgar was angry enough to kill her?"

"That'd be a definite *yes*." Virginia returned her chair to upright. "It's getting late. I'm going to throw something together for dinner."

As she passed in front of him, Emory said, "I can help with the cooking."

"That's okay." Virginia put out her hands like she was picking up vibes. "I sense you two have something to work out. Whatever it is, don't bring it to the dinner table."

Once Virginia left, Jeff popped out of his chair and glanced around the room. "Let's move on."

Emory sighed in relief and stood before his partner. "Good. I really am sorry."

"I meant to the next floor."

"Oh. I think there are three or four rooms on the other two levels we haven't seen yet, including Blair's bedroom."

"We can forget about that one until Eden decides to leave the house."

Emory headed for the stairs. "I haven't seen her leave the house yet. Doesn't she work?"

"Bereavement leave, I'd imagine."

The PIs left the theatre and ascended the front stairs to the main level hallway. Emory tried the first door on the right, across from the locutorium, and found it to be a bathroom. Jeff opened the door a few feet away on the other side. "Nice!"

"What is it?"

"A library."

Emory followed Jeff inside to see a spectacular room with expansive, floor-to-ceiling bookshelves recessed into each rust-colored wall. The shelves were full of books, the highest ones accessible via a sliding ladder attached to a rail that circled the top of the room. On the wall opposite the door was a large picture window overlooking the evening woods east of the driveway. The room was divided into three distinct reading areas, distinguished by rugs and furniture tone. Built into the wall behind one reading area was a clock four feet in diameter with independent silver numbers adhered between two concentric circles around spike-shaped hour and minute hands.

As they walked around the room, Jeff called attention to the clock. "That's interesting."

"Are these walls metal?" Emory felt the one surrounding the window. "They look rusted."

Jeff ran his palm along the wall. "I've seen this treatment before at the house of one of my parents' friends. You paint the walls with a liquid metal primer and then spray it with an activating solution that gives it the look of rusted metal. It's covered with a sealant to keep it from rubbing off." He jumped onto the ladder and pushed off the floor with his foot, riding the ladder down the wall and halfway down the adjacent one.

"You're going to break something."

Jeff jumped off the ladder and held his hand out to Emory. "Let me see your license."

"What are you talking about?"

"You act too old to be twenty-three. I think you lied to me."

Emory rolled his eyes, jumped on the ladder and rode it quarter of the wall's length before jumping off again. "Happy?"

"Happier." Jeff headed for the door. "Are we done with this floor?"

Hearing low-pitched chimes, Emory turned his head to follow the sound back to the wall clock, which read two minutes past eight. "That clock's strikes are a little off." He returned his attention to Jeff. "We passed by a room across the hall, next to the locutorium, when we first came here. I think it's a living room or a den."

"What's the difference?"

"Living rooms are more for entertaining. Dens are more personal. Family-centric. Less formal."

Jeff scoffed. "That's like distinguishing between a couch and a sofa."

"There are differences with those too." Emory walked across the hall and opened the door to a wood-paneled room with a stone fireplace, burgundy fainting couch and white area rug under two houndstooth sofas facing an oversized coffee table. A lacquered cherry secretary desk with hand-painted floral designs and matching chair stood before the far wall, a few feet from the only window.

Jeff waved his hands around the room. "Is this a living room or den?"

Emory noticed the framed vacation pictures hung on the lone wall with white and periwinkle fabric in place of wood paneling. "Den."

While Emory looked around the room for any sign of the Pangram Box, Jeff took a seat. "Couch or sofa?"

Emory noticed the delicate fabric and sturdy back. "Sofa."

Jeff laughed at him. "You're just making this crap up, aren't you?"

"I'm totally serious." Emory inspected the desk.

"You're a mountain boy. Why on Earth would you possibly know these fancy nuances?"

Emory opened each drawer. "Completing TBI reports. I wanted to be as accurate as possible, so I learned."

Lying on the sofa, Jeff pointed to a black spot about the circumference of a basketball on the ceiling near the window. "Is that water damage?"

Emory looked up at the spot, glimpsing the rising gibbous moon in the window. "I'm not sure. It looks like it."

Jeff pushed up from the sofa and joined his partner for a closer look. He tapped the floor with his toe. "You're stepping in it."

Emory jumped back to see a similar dark spot on the white hardwood floor. "It went all the way through." He stooped to feel it. "It's not even a little wet, but it has to be relatively new. From what we've heard of Blair Geister—"

Jeff finished his thought. "She would've insisted Tommy fix it right away. Is there a bathroom above here?"

"I think it's about where the master bath would be."

Jeff fixed his gaze on the ceiling. "What was Eden doing in there?"

Emory caught a light in the corner of his eye – something moving on the other side of the window. "Did you see that?"

"See what?"

"I think someone walked by the window."

The PIs ran to the locutorium to look out the room's many French doors. Jeff opened his mouth but took seconds to speak. "What the hell…"

Emory shook his head. "I have no idea."

Gathering on the lawn were no less than two dozen people in dark, hooded cloaks carrying lanterns.

Virginia appeared behind her partners. "I think they're witches."

Emory asked, "What are they doing here?"

Jeff opened one of the French doors. "Let's find out."

The PIs piled onto the walkway by the pool, but Virginia stopped them from proceeding. "Wait. It looks like they're about to do something."

The witches began to chant as they fell into formation. Three by three, they circled around an imaginary axis like spokes in a wheel. Their movements synchronized into a dance as their chanting turned to song. The ritual seemed to summon a swarm of lightning bugs, adding flares to the witches' lantern lights.

Jeff muttered, "It's beautiful."

The dancers twirled, stretching their arms to the moon as if it were within reach.

Emory found himself mesmerized until he heard Virginia shout, "There's the light!"

Jeff side-eyed her. "Uh, there are lots of them."

"No." Virginia pointed toward the boathouse. "In the river!"

Emory could see it now – a glow of light under the water's surface.

Jeff took off running. "Come on!"

The three investigators ran around the witches and darted toward the water. Once they reached the riverbank, Virginia stopped and pulled out her phone. "I'll stay here and record it."

Her partners slowed their pace as they stepped onto the creaking slats of the pier. Emory could see the ball of light still under the boathouse, near where it connected to the six-foot pier. Jeff placed a hand on the boathouse door and crouched to look over the edge of the pier.

The light disappeared.

Jeff looked up at his partner. "What the hell was that?"

CHAPTER 14

EMORY PULLED MARGARINE and a carton of free-range eggs from an oversized refrigerator and searched the quilted-maple cabinets for spices. From the custom-made appliances, like the *La Cornue* stove in the expansive island, to the blue granite counter-tops and silver-lined cookware, Blair Geister's kitchen would be any gourmet's happy place.

He found a pepper grinder in an overhead cupboard, next to a matching salt shaker. Behind them were boxes of whole white pepper and Fo-Salt. Emory checked the ingredients of the salt sub-stitute and found the main one to be potassium chloride – just like Cathy Shaw had told him a person with hypertension might use. He turned around to find a shirtless Jeff seated at one of the island's barstools. "Good morning."

"Morning," Jeff muttered while looking out the window.

Emory placed the ingredients next to the stove. "I'm making breakfast. Any special requests?"

"Frittata and French toast with sliced banana."

Emory grinned. "Is that a challenge? I'm no Kenn Marty, but I can get by if the fixings are here."

"Why do you know how to cook? I mean, who do you cook for? You're alone."

Emory's face dropped. "I cook for myself, and I like leftovers." He rounded the island to sit next to his partner. "We need to talk."

"About what? How you don't trust me after all we've been through together?"

Emory placed an arm around Jeff's shoulders. "I didn't mean to say that to you."

"Oh? You meant to yell out, 'I trust you!' instead?"

"No."

A corner of Jeff's lips pinched. "Is this your first time trying to comfort someone? Because you're *really* good at it."

"I just meant there are things about you I don't know. Things I need to know before I could possibly consider completely opening up to you."

Jeff turned and stepped away from the barstool, letting Emory's arm drop. "See, that's what I don't get. Sure, I haven't filled you in on every single moment of my life up until we met, but you should be grateful for that. Life without mystery is boring. If you know everything about me, there's nothing more to learn. You graduate and move on."

"Okay, but there are particular moments I need to know—"

Jeff jabbed a finger in Emory's shoulder. "You need to even the scales first." He crossed his arms and waited.

Emory knew he was right. Jeff didn't know anything about him that he hadn't volunteered, and he knew way more about his green-eyed partner – thanks to the information Anderson Alexander had given him. "Once this case is over, we'll talk."

"Promise?"

"Promise."

Jeff lurched forward and kissed Emory just as Virginia entered the kitchen. She smiled at them and said, "I'm glad to see you two made up."

Jeff plopped down again on the barstool. "I wouldn't say we've made up, exactly."

"If that's mad at each other, save the arguing for the bedroom."

Emory returned to the stove. "How'd you sleep?"

"Okay, once the witches stopped singing." She sat next to Jeff. "They were out there until at least midnight."

Emory sliced a pat of margarine into a pan on the stove. "You should ask Juniper what that was all about. They acted like they were at home here, so I assume they've visited before."

"She actually texted me this morning. She spread Blair's ashes and is on her way to Phoenix to catch a flight home. She said she'd meet us at The Monolith open house."

Emory cracked eggs into a pan. "Speaking of which, I want to leave early so we can stop by Dr. Sharp's lab."

Jeff scoffed. "I'm sure you do, but I'm thinking you should pursue hobbies when you're not on the clock."

Emory dropped his spatula. "This *is* business. He could tell us more about Blair Geister and her foundation, which could point us in the direction of a suspect in her death."

"That's not why you want to go."

"The fact that I'm interested in his research is beside the point."

"Guys!" Virginia raised a palm to both men. "We'll go to the lab on the way to The Monolith. Now, I have a question. Were either of you in my room – the office – last night?"

"Not me," answered Jeff.

Emory replied, "Me neither. Why?"

"The past two nights, I've woken up with a feeling someone was in the room with me. This morning, I couldn't reach my phone."

"What do you mean?" asked Jeff.

"I've been charging it on top of this file cabinet by the sofa because I can reach it while I'm lying down. This morning, I couldn't reach it – like the file cabinet had scooted a few inches away from the sofa."

Emory slid the eggs onto a plate. "It's a long sofa. Isn't it possible you just moved down it in your sleep?"

"I'm not an idiot."

Jeff laughed. "You're not seriously thinking Blair Geister's ghost played a prank on you, are you?

Virginia slapped his arm. "I didn't say that. But someone did move it."

Jeff opted to cede the passenger seat to Virginia when they left Geisterhaus, but now he was regretting that decision. He questioned whether his lingering anger at Emory over his "trust" revelation was worth taking a backseat to the primary conversation. Eyes hidden behind frosted Dillon sunglasses, he watched as Emory turned down the private road to Oak Ridge National Laboratory and pulled into the security station, a green-roofed building spanning both lanes. A young, mustached security officer with a red snake tattoo peeking out under the cuff of his shirtsleeve greeted them from the booth window. He asked for their IDs and checked his computer before directing Emory to drive to the visitor center.

After Emory parked, Jeff stepped out of the backseat and checked his phone. "Guys, I have to stay in Knoxville tonight. You can drop me off at the office after The Monolith."

"What?" asked Virginia. "Why?"

Jeff pocketed his phone and took the lead. "My cat-sitter said Bobbie isn't eating, so I'm going to see if I can help her regain her appetite. If not, I'll have to take her to the vet."

Emory asked, "Where did you even find someone to cat-sit your bobcat?"

Jeff opened the front door to the visitor station. "Yelp."

Virginia smirked at him. "You're just using that as an excuse not to stay in the haunted house."

"It's only for one night. I'll drive my car back down in the morning." He noticed Emory grinning at him. "What?"

"I just realized I get to sleep in the guest room tonight."

After a run through the metal detectors, Emory told the security officer behind the front desk who they were there to see. They received ID badges on lanyards and made small talk until Dr. Barry Sharp arrived to escort them.

Dr. Sharp gave Emory's hand a vigorous shaking. "Good to see you again. I'm glad you took me up on my offer."

"I've been looking forward to it." Emory waved toward his companions. "You remember my partners, Jeff Woodard and Virginia Kennon."

"Of course." Dr. Sharp gave a quick handshake to each before leading them outside to a golf cart. "My lab is just down the road. Hop in." Dr. Sharp got behind the wheel with Emory riding shotgun, and Jeff and Virginia in back. "Let me start the tour by giving you some background on the Oak Ridge National Laboratory. You might know it was built to help develop the atomic bomb in 1943. Since then, it's been dedicated to other research, not only in nuclear physics, but also environmental sciences, computer sciences and a wide range of other disciplines. In fact, we have the world's most powerful supercomputer, which I use for my computer simulations." Dr. Sharp parked in front of a small, red-brick building. "We're here."

Emory stepped from the golf cart. "Thank you for the invitation to see your lab. I've always been curious about Oak Ridge, but this is my first time here."

Dr. Sharp beamed. "Absolutely. I love sharing my work with a kindred spirit." He glanced back at Jeff and Virginia, who were a couple of steps behind, and he added an "s" to the end of his last word.

He led them to a door with a sign that read "Fulminology Laboratory" and a warning sign about high voltage.

Dr. Sharp swiped his badge and opened the door. "Welcome to my laboratory."

Jeff whispered to Virginia, "What's fulminology?"

She pulled out her phone. "I'll look it up."

They entered a rectangular control room with a row of thick windows on one of the long sides. The windows faced a much more sizeable room, which housed large and unusual devices straight out of a *Frankenstein* movie. Underneath the control room windows were several stations staggered with computers or control panels. Stacked two-by-two on the far wall were four large monitors, each displaying satellite video feed of different parts of the world. Aside from the doctor and the PIs, the room's only other occupant was an attractive young woman with long black hair sitting at one of the computers.

Dr. Sharp waved toward the woman. "This is my assistant, Ann Webber. She's a doctoral student from UT."

Keeping her hands on the keyboard, Ann acknowledged the group. "Nice to meet you."

Dr. Sharp stood in front of the monitors. "Here we have live feeds of weather from the four corners of the globe, coming from NOAA satellites – the National Oceanic and Atmospheric Administration. I'm sorry, but I have a tendency to speak in acronym." The last comment elicited an awkward chuckle from Dr. Sharp and a polite one from Emory. The doctor pointed at flashes of light just east of the Mississippi River. "Here's a thunderstorm that's going to hit us tonight."

"It's raining tonight?" asked Jeff. "I thought it was scheduled for tomorrow."

Dr. Sharp shook his head. "It's been gaining momentum. Our research in this lab is two-pronged. We're trying to provide indisputable evidence to the climate-change naysayers, and we're looking for a viable, cost-effective way to harness lightning and convert it into usable energy.

"Lightning is a bellwether for climate change. I think I told you every degree increase in global temperature can cause as much as twelve percent more lightning. This in turn sparks more wildfires, further devastating the environment." He put a hand up to the monitors. "We use the satellite data to count the number of lightning strikes all over the world over the course of the year, and we compare that to the average global temperature. Then we use the supercomputer to create models of the future impact."

"That's incredible," said Emory. "You're also trying to convert lightning into an energy source? How could you possibly predict where and when it will strike?"

"We can't." Dr. Sharp walked to the nearest window and looked into the other room. "That's why we're studying manmade lightning – something we can control. Unfortunately, with our current technology, the cost of creating this lightning outweighs the value of the energy we can capture. Another problem is that lightning produces such a massive energy output almost instantaneously, it's difficult to convert it into lower-voltage energy for storage quickly enough."

Dr. Sharp pointed to a device that looked like a car-sized donut on its side atop an eight-foot-tall pole. "That's a Tesla coil, similar to what you've seen in those toy plasma balls, but this one is much more powerful. We don't really use it much, but it looks impressive. Ann, could you turn it on?"

Ann replied, "I'm not sure how to do that."

"It's okay. I'll show you." He told the PIs, "Ann started last week." Dr. Sharp stepped over to the control panel beside her and showed her how to turn it on. The Tesla coil emitted white-blue lightning in every direction.

Emory's eyes widened above a broadening grin. "That's amazing."

Dr. Sharp admired the light show as if he were seeing it for the first time. "It's beautiful, isn't it? Hard to believe lightning is basically static electricity on steroids." He pointed out two metal pylons of differing heights, each topped with a large metal sphere. "You see the two Marx generators?"

Emory asked, "The ones that look like the Sunsphere?"

"That's what we use for the bulk of our research into energy conversion." Dr. Sharp explained how the process worked, and Emory hung on to every word.

Several feet away from the others, Jeff muttered to Virginia, "Emory is certainly in his element."

She smiled. "It's like glimpsing the future."

"What do you mean?"

She nodded toward Emory and Dr. Sharp. "Don't you see it?"

Jeff watched the men talking for a few seconds, noticing their similar mannerisms. They had the same smile, same lilt in their voice, same professorial air and even the same tendency to avoid direct eye contact while talking. "You're right. That's Emory in ten years, if his hair turns prematurely gray."

Virginia grinned. "Now that you notice it, you can't un-notice it."

"Honestly, it does make me like the doctor a bit more. It almost makes me feel bad for what I have to do next."

"What do you have to do?"

Jeff didn't answer. Instead, he charged ahead and broke up the conversation. "Dr. Sharp, why was Blair Geister planning to extend the escrow on your grant?"

Emory gasped. "Jeff!"

"What are you talking about?" the doctor asked.

Virginia cut in between Jeff and the professor. "Dr. Sharp, I don't know if Juniper told you, but she hired us to investigate Blair Geister's death."

"I wasn't aware there were any questions concerning her death." Dr. Sharp turned to Jeff. "And what do you mean she was planning to extend escrow?"

Jeff said, "You showed up at her house the day she died to discuss it with her."

"No, I didn't. I mean, I did stop by her house that day, but it was to let her know my departure from here was happening sooner than anticipated."

"I don't understand," said Emory. "Your departure?"

Dr. Sharp sighed and crossed his arms. "Oak Ridge is run by the U.S. Department of Energy, which means we're federally funded. It also means the value of particular fields of research sways with the political pendulum."

Emory asked, "Did Ms. Geister know you would be leaving this facility?"

"Of course. I've known it was coming for months now. It was just a matter of when – and that's now at the end of the month. I had applied for the EARTH grant to start my own, independent lab a few miles away, in Claxton. I went to see her to ask if she would agree to close escrow early. I was trying to eliminate any interruption in my research. It takes time to set up a new lab, particularly with the specialized equipment I need. I can't simply order it on Amazon." He asked Jeff, "Were you serious? She was going to delay the grant money?"

"That's what we heard."

"But why?"

Emory told him, "We don't have a clue."

CHAPTER 15

AT FORTY-FOUR FLOORS, The Monolith was now the tallest building in Knoxville. Unlike most of its comparables, however, the solid black building – four times wider than deep – had been constructed outside the downtown area, in a community known as Old North Knoxville.

"Very cool," Virginia said. "The last time I was on this side of town, they still had the cranes going."

Emory turned right onto the drive leading to Leland Cinema but pumped the brake when Jeff spoke up from the backseat. "Whoa! Are we seeing a movie?"

Emory nodded toward a sign next to the mechanical arm in their path. "The underground parking here is $5. Who knows how much it is at The Monolith."

Virginia said, "I don't want to walk."

"It's like a block and a half," Emory replied.

Jeff slapped Emory's shoulder. "We charge the client for expenses, so it doesn't matter."

"Fine." Emory backed out and headed once again toward The Monolith.

Jeff tilted his head to see out the windshield. "It looks exactly like the monolith from *2001: A Space Odyssey*. I wonder if that's why she chose the name."

Once he drove in front of the building, Emory had to wait several minutes in line for valet parking. "Why don't they just let me park my own car? I never do valet."

Virginia replied, "An event like this, they probably want to make sure everyone enters through the lobby instead of taking an elevator up from the parking levels. I'm sure the lobby is spectacular."

Jeff tapped his window. "Hey, look across the street."

Emory turned to see a block-sized tract of land hidden behind an eight-foot-tall wood-plank fence. A sign posted on it read, "A Godfrey Construction Development."

"Myles Godfrey," said Virginia.

Jeff smirked. "I bet he's going to make sure to add at least one more floor to his building."

Even before the elevator opened to the fortieth floor of The Monolith, Emory could hear the music and chatter of a party. When the doors withdrew, Juniper was nearby to greet them with a broad smile and twinkling eyes. *This is a different Juniper than we've encountered before. She seems relaxed, happy even.*

She gave Virginia a quick hug. "I'm glad you all could make it. I have lots to tell you."

Virginia patted her on the back before disembracing. "You look good. That desert air must've agreed with you."

Juniper laughed. "I think I'm just relieved. It's finally over."

"What do you mean?" asked Emory.

Juniper looked to the same picture of Blair Geister used at her memorial, now placed near the elevator bank. "When I was spreading her ashes, I could just feel it. I was tucking her soul in. I'm pretty sure it's at rest now." She opened her arms. "But her legacy lives on. What do you think of The Monolith?"

Emory looked around the expansive reception area of Geister Innovations & Engineering. From the holographic sign on the wall and the uninterrupted, wall-to-wall window overlooking Knoxville to the copious plants sprouting from just about every surface, the space was a seamless melding of business and nature.

"It's breathtaking," replied Jeff.

Virginia agreed. "And I love all the greenery in the lobby and that amazing waterfall. I don't think I've ever seen an indoor one so high."

"Eighteen feet," said Juniper. "She wanted the lobby to represent how people and technology can coexist with nature without one destroying the other."

Jeff pointed his thumb in the direction from which they had come. "I noticed in the elevator there are forty-four floors. Why did she put her business headquarters on the fortieth?"

"Taking the top floor would've been perceived as greedy and selfish. She was all about perceptions. Actually, the company only takes up half this floor. There's a door in Ms. Geister's office that leads directly to a large apartment she had built for herself."

Emory asked, "Was she moving up here?"

"Oh no. She just wanted to have a place in the city so she wouldn't have to drive home if she didn't feel like it. She had been staying here quite a bit recently, though, overseeing final preparations on the building. She took advantage of that time away to have her bedroom renovated. The weekend she died was the first time she had stayed at the house in two weeks, since the renovation began."

"Really?" asked Emory. "How many people knew she wasn't staying at the house?"

Juniper thought for a moment. "I'm not sure, but quite a few. We had a lot of construction workers at the estate due to the tight turnaround time she insisted on. I had to leave the gate open the entire time because people were coming and going at all hours of the day and night."

"Was the renovation to repair the water damage?" asked Jeff.

"What water damage?" Juniper's attention didn't wait for an answer, instead diverting to raised voices a few feet away. A forty-year-old blonde woman with soft features and a fifty-something, well-groomed man with thick brown hair were having a discussion that had elevated in tone. Juniper tightened her features as she told the PIs, "That's Myles Godfrey."

The blonde woman in the tailored midnight blue suit said, "This event is just as much a commemoration to Blair Geister as it is an open house for her crown jewel. It's certainly not the time to discuss selling her company!"

Myles responded, "It's a very generous offer – one that shouldn't be dismissed without careful consideration."

"Turn from me now, and walk away."

Myles huffed but complied, heading toward the extravagant buffet.

Juniper stepped closer to the woman. "Should I call security to have him removed?"

She shook her head. "No, this isn't the place for a scene."

Juniper turned her attention back to the PIs. "Rue, I'd like to introduce you to Virginia Kennon, Jeff Woodard and Emory Rome from Mourning Dove Investigations. This is Rue Darcé, the interim CEO of Geister Innovations & Engineering."

Rue scowled at Juniper. "Investigations?"

"They're doing some consulting work for Ms. Geister's estate."

Rue smiled at the trio. "Lovely to meet you. Pardon us for just a moment." She turned her back to the PIs and whispered to Juniper, "We found something else this morning."

"Oh no. Anything major?"

"It could've been if we hadn't caught it. The penthouse elevator."

"I thought they had stopped."

"We all did, and they actually might have. No one's worked on that elevator for at least two or three months, which means it very well could've been done then and we just now noticed it."

"Thank goodness for that."

Rue turned back to the PIs, "Please excuse me."

Once the interim CEO had walked away, Virginia said, "I thought Blair made you the CEO."

Juniper shook her head. "Of her EARTH Foundation, but not her construction company. She had a succession plan in place here. Ms. Geister announced a while back that she would be grooming Rue to take over as the next CEO. She felt the company's strongest growth potential lay in the Innovations division, and since Rue was the vice president of that area, she would be the best one to lead the company once Ms. Geister stepped down. Of course, that wasn't supposed to be for another five years or so, but here we are."

Jeff glanced at his partners. "That fast-forward is rather fortunate for Rue Darcé, wouldn't you say?"

Virginia asked, "She doesn't own the company now, does she?"

"No one does right now." Juniper's eyes darted to the guests arriving from the elevator, but her words stayed with the conversation. "It wasn't specifically bequeathed to anyone in the will, so it'll be part of the residuary clause." Her face dropped. "Or it's part of the Pangram Box, but surely Ms. Geister wouldn't hand her company over to that man. She wouldn't."

Emory told Juniper, "We couldn't help overhearing your exchange with Ms. Darcé. What's going on?"

Juniper checked for Rue, who was now engaged in a conversation several feet away. "We've been trying to keep it quiet, but during the construction of this building, there have been various incidences of apparent sabotage. Ms. Geister was convinced Myles Godfrey had planted someone on her crew, who was actively working to slow down construction. Keeping construction going twenty-four hours a day is the only reason the building is actually opening on time."

"Did she ever find the saboteur?" asked Emory.

"She had a few suspects, so she moved them off the team."

Jeff asked, "She was certain Myles Godfrey was the one behind it?"

"It was a safe bet."

Emory nodded toward an office with Blair Geister's name on the door. "What is he doing?"

They all turned to see Myles Godfrey standing in front of the door with his hand on a flat panel next to it before walking away.

Juniper shook her head. "He's trying to get into Ms. Geister's office for some reason. Fortunately, every door on this floor as a security panel, and his handprint's no good here."

"No keys?" asked Jeff.

"None needed."

Virginia waited for a guest to pass them. "There's something else we wanted to ask you about. Last night, a group of people showed up at the house and performed some kind of ceremony on the lawn. They looked like—"

"Witches." Juniper finished her thought. "It must've been a Wiccan holiday. I'm not sure which one. Ms. Geister has let a local coven use the property for their celebrations ever since they lost access to the Ocoee Woods. People didn't want them there. She had a soft spot in her heart for persecuted groups who practiced harmony with the environment. They celebrate just about all of their holidays and full moons on the property. They usually stay in the woods, so you don't see them much."

At the other side of the room, Rue Darcé tapped a microphone from behind a glass podium. "Could I have your attention please?" She waited for the crowd to quieten before continuing. "Thank you all for being here. I think Blair Geister would've been gratified to see you all gathered here today – some who stood by her as a struggling architect but all who knew her as an inspirational business leader and visionary. We stand here in The Monolith, the building she hoped would serve as a testament to human advancement through conscious environmentalism. A company's success more often than not directly correlates with the resources it uses, repackages and sells. Blair Geister believed the future would measure success not on the size of our carbon footprint but rather the absence of it. I'm very proud to announce that The Monolith is now the greenest commercial building inch-per-inch in the world!"

Rue smiled as the attendees applauded – all except Myles Godfrey, Emory noticed.

"The Monolith is made from one hundred percent recycled material – from the repurposed wood in the furniture to the reclaimed steel at its bones."

The attendees again applauded.

Rue waved toward the picture window. "The windows you're looking through are actually transparent solar panels. When they're brought online, they will provide all the energy that will ever be used in this building." She waited for the applause to subside before continuing. "Each floor is a separate grid with the panels feeding direct current electricity to an inverter that converts it into usable energy. There's an inverter on every floor except the bottom ten, which don't receive enough sunlight. Fortunately, the top thirty-four receive more sunlight than needed, so the excess energy is sent to those bottom floors.

"Yes, Blair Geister was a visionary, and through her eyes we can see a future of coexistence with one another and with the planet we call our home. Thank you." Rue left the podium to a final outbreak of applause.

As conversations picked up again, Emory asked Juniper, "Rue said when the solar array is brought online?"

"Yes. That'll be Monday, when the building officially opens."

Emory raised his palms to his side. "Where's this electricity coming from?"

Juniper tightened her lips and looked around before whispering,

"Don't tell anyone, but we're actually on city power right now. That will be turned off Monday morning, and we'll have some downtime during the transition to the solar array."

Jeff asked Juniper, "Are you staying with your daughter tonight?"

"I am. Why?"

"Would you mind giving me a ride to our office? I'm staying in town tonight as well."

"Of course, but aren't all…" Juniper stopped herself. "I'm sorry. I must have a little jetlag. I should've told you all that you could pack up and save yourselves another trip to Calhoun."

"What do you mean?" asked Jeff. "Are you firing us?"

"No, of course not. You know I hired you at my daughter's behest to see if there were possibly some other explanation for what I saw the night Tommy and Ms. Geister died, but it's a moot point now. I no longer have to worry about Ms. Geister's spirit coming for me. She's at peace, and now so am I. Your work is done, and I'm just so appreciative."

Emory held up a hand to put the brakes on her logic. "All due respect, Ms. Crane, but our work isn't done. We're convinced that Ms. Geister and Mr. Addison did not die natural deaths."

"I know Tommy didn't, but do you have any proof at all that Ms. Geister didn't die of a heart attack like the doctor said?"

"We're close."

Juniper pursed her lips. "Okay. I'm returning to Geisterhaus this weekend to start executing the terms of Ms. Geister's will. You have until then to show her death wasn't natural, or I really will need to move on, as will you."

CHAPTER 16

WHILE DUSK SET in around Barter Ridge, Sheriff Rome rested his forearms atop the split-rail fence bordering his property and stared at the woods on the other side. He inhaled a puff from his pipe before lifting his eyes to the mountain rising above the canopy.

Crown-of-Thorns Mountain was wrapped in the green of life up to a ring of twisted dead trees encircling its barren peak. The locals had come up with several theories for the bleakness of the peak so far beneath the natural timberline. Some blamed acid rain, but those prone to superstition called it the Devil's Sacellum – where Satan himself seduces Christian women into witchcraft.

The sheriff inhaled another breath of burning tobacco. His ears perked up at the whisper of approaching footsteps in the grass, but he didn't turn to see who it was.

"Nick." Lula Mae placed a hand on his arm. "I turned on the air. A big thunderstorm's rolling in tonight so we can't keep the windows open."

"We probably shouldn't have the windows open now anyway, with all that's going on."

"I know. I've been thinking we should get a security system for the house. Maybe we should change the locks too."

Sheriff Rome exhaled smoke away from his wife. "Lula Mae, intruders don't have the door key."

"Well, I'd feel safer."

"I'll take care of it tomorrow."

"Thank you." Lula Mae rested her hands on the fence beside her husband.

As if waiting for lines to be added to their script, the couple entered an inflated moment devoid of words. A chorus of wind-sifted trees, chattering insects and avian song took center stage until disquieted by the discordant whistle of the sheriff's next pipe-filtered inhalation. Perhaps annoyed by his own intrusion, Sheriff Rome jabbed the pipe's stem into the air before him, aiming it at the mountain. "That's where it happened."

"I know." Lula Mae stared at the lifeless peak. "Do you think it's true, what Wayne said?"

The sheriff clenched the pipe with his teeth. "I can't rightly say."

Lula Mae turned to face her husband's profile. "I can't imagine he'd make it up." Silence. "We should call Emory."

"Why?"

"To ask him."

"Lula Mae, you can't just ask him something like that. He chose not to tell us for a reason."

"What do you mean? What reason? You think he's afraid of how we'll respond?"

"How *are* we going to respond?"

CHAPTER 17

WHILE A DECADES-OLD slasher movie played on the wall-mounted TV, Emory kicked back on the bed in the guest room, thumbing through case photos on his phone. He had muted the TV volume, allowing the intensifying claps of thunder from the approaching storm to rewrite the movie's score. The overhead light flickered. Emory, barefoot and wearing gray pajama bottoms and a V-neck T-shirt, turned his eyes to the ceiling and waited in vain for the light to settle. The TV picture froze on a glistening hook held high above a soon-to-be victim.

"What's going on?"

He rose from the bed and stepped closer to the TV, fixing his eyes on the frozen picture. He reached up and touched the hook in the killer's hand. The hook came down!

Emory jumped back, tripping over his feet and landing on the floor before he realized the movie had started playing again.

Following a few gasps of air, he climbed to his feet and backed out of the room. "I wonder what Virginia's up to."

He headed down the hall and looked into Virginia's makeshift bedroom, Blair Geister's office. The room was empty.

"Maybe she's in the kitchen." He descended the back stairs to the main level. The kitchen light was off and the hallway unlit. He heard voices coming from the other end of the house, and he proceeded toward them.

A lightning strike outside the kitchen window flashed across his pale cheeks. He noticed the chandelier flickering in the dining room. *Why is that light even on?*

The voices grew louder as he approached the locutorium. He walked in on a conversation between Virginia and Eden, of all people. They were seated on the sofa nearest the fireplace, each holding a glass of red wine and sporting smiles.

Eden told Virginia, "He said his experiment proved conclusively that his roommate's flatulence was chemically identical to swamp gas."

"Eww." Virginia scrunched her face as if she could smell it. "Did you fail him?"

"I had to. Not because of the subject but because his data-gathering technique stank."

While Virginia laughed, Emory took the opportunity to make his presence known. "What's going on?"

Virginia replied with a slight slur, "Eden was just telling me about her work. She's a microbiology professor at UT Chattanooga. Ooh, and she's researching bacteria that can eat coal slurry."

"What's coal slurry?"

Eden replied, "Coal is washed after mining to remove impurities, creating a toxic mixture called coal slurry."

"And how do they dispose of that?"

"Manmade ponds, usually. The problem is sometimes they leak into the ground water, rivers, lakes. If my research pans out, we can eliminate many of the contaminants, except for the heavy metals of course, before they become a problem."

"That sounds fascinating," Emory said in all earnestness. "Is that the same research you submitted for an EARTH grant?

The smile left Eden's face. "It is."

Emory sensed the shifting tone, but he pushed forward now that the subject had been broached. "Why was it turned down?"

"Obviously, my cousin lacked faith in me." Eden stood and turned to Virginia, "Nice chatting with you, but I'm going to bed." She walked past Emory on her way out, muttering, "I miss the looker."

Virginia scoffed. "Way to go. She was just warming up to me."

"Sorry. What did she mean by that?"

The darkness beyond the locutorium's French doors retreated for several seconds as lightning struck nearby and lingered.

Virginia gasped. "Whoa! That was close."

Emory sat on the gold sofa. "I was surprised to see you chummy with her."

Virginia held up her glass. "Wine and girl talk. No better way to get someone to open up. Want a taste? It's Malbec."

"Sure." Emory took a sip and handed it back to her. "That's nice. What do you know?"

"We were just getting started, but I found out that she had her lawyer file an injunction today to stop the execution of the will. She's contesting it."

"I guess she wasn't bluffing."

"I also learned a little more about her lover."

Emory's eyes widened. "She admitted she's seeing the gardener?"

"No, but I tried. I brought him up, saying how beautiful the yard is, and then she told me he used to tend the grounds at UT Chattanooga, and she recommended him to her cousin."

"Why would she want her lover to leave a job where she works to come here – where, according to Juniper, she rarely visited?"

"I thought of that too, but I couldn't ask her about it. She doesn't know we know he's tending her garden."

"I'd love to look inside that master bedroom."

Virginia frowned at him. "Strange segue."

"I don't mean to watch them. I know in my gut that Blair

Geister's ear bleed means something, and the evidence we need could be in the room where she died."

"Maybe I could distract her tomorrow while you look."

"That would be perfect. We're running out of time. I also really want to find that Pangram Box." He checked his phone. "Eighty-two hours until the deadline."

Thunder rattled the panes in the French doors.

"I've been thinking about that too, and I have an idea."

Emory's ears perked up. "What is it?"

"The desk in Blair's office is locked. Gotta be a reason. Maybe it's in there."

"Okay. Maybe the key to her desk is in the office somewhere. Let's go search for it."

The two raced up the front stairs to the office on the upper level. After searching for half an hour, Virginia suggested another option. "I should just pick the lock."

"We can't break it open. Remember the will stipulates nothing in the house can be damaged."

"Trust me. I won't leave a trace."

Emory inspected the desk. "Are you sure you can do this?"

Virginia searched her purse, which she had left on the sofa, her makeshift bed. "I was taught by an expert."

"Jeff?"

"You guessed it." She pulled out an L-shaped strip of copper and a pick with a tulipwood handle and aluminum blade. "He actually made this for me."

Emory glanced out the window when another lightning bolt illuminated the boathouse. He followed Virginia around the desk, where he saw brass key locks above each column of drawers, including the lone drawer in the middle. "Maybe we should wait for Jeff or at least until you're one-hundred-percent sober."

"Trust me."

"Well, be careful. I don't see scratches on any of the locks."

Virginia took a deep breath and got to work. Emory soon realized he worried for naught. She spent less than twenty seconds clicking open each of the three locks, leaving not a scratch. "Done!" She placed her toolkit on the desk and smiled at her partner.

"Great job."

The two PIs took sides and searched the drawers, working from the bottom up. Emory thumbed through folder after folder. "I'm finding nothing but work files on my side."

"Same here." Virginia jumped ahead to the middle drawer. "Here's something that could be helpful."

"What is it?"

Virginia pulled out a folded, tabloid-sized paper. "It's a rendering." She underlined the header at the top of the page with her finger. "Master bedroom."

"Plans for the renovation of Blair Geister's bedroom."

"Look at all the detail. Her bed, the furniture, even where the paintings were to be hung."

Emory took the rendering from her. "I could use this for comparison when I search her room tomorrow."

"Of course, Eden's been in that room for days. She could've moved everything around."

"True, but it's something." Emory folded the rendering.

"I'll lock the drawers back."

"Sounds good." Emory headed for the door but stopped short of leaving. "Hey, would you want to open another bottle of wine and help me search the house for the Pangram Box?"

Virginia grinned. "You had me at wine."

"I'll meet you in the cellar." Emory left for the guest room, placing the rendering in his suitcase. Lightning drew his eyes to the window, and he noticed something outside. Twin lightning strikes lit up the woods to the west of the house all the way to the barrier fence. Emory thought he detected movement. Another strike confirmed it.

He ran from the room and down the front stairs.

As soon as he threw open the front door, the chilled rain pelted his face. *I should've put something on.* His bare feet sloshed over the flooding grass. By the time he reached the woods, his T-shirt and pajama bottoms were clinging to his body like a wetsuit.

Once in the trees, he lost any light coming from the house. *Should've brought a flashlight.* Emory felt his way through the darkness, bolting ahead whenever lightning showed him the way forward. He was almost at the fence when he heard grunting. Lightning struck, and he saw its source.

A man in a vinyl mask leaned against the historic cedar tree, resting his right hand atop the handle of a shovel. Emory wasn't certain, but he seemed to be facing down and perhaps hadn't spotted the PI.

Emory stepped into the clearing around the historic cedar. As he stepped over the low chain fence surrounding the tree, lightning struck again.

The masked man lifted his face toward Emory. He grabbed the shovel and darted into the woods.

"Mr. Drake! Wait!" Emory gave pursuit.

Between the flashes of lightning, Emory tried to follow the stomping of the man's boots against the muddy ground, but the intensifying downpour and blasts of thunder drowned out the sound. A double strike provided a glimpse of the man escaping the woods and heading toward the property's front gate. Emory no longer saw the shovel in his hand, but he soon discovered why when the toes of his right foot kicked the wooden handle.

Emory tumbled into the mud. His toes throbbing, he forced himself to his feet and continued the pursuit. By the time he reached the gate, the man was climbing into the cab of a small moving truck parked on the road. As he watched the truck drive away, Emory stopped running.

With a slight limp, he hiked the long driveway to the house.

He patted the hood of his car as a tremendous bolt of lightning streaked overhead, followed by two more. Emory ducked and put his hands at his side. *Probably not the best time to touch metal.*

A horrifying shriek pierced through the thunderstorm.

Emory bolted through the open front door of the house and followed the screams upstairs. Through the unlit hallway, he saw light slicing out from underneath the closed door to the master bedroom. He twisted the knob and shoved the door open.

The wet hair on his arms jumped to attention as he tried to make sense of what he beheld. "Holy crap!"

Eden Geister knelt in the middle of the gold bed, screaming with her arms crossed at her chest. Streaks of electricity danced up and down the head and foot of the bed and snapped between the posts on both ends. Caught in the middle of the erratic lightshow, Eden cried to Emory, "Help me!"

"Oh my god!" Emory heard behind him, and he turned around to see Virginia in the doorway.

"We have to get her off of there!" Emory shouted over Eden's screams and the sizzling electricity. He stepped toward the bed, and the hair on his neck joined that on his arms in standing. Streams of electricity wriggled between the gold posts at all four corners of the bed, blocking both sides and preventing Emory from reaching the terrified woman kneeled in the center of the mattress. Seconds later the current on the other side of the bed broke. Emory pointed. "Eden! Jump off that way!"

Eden scurried to the other side of the bed but stopped short of jumping to safety. She screamed again and backtracked.

Emory wondered why until he saw the reason. Standing on the other side of the bed was a hulking ghoul of a man. Frazzled black hair topped an anguished face – lacking a nose and left cheek and with a scraggly beard half-hiding the other cheek. *Zyus Drake!*

Zyus approached the bed and reached for Eden.

Eden screamed again and scooted closer to Emory, where a single bolt of electricity continued to stretch the length of the bed.

When the stream flickered away a few seconds later, Emory started to reach for her, but it sparked to life again inches from the top of his head. The hair on his head rose and reached for the electric stream, causing pops where the ends made contact. His skin tingled as the sensation permeated the thin layer of rainwater covering his body. He felt energy tentacles from the stream scratching paths in the air toward him.

The stream stopped again.

Emory reached for Eden, who jumped into his arms. The shaking woman grappled his shoulders and buried her face in his damp chest.

POP! The stream sparked to life once more before the electricity fizzled from the bed, leaving the room in darkness.

Virginia hit the light switch. "Is anyone hurt?"

Emory noticed Zyus was no longer in the room. "Where did he go?"

Eden lowered her legs to stand on her own. "You're wet."

He scoffed. "You're welcome."

The older woman looked at the bed and backed away. "What the hell was that?!"

He wasn't sure if she were talking about the electric bed or Zyus Drake, but he didn't respond to either. Instead, he walked over to where Zyus had stood a moment earlier.

Virginia placed a hand on Eden's back. "Are you okay?"

"I think so, but I'm not sleeping in this room ever again." Eden held her own shoulders as she scurried into the hallway.

Virginia joined Emory, whose eyes were on the floor. "What is it? And why are you wet?"

"I have a better question. Why wasn't he?"

"What do you mean?"

Emory pointed to his own wet footprints on the bedroom

floor. "I just encountered Zyus Drake in the woods, but look where he stood."

"There's nothing there."

"Exactly. He couldn't possibly have dried off and changed in time, and I walked directly here from the gate, where I last saw him driving away in a truck. I would've seen him if he came back."

"You're not making any sense."

"Virginia, I saw someone in the woods with the same mask that Zyus wore to the will reading, but the guy who was just in this room had to be Zyus, right?"

"I guess his face could be described as *disappearing*."

Emory asked, "So who was in the woods?"

CHAPTER 18

EMORY AWOKE JUST before dawn, anxious to investigate the events of the previous night. Plus, the fact that Eden had commandeered the guest room, relegating him to the fainting couch in the den, didn't help him sleep longer than necessary. He could have slept in Tommy's room again or even on a luxurious recliner in the movie theatre, but he felt an uneasiness as he descended the stairs so opted not to go beyond the main level. He glanced at the luggage by the secretary desk. *I guess I should be grateful she let me get our stuff before locking me out.*

He threw on some fresh clothes, grabbed the rendering Virginia found in the office desk and hurried up the stairs. *At least now I won't need a distraction to check out Blair Geister's bedroom.*

When he opened the door to the master bedroom, he noticed an odd scent in the air. *Is that ozone?* He unfolded the rendering and checked it against the placement of everything in the room. *Looks like all's where it should be.*

He approached the gold bed but hesitated to touch it. He gave the nearer foot post a quick tap with his knuckles. Although he felt nothing, he opted to avoid contact with any of the metal.

He placed the rendering on top of the comforter and scanned every inch of the bed but saw no wires or mechanisms to explain the electrifying display from the night before. *The only thing in contact with the bed is the floor.* He dropped to his hands and knees to get a closer look at the hardwood floor, focusing on the areas around the bed posts. All seemed fine until he reached the left post of the headboard. He spotted a small deviation in the wood, something that would've gone unnoticed had he not been on his hands and knees looking for it. The slat under the post was shorter than the other slats in the floor – about six inches long. Emory tapped the short slat with his fingernail and heard a slight *ting*. He tapped the surrounding slats, and they all thumped. *It's definitely different.*

"What are you doing?" a voice asked from behind him.

Emory jerked up, hitting the back of his head on the side rail of the bedframe.

Virginia winced in sympathy. "Ooh, sorry. Are you okay?"

"I'm fine." Emory stood and rubbed the back of his head. "I need to move this bed."

"How heavy is it?" Virginia reached for the left post of the footboard.

Emory stopped her before she made contact with the metal. "Don't touch it!" He went to the other side of the bed and pulled the sheet from under the bedspread. He looped it around the far-right post of the headboard and handed one end of the fabric to Virginia. Together they scooted the heavy bed a couple of inches. "That should do it." He returned to the short slat in the floor. "Can you find something I could use to pry up this floorboard?"

Virginia scanned the bedroom before disappearing into the bathroom. She came back a moment later with a stainless-steel Mac cosmetic spatula. "Will this work? Uh, what happened to your shirt?"

Emory's shirt was now wrapped around his left hand. "I don't want to get electrocuted." He took the spatula from her. "It should work." Within a few seconds, he had pried the piece loose. He pulled it up with his shirt-wrapped hand, but something prevented lifting it more than a few inches. He turned it over to reveal electrical wires running from inside the floor to the slat. "It looks like wood on top, but it's metal."

"You need to cut the wire. Hang on." Virginia ran into the bathroom and came back with grooming scissors.

Emory snapped pictures with his phone before taking the scissors and cutting each of the wires. He handed the metal slat to Virginia, and stood to put on his shirt.

"It's copper," she said. "This means you were right."

"Blair Geister was murdered." Emory looked at the cut wires in the floor. "When this room was renovated, someone took the opportunity to plan an electrocution for her."

Virginia knelt for a moment to inspect the hole in the floor. "Look at the black sheath on the wiring. Standard house wiring has white sheathing."

"How do you know that?"

"My dad was an electrician. During summers, he'd sometimes take me on jobs, and I'd be his helper."

"It must be controlled by a switch somewhere. How long do you think it would take to rig something like this?"

Virginia thought for a moment. "Maybe an hour."

"For you, but you have some experience."

"That doesn't matter. You can find tutorials online."

"Which means anyone could've come into this house during the two weeks the bedroom was being renovated and spent an hour setting this up to kill Blair Geister."

"And used the rendering to know exactly where the bed would be."

Emory sighed. "That leaves a wide window of opportunity, which means really no one has an alibi."

Virginia felt the wall above the opening in the floor. "We need to see what the wiring is connected to so we can figure out how it was controlled."

Emory agreed. "There has to be a toolbox around here somewhere."

A few minutes later, the PIs were back in the room with a hammer. Emory aimed the head at the wall and was about to swing but stopped himself. "We're not supposed to damage the property."

Virginia scoffed. "We're not looking for that stupid Box. We're looking for a murderer."

"You're right. Hopefully, this won't count." Emory pounded a hole into the wall above the one in the floor and pulled away a chunk of the drywall.

Virginia pointed to the white horizontal wire that passed behind the vertical black wire. "See, there's the standard wiring there."

Emory hammered more holes into the wall, following the black wire up to the bottom of the Cathedral ceiling. "The black one continues up."

Virginia eyed the ceiling. "The only thing above this room is the roof."

Emory dropped the hammer on the bed. "I need a ladder."

"Maybe there's one in the garage?" The PIs headed downstairs and found the garage door on the main level near the kitchen. Virginia opened the door to a spotless eight-car garage, home to several luxury electric vehicles. "Look at these cars. Ooh, one of these things is not like the other."

Emory spotted it too. In the far space was a twenty-year-old gas-engine utility truck. "Why would she have that?"

"Maybe she needed it for taking supplies to construction sites. Virginia waved toward the electric cars. "These aren't really for hauling."

Emory spotted a telescoping ladder hung from two bicycle hooks on the wall beyond the truck. "There it is." He glanced inside the cab of the truck and spotted a silver, rectangular box on the passenger-side floor. "Hang on."

"What is it?"

He opened the door, reached for the box and popped its lid. His shoulders slumped. "Just a toolbox."

Virginia smirked at him. "You thought that was the Pangram Box, didn't you?"

"Not really, but I had to check." Emory picked up a credit-card-sized paper from the floor mat. "She went to see a movie in Knoxville a couple nights before she died." He held it up for her to see. "Parking stub for Leland Cinemas."

"I hope it was good – last movie and all." Virginia opened the ashtray. "Look what I found." She held up a joint.

"Huh. I wonder if Juniper gave it to her."

They closed the doors and returned their attention to the ladder. Virginia helped Emory get it down from the wall. "Hey, before we go climbing on rooftops, how about some coffee to wake up?"

Emory assumed the full weight of the ladder. "I'm good."

"Let me get a pot started for myself, and I'll be right out. Don't start climbing without me."

Virginia headed to the kitchen but caught the aroma of fresh coffee before she entered. She found a red-eyed Eden sitting at the island bar and clutching a mug with both hands. "Eden, are you okay?"

Eden wiped her eyes. "Oh, yes. Just didn't sleep well. I perked some coffee. Enough for us all."

"I understand." Virginia poured herself a cup. "You could've died last night."

"What the Bell Witch was that?"

Virginia sat on the barstool next to her. "I'm not sure."

"The other night, I thought I heard humming coming from the bed, but I couldn't figure out why."

Virginia sipped her coffee. *That's what she was doing under the bed.*

"Do you think that's what happened to Blair?"

Virginia didn't answer because she saw a ladder go by the window. "Actually, I need to—"

"On top everything else, the man I've been seeing broke up with me this morning."

I wonder if Emory was right. If so, why would the gardener break up with her? Virginia placed a hand on her back. "I'm sorry. Why?"

"He said we had become too serious and he wasn't ready for that."

Virginia shook her head. *More likely, he found out how comparatively little she's getting in the will.*

Emory carried the ladder around the house and propped it against the wall near the den window – above which was Blair Geister's bedroom. He stood the ladder up on the narrow walkway between the wall and the edge of the pool but didn't like the resulting angle. "Too steep."

He looked to the right, at the rounded exterior wall to the locutorium. It had a circular roof that didn't connect with the one above the master bedroom. He glanced at the pool, which extended the length of the wall, and he realized he had no optimal place to position a ladder on this side of the house. He grabbed the ladder and continued walking around the house. Once he turned the first corner, he noticed the property line fence just behind the thick hedge of skip laurel. Beyond that stood one of the walls of Edgar Strand's house.

"The houses are so close on this end." He looked up at Geisterhaus. "No wonder she has no windows on this side." He craned his neck to try spotting the purported gargoyles on the slope of the roof without success.

He continued to the south side of the house and stood the

ladder in a spot he estimated would be across the house from the master bedroom. "I think that's the last gym window before the sauna." He thought about waiting for Virginia, but his curiosity proved impatient.

Emory ascended the ladder to the grey-tiled roof. Once his hand clasped around the top rung, the metal gutter at his waist, he glanced at the lawn two stories down. "Oh, this is a bad idea."

The words didn't keep him from stepping off the ladder and crawling onto the roof. He soon discovered he couldn't get far from the edge, however, because solar panels covered the entire slope of the main southern roof. "I can't walk on those. I'll have to go around."

He began crawling eastward, toward Edgar Strand's house, but he stopped after several feet. "These tiles are killing my knees."

He took a deep breath and pushed himself to his feet, hunching over to keep his center of gravity low. The path before him, between the solar panels and the gutter, was no more than two-feet wide. "Just don't look down." He started walking, his arms out for balance.

The solar array continued unabated until he reached a pronounced edge in the roof. He stepped over the edge to the slope facing the Strand house, and there he saw the backs of the three gargoyles. He continued to the next edge and scooched onto the slope over the office and master bedroom.

In the distance he saw the large antenna he and Jeff had spotted during their walk along the river, and he realized it was above the bedroom. Once he reached it, he crawled down to the gutter and popped his head over the edge to ensure he was in the right place. He saw the pool and the spot he had first propped up the ladder. "This is it."

He estimated where the black wire that ran up the bedroom wall would've come into contact with the roof. Two inches from his estimation, he spotted an aluminum cable concealer stretching all

CHAPTER 19

SLIDING DOWN THE roof, Emory grasped at anything but found nothing until his fingers hooked on the gutter. He looked down at his feet dangling over the walkway between the house and the pool.

Virginia came running into view. "Emory! Hang on! Where's the ladder?"

Emory shouted down, "Other side of the house!" The gutter creaked. "Hurry!"

While Virginia raced around the house, Emory heard the clang of heavy metal on hollow metal and felt a vibration in his hands. He looked to the right and saw the axe had slid from the roof into the gutter. The handle pointed away from him, but the foot-long, curved blade was mere inches from his fingers. "Crap!"

Emory looked down and tried to calculate a trajectory to the pool. *Maybe if I push off the house.* He placed the soles of his shoes against the wall and contemplated jumping. *I need to wait for Virginia.*

The gutter, however, had other plans. The brace to his left began to pitch, allowing the section to which he clung to droop under his weight.

The axe inched toward his fingers.

Okay, I need to move. He dropped his feet, causing another droop in the gutter.

the way to the antenna. He walked back to the antenna and tapped it with his knuckles. No shocks. He clasped it with his left hand, and the tip of his middle finger just met the tip of his thumb. "I think this is too thick for an antenna."

Emory heard a crash to his left, like broken glass. He hurried across the roof to investigate and slowed when he reached the edge, looking over at the slope with the gargoyles. He heard a whooshing sound and saw an executioner's axe flying right at his neck!

Emory fell back and lost his balance. He slid down the slick tiles, trying to grip something, but there was nothing to hold on to. He couldn't stop.

The axe grinded closer.

Emory scooted his hands left, faster and faster.

The gutter continued to angle down, speeding the axe on its screeching path to Emory's fingers.

"Now or never!" Emory raised his feet to the wall, but they just kicked air. "What?"

"I'm here!" Virginia yelled, running while dragging the ladder.

"I'm not going to make it!"

Emory felt something tighten around his waist.

The gutter brace snapped!

Emory's fingers slipped, but he didn't fall.

The axe completed its journey down the gutter and fell to the walkway below – just missing Virginia.

"Help me out here, kid!" grunted George Henry, his hands vise-gripped around Emory's belt from Blair Geister's office window.

Emory grabbed the window ledge and, with the gardener's help, pulled himself through the opening. He dropped to the floor, panting. "Thank you."

George grinned at him and coughed in his face. "You okay?"

"Yes." Emory pushed himself to his feet as the gardener continued coughing. "Are you?"

The older man coughed out an answer. "Yeah."

Virginia bounded into the room and grabbed Emory. "You idiot! You were supposed to wait for me." She glanced at George. "Thank you."

The gardener tipped an imaginary hat. "No problem. I better get back to work."

Once the gardener left, Emory said, "I wonder what he was doing in here."

Virginia laughed. "Don't look a gift horse in the mouth, you klutz."

"It wasn't my fault. I slipped dodging an axe."

"What? You mean that axe that almost hit me? Where did it come from?"

"Someone threw it at me, over by the gargoyles. I didn't see who. But listen to this." Emory stepped over to the sofa to sit. "I know how Blair Geister died."

Virginia joined him on the sofa. "You found the switch the wire led to on the roof?"

"It wasn't a switch. It's attached to a lightning rod."

"What? Someone installed a lightning rod to kill someone? That's an awful lot of trouble to go through." Virginia grabbed Emory's forearm. "Hey, do you think maybe Tommy Addison tried to help Blair get out of the bed, and that's how he died?"

"If so, that means Juniper lied. She said he was on the lower level when he died."

"Why would she lie about that?"

"I don't know. Fortunately, we now have definitive proof Blair Geister was murdered, so Juniper should support our continuing the investigating."

"You can prove Blair was murdered?" Jeff asked from the doorway.

"You managed to miss all the action." Virginia jumped up and headed toward him.

"What did I miss?"

"I'll let Emory fill you in. I have to check on something." Virginia patted him on the chest and whispered something in his ear before leaving.

Jeff plopped on the sofa beside Emory. "What's your proof?"

"I found a metal pad under one of the posts of Blair Geister's bed. It was connected to a lightning rod on the roof."

"Seriously? Well, that's elaborate."

"Virginia actually said she could've wired the bedroom in under an hour. Of course, that didn't include installation of the lightning rod on the roof."

"Ah." Jeff smiled. "That's what she was talking about."

"What do you mean?"

"You climbed on the roof and almost fell off, didn't you?"

"Did you see me?"

"No. Virginia told me to take it easy on you, so I figured something must've happened. You have become quite the danger-prone Daphne."

"I have not!"

Jeff started counting on his fingers. "You drank drugged water—"

"Which *you* gave me!"

"You fell off the Godfrey Tower."

"I was pushed!"

"And now you almost fell off this roof."

Emory threw his hands up. "Someone threw an axe at me! How is that my fault?"

"Who would throw an axe at you?"

"Someone who didn't want me to find the lightning rod."

"You're saying whoever killed Geister is after you now, putting you in more danger."

"Fine. But I could say the same thing about you."

"What are you talking about?"

"In the short time I've known you, you've been in two car accidents."

Jeff waved off the statement. "Neither of which was my fault."

"You got tazed, tied up, suffocated and almost blown up—"

"Because *you* didn't blow out all the candles."

"You provoked a knife-wielding bully and almost got your throat slit."

"That was just fun."

"You were caught breaking into someone's home and ended up in jail."

"All right!" Jeff held up his hands in surrender. "Enough. I guess we're both danger-prone Daphnes. What does that make Virginia? Fred? Shaggy? Velma?"

They looked at each other and agreed. "Velma."

Emory smiled and relaxed into the sofa. "How's Bobbie?"

"Eating now. I think she just missed me."

Emory rested his hand on Jeff's. "I might've too. Just a little."

Jeff acknowledged the statement with a micro-smile before changing the subject. "One thing I don't understand. Wouldn't Blair Geister, world-famous architect and construction tycoon, have noticed a lightning rod on her house?"

"Lightning rod?" Eden stopped in the hallway as she walked by the door.

Emory pointed up. "I found one on the roof."

Eden stepped into the room. "Blair installed one on every house she's ever owned. Wouldn't move in before it was done."

"Seriously?" asked Jeff. "I thought those were only for tall buildings."

Eden rolled her eyes. "Most definitely overkill, but you can understand why."

Emory looked at Jeff and turned back to her. "Why?"

Eden smirked. "I assumed you *investigators* would know every-thing about Blair. My cousin, Adrick – Blair's little brother – died when we were kids after being struck by lightning."

Jeff muttered, "Oh wow."

"Their parents took them on a family trip to Gatlinburg, and they stayed at an antique cabin in the mountains. It was Adrick's birthday, August 2nd. Story goes, Blair had claimed the loft bedroom for herself, leaving Adrick to sleep on the couch. Their first night there, the mist turned to rain, and the lightning came. Blair caught Adrick in her room. He was scared of the storm and didn't want to sleep by himself, but she wouldn't have it. She sent him back down the little metal ladder from the loft. He had only descended a couple of feet when the lightning struck. Tore right through the ceiling and hit the ladder."

Jeff asked, "Did he die?"

"Not right off. He held on for a few days and then just faded away. Of course, Blair blamed herself for the longest time. She was in therapy until around thirty. I guess it did help her get over the guilt. Kept the fear, though."

"That's horrible," said Emory.

"Yeah, but it doesn't explain why the lightning rod was hooked up to her bed."

Eden's face contorted in confusion. "What are you talking about?"

Emory replied, "That's what killed her and almost killed you last night."

"That doesn't make any sense. Lightning rods are connected to a grounding system. If it had been improperly wired, she would've died long before now."

Jeff said, "Then someone must've rerouted it from the grounding system recently."

Eden turned away from them. "Blair was murdered. And now they're trying to kill me!"

Virginia knocked on the front door to Edgar Strand's house. "Mr. Strand!"

She heard a growl coming from the side yard, between Edgar's house and the fence he shared with Blair Geister. She poked her head past the corner of the house. Scattered over the narrow lawn and house-hugging jasmine were shards of flat glass. She heard a voice from above and tilted her head upward to see one of the windows to Edgar's office – the room he said he could no longer use because of Blair Geister's gargoyles – was now broken.

She heard Edgar yelling from the broken window. "Damn demons taunting me! Tearing at my life!"

"Mr. Strand!" Virginia ran to the back of the house and found an unlocked sliding door.

As soon as she entered the living room, she heard a gunshot. She jumped but hurried up the stairs, slowing her pace as she ascended. Through the second-floor railing, she detected motion. *He's not dead!*

"Mr. Strand." She left the final step and turned toward the office. She peeked inside and saw Edgar Strand in blue flannel pajamas and matching robe, aiming a rifle out the broken window.

Before Virginia could speak, he fired another shot, blasting half the face from one of the gargoyles on Blair Geister's roof. She plugged her ears. "Mr. Strand!"

"Who's there?!" Edgar swung the gun toward the doorway.

Virginia yelped and ducked behind the couch. "It's Virginia Kennon. We met the other day." She lifted her head so he could see her face.

"You. What do you want?"

"First of all, for you to put that gun down." Virginia rose to standing as he lowered the barrel toward the floor. She stepped from behind the couch, hands up midway. "Mr. Strand, what's going on here?"

"It's over." He nodded to his desk.

"Do you mind if I look?"

"Everyone's going to know about it now."

She went to the desk and saw unfolded court papers under a light bottle of Jack Daniels. She didn't have to move the bottle to see the word *Divorce* at the top. "Oh, I'm sorry."

"It's because of her!" He turned around and fired another shot at the gargoyles. "She was the worst neighbor ever! Drove me so crazy, my wife couldn't take it no more." Edgar steadied himself with the gun as he dropped to a seated position on the floor. "Lost my wife. My view. My peace. Lost my axe."

Virginia glanced over at the hooded mannequin and saw it no longer held an axe. She pried the gun from him and placed it on the couch before joining him on the floor. "Mr. Strand, I'm sorry. I promise, if you stop shooting, I'll do everything in my power to make sure all that ugly over there goes away."

"You can do that?"

"I have some pull with the person who's running things now. I really believe she'll do the right thing."

Edgar took her hand. "Thank you."

"Now, is there anyone I can call for you? I don't want to leave you alone like this."

He pulled his cell phone from the pocket of his robe. "That's okay. I better call the reverend myself. I don't want him to think I've moved on to another woman already."

Virginia laughed and gave him a parenting stink-eye. "Okay, you take care of yourself." She headed for the door but stopped to say, "No more guns. Or axes."

CHAPTER 20

WAYNE BUCKWALD AND Steve Linders showed their TBI badges to the uniformed police officer at the front door before entering the modest blue-paneled home. Wayne spotted a police detective standing in the middle of the living room typing on his phone. "Hi. We're TBI. I'm Wayne, and this is my partner, Steve."

The detective shook hands with both. "Barry. Nice to meet you. You beat the ME."

Wayne asked, "What do we have?"

The detective led them to the bathroom. "Watch your step. Floor's slippery."

The warning came too late for Wayne, who slipped on wet tile but was kept from falling by his partner's sturdy grip and quick reflexes. With a sneer toward the detective, he grunted his thanks to his partner.

Wayne's eyes went from the nude body of a young woman on the floor to the water in the tub. On the bathroom counter were three red puddles of hardened wax – the remnants of candles allowed to burn themselves out. The mirror bore the phrase, "Tired of even trying," in rose-colored lipstick.

Barry explained the scene. "Lynn Pinter, 23. Her best friend came by when she hadn't heard from her, pulled her out of the water and tried to resuscitate her. There's an empty bottle of Percocet on her nightstand."

"Suicide?" asked Steve. "Why'd you call the TBI?"

"She worked for the state parole board."

Wayne glanced at Steve while heading for the bathroom door. "I'll check out the bedroom while you get the details from the detective." He proceeded to the next room and found the pill bottle as described, but a framed picture behind a lamp stole his attention. It was a shot of the smiling victim with a scenic view of the Smoky Mountains behind her. He stared at the photo for a moment before Steve entered.

"Everything okay, Wayne?"

"Yeah. It's just… She looks like my daughter. Little bit older. What would've made her do this?"

"Maybe she suffered from clinical depression. I got the parents' information. We can ask them."

"The parents. I don't know what I'd do…" Wayne headed for the door. "Do me a favor. Catalog the scene. I have to make a phone call."

Once outside on the front lawn, Wayne pulled his phone from his shirt pocket and dialed.

Sheriff Rome opened the door to the Barter Ridge Sheriff Station, but he didn't enter alone. A bird flew in over his head, prompting him to duck. "What the devil!"

Deputy Harris grinned at him from behind his desk. "Morning Sheriff. Who's your friend?"

"Very funny." The sheriff watched the gray bird with a red-tufted head flutter around the station. "Help me get this pigeon out of here." He removed his hat and waved it at the bird.

The young deputy with the farm-boy face scooted back from his desk. "That's not a pigeon. It's a pileated woodpecker. Your phone's ringing."

"Dang!" The sheriff hurried to answer his office line. "Get that bird out of here before he starts putting holes in the wall." He pushed open the glass door to his office. "I'm coming. I'm coming." He picked up the receiver. "Hello?"

"Sheriff, this is Wayne Buckwald."

"Wayne?" Sheriff Rome's tone did little to conceal his contempt. "What do you want?"

"I wanted to apologize to you, first off. I had some major differences with Emory, and I took it out on you and your wife. I'm sorry about that."

Sheriff Rome sat at his desk. "Thank you. I appreciate it."

Wayne paced around the lawn. "I have children too, and there's nothing I wouldn't do to keep them safe, so I know where you're coming from. I want to help."

"For real?"

"For real." Wayne spotted his partner exiting the suicide victim's house. "I'll call you later to get all the details."

"That'd be great."

"One more thing. My help is conditional."

The sheriff sighed and rested his elbows on his desk. "On what?"

"Don't tell Emory I'm helping you."

CHAPTER 21

EMORY PACED IN Blair Geister's office as he talked on his phone to the local sheriff. "I definitely will."

Jeff waved him over to one of the framed photos on the wall – Blair when she was young, with her parents and brother in Gatlinburg. "Bet it's their last picture together."

"We'll see you then." Emory hung up and turned to his partner. "Sheriff Flynn is out of town and won't be back until tomorrow. He wants us to seal off the bedroom for him."

Jeff spun the standing globe adjacent to the desk. "Where's Eden going to sleep?"

"Oh, I haven't told you. She kicked you out of the guest room. Your stuff is in the den."

"Ugh. I've been relegated to steerage."

Emory smirked and touched his shoulder. "You'll survive."

Jeff ran his fingers over the smooth, white surface of Blair Geister's drafting table. "You know, since we have a definite murder and a long list of suspects, we need to start a murder board."

"We can't display a murder board in full view of poten-tial suspects."

"I know." Jeff adjusted the drafting table, tilting the top to almost ninety degrees. He turned the table around to Emory, exposing the underside of the tabletop. "We'll use this and tilt it back into place when we're done."

Emory inspected the table. "Great idea."

Virginia bounded into the room. "Good news, Emory. No one's trying to kill you."

In his excitement, Emory pushed on the drafting table, clocking Jeff in the face as it tilted up. "You know who threw the axe?"

"The neighbor. I talked to him. He was aiming for the gargoyles, not you."

Jeff massaged his jaw, straightening himself. "I'm fine, by the way. It's good to know your attempted murder has been plea bargained down to attempted manslaughter. Virginia, we're starting a murder board. Would you mind—"

She anticipated his request. "Finding online pics of everyone involved in the case. No problem."

Jeff turned to Emory. "Before we hunker down on this, let's select an expensive sipping wine from Blair's cellar."

"Is it even noon yet?" Emory looked for a clock on the walls.

"It's already happy hour in my head."

Virginia laughed as he passed her. "When is it not?"

Emory followed Jeff out the door and down the stairs to the lower level, discussing the case along the way. "I'm glad we didn't let Eden throw away the original mattress. Remember the outline, the way the hand was up above the head?" Emory mimicked the pose.

"I remember."

"I think Blair Geister's hand was touching the metal headboard. She probably died instantly."

Jeff held the door to the wine cellar open for Emory. "Best way to go."

"Something else odd happened last night." Emory walked to the right of the table in the center of the cellar.

Jeff perused the wines displayed along the left wall. "Something else? I picked a bad night to leave."

"You did." Emory checked out the bottles racked along the wall. "There was a man in the woods, standing by that historical cedar tree."

"He was just standing there?"

"I think he was about to dig for something. He had a shovel in his hand."

Jeff picked up a bottle and inspected the label. "Could the Pangram Box be buried on the property?"

"Digging up the property would go against the directive in the will not to damage anything while looking for the Pangram Box."

"Are you in the mood for a merlot?"

"I'm not picky." Emory reached a section devoted to red blends. "The guy I saw was dressed like Zyus Drake."

"It was Zyus?"

"No, he was dressed like Zyus."

"Seriously? Why dress like Zyus and stand by a tree waiting for you to notice?"

"I didn't get the impression he wanted me to see him. I think he was disguised as Zyus in case anyone did."

"But why?"

"I have no idea."

"It had to be Zyus. Hey, look at this." Jeff held up a dusty wine bottle. "It's a 1982 *Chateau Petrus Bordeaux*. This is worth like five grand."

"Put it back. I'm not going to take expensive wine from a deceased woman's collection."

"Why not? Juniper told us to make ourselves at home."

"It's unseemly."

Jeff returned the bottle to the rack. "I think it's very seemly, but fine. I wouldn't want to sully your morality."

Emory ignored his comment because the label on a particular bottle caught his eye. *La Fleur's Winery. California. Coyote Red.* Under the words was a water color of a red coyote. He glanced at the painting on the wall, past the gaunt figure of Hugo Hickory to Waya'ha, the red coyote watching the murderous soldier from behind a tree. He looked back at the painting of the red coyote on the wine label. "It's uncanny."

"What is?" asked Jeff.

"The coyote on the wine label looks so much like Waya'ha in that painting." He picked up the bottle to show Jeff, and he felt something click. He looked at the cradle that had held the bottle and saw a black trigger inside it. "Huh. Do they all have that?" He picked up the bottle next to it and saw no such trigger, nor did he find one in two other cradles. "Hey, Jeff, come look at this."

Jeff cleared his throat. "No, you look at *this.*"

Emory turned around to see his partner now standing by the painting, but it wasn't where it had been when he last looked. Instead of being flat against the wall, the frame now protruded from the wall at ninety degrees, with the left side of the frame still touching the wall. "What did you do?"

Jeff threw a hand to his chest. "It wasn't me. It must've been something you did."

Emory pushed down the trigger in the wine cradle. The painting started returning to the wall. He released the trigger, and the painting again protruded. He looked at the coyote on the wine label. "You are Waya'ha."

"That's not all." Jeff beckoned Emory with his index finger.

Emory placed the wine bottle on the table and walked up to the front of the painting.

"This side."

He joined Jeff behind the painting and followed his gaze. Built into the wall, behind where the painting hung, was a steel box about the size of the artwork, minus the frame. "A safe."

"Notice anything strange about it?"

Emory focused on the safe's most prominent feature – the

standard safe handle to turn after inputting the combination. That's when it hit him. "There's no lock."

"Exactly. What kind of safe has no lock?"

"No such thing." Emory gasped. "It's the Pangram Box!"

"It has to be, right?"

"Do we open it?"

"Don't be stupid." Jeff turned the handle and opened the safe door.

Emory caught a glimpse of something inside the safe before it disappeared. "Did you see that?"

"I did. What the hell?"

"It was the Box, right? I couldn't tell what it was made of, but I think I saw writing on it."

Jeff felt around the inside of the empty safe, which was about large enough to store a carry-on bag. "I feel something." He pushed on the bottom, and it opened down, inside the wall. "The bottom is a flap. It must've released when I opened the safe door. But why?"

Emory heard a continuous whooshing sound that began when Jeff pushed the bottom down. "What's that noise?"

"It feels like a fan blowing. When Jeff drew his hand out of the safe, the bottom flapped back into place, and the whooshing stopped.

Emory stepped forward and pushed the bottom down again. He could feel the air blowing on his fingertips. "It's not a fan. It's one of those pneumatic tube systems."

"A what?"

"Juniper told us this room was a pharmacy when the house was a convalescent home. I worked one summer in a hospital pharmacy. They used a pneumatic tube system to send pill bottles up to the floors. They probably used it here for the same reason. Blair Geister must've modified it."

"The Box was sent somewhere else in this house?"

"Well, I don't think the safe was rigged to just drop it behind the wall, where no one could reach it without damaging the room."

"But why?"

Emory tried to think of a reason. "I don't know."

A voice behind them said, "You found it!"

Emory and Jeff jerked around to see Zyus Drake entering the room. He was wearing the same mask as before, with jeans and a maroon pullover that accentuated his massive frame. "The Pangram Box. Is that it?" Zyus walked around the table to stand before them. "It's empty. Did you take what was inside?"

Emory heard the knuckles cracking in Zyus' clenching fists. "We didn't take anything."

Jeff interceded. "This is how we found it. Completely empty. What were you expecting to find?"

Zyus pounded a fist on the table. "How the hell should I know? You guys were there. I don't know nothing more than what was said."

Emory raised a hand. "Wait a minute. Do you know this is the Pangram Box, or were you assuming it was?"

"Assuming, I guess. That's not it?"

Jeff waved to the empty safe. "If it is, it isn't much of an inheritance."

Zyus looked at Emory. "Sorry about scaring you last night. This mask isn't the most comfortable, so I only wear it when I know I'm going to run into people. I try to stay out of sight."

"You don't need to apologize, and you didn't scare me."

"I scared Eden."

Emory gave a polite laugh. "Well, she had a lot going on at that moment."

Jeff stepped between them. "Zyus, what do you think Blair Geister would've left you in the Box?"

Zyus shrugged his massive shoulders. "I couldn't begin to guess. I was surprised I was even in the will."

"Why the hoops?" asked Jeff. "Why not just give it to you, whatever it is?"

Zyus sighed. "I guess she wanted to challenge me."

"Uh-uh. That's bull."

Emory grabbed his partner's arm. "Jeff—"

"No, I'm not going to pussyfoot around." Jeff held a finger to Zyus' chest, just a breath shy of touching him. "She said in the will that you like to play games. What did she mean by that?"

Zyus crossed his arms and filled his chest with the palpable air of disdain. For a moment, Emory feared the masked man was going to headbutt his partner. "Our relationship's none of your business."

Emory wedged a shoulder between them. "Mr. Drake, Blair Geister alluded to a feeling of guilt. Is she responsible for... uh... the mask?"

Zyus bore into Emory with his light brown, almost golden, eyes. He turned away and took a seat at the table. "Blair invited me to one of her parties – something she hadn't done before."

Emory and Jeff sat at the table across from him.

"I don't know why, but I was nervous. I started going through the drinks pretty good. I guess I was embarrassing Blair. She wanted to get me away from the party. She made her assistant give up her room so I could sleep it off."

"Not Blair's room?" asked Jeff.

"We didn't have that kind of relationship. Anyway, I could tell that Juniper wasn't thrilled about having to give up her room. I don't remember exactly, but I guess I wasn't happy about it either. Apparently, I left and went upstairs, probably looking for Blair's room. I ended up crashing in the guest room, even though it was under construction at the time and didn't have any furniture."

"You slept on the floor?" asked Emory.

"I had a pillow. Must've taken Juniper's." He inhaled a nervous breath. "I... uh..." He clenched a fist on the table. He started to speak again, but his voice carried a different, much more vulnerable tone. "The drywall had been torn out, so there was nothing but old exposed wood all around."

Zyus lowered his head. "While I was passed out on the floor, spi… spiders… brown recluses came out of the wall." He choked up and couldn't speak for several seconds. "I woke up. I had three, four… I don't know how many spiders on my face. I freaked out, and they started biting me."

Jeff gasped. "Oh shit."

"Their venom kills the skin. Necrosis. I lost half my face!"

Emory asked, "Is that why you sued her?"

"Of course, I sued her!" Zyus ripped off his mask. "*This* happened here, at her place! I got drunk at a party. I didn't deserve this!"

Emory steeled himself when he realized what Zyus was about to do, but he couldn't suppress micro-expressions of horror.

Jeff, who was seeing Zyus' face for the first time, winced but maintained eye contact. "I'll bet she blamed you. Said it was your fault for not staying in Juniper's room."

Tears ran down Zyus' good cheek but dripped into his mouth on the other side. "That guest room door should've been locked. No one should've been allowed in there." He buried his head in his hands and sobbed.

Jeff looked at Emory. "We should go."

As the PIs scooted their chairs back, Zyus growled, "Wait! I need your help."

Emory asked, "What do you need?"

"You guys are private investigators. I want to hire you to help me find what Blair left me. The Pangram Box."

Emory sighed. "We're already working for Ms. Crane. Working for you too might pose some ethical issues."

"Then just help me find it because it's the right thing to do. Look, you don't have to do anything, really. If you find it, you could maybe point it out to me."

Emory looked at Jeff, who replied, "We'll think about it."

CHAPTER 22

IN BLAIR GEISTER'S home office, the three partners prepared a murder board on the underside of the drafting table. While Virginia stretched out on the sofa, laptop parked on its namesake, Jeff took a piece of paper from the printer and Emory made sure the door was locked.

Jeff taped the paper onto the right side of the board, and stared for a second at the faculty picture of Eden with her name underneath. "The way I see it, Blair Geister had three separate lives, giving us three primary pools of suspects: *Business, Foundation* and *Personal*."

Emory joined him at the board. "Sounds good to me."

Virginia agreed. "Me too. I have another picture printing now."

With a red sharpie, Jeff wrote the three categories onto separate Post-It notes, sticking each at the top of a column on the murder board. He posted Eden's photo in the *Personal* column and wrote the motive on the paper under the photo. "Eden could've sought revenge for turning down her grant, but her primary motive would've been greed, since she assumed she would receive a much greater inheritance than she actually did."

Emory said, "Okay, as far as means, Virginia pointed out that anyone could've bought the materials needed to reroute the lightning rod grounding wire and learned how to do it on YouTube, meaning everyone could've had the means to commit the murder."

"And the opportunity," noted Virginia. "Juniper said the house was basically open 24/7 for two weeks, while the bedroom was being renovated."

Emory tapped Eden's photo. "Getting back to Eden, she wouldn't have slept in that bed if she had known it was rigged to kill."

Jeff shook his head. "I don't agree. Remember, we've had someone put herself in danger before just to throw off suspicion."

"True, but you didn't see the lightning dancing all around that bed. There's no way Eden could've been sure she'd survive."

Virginia glanced up from her laptop. "I'm with Emory. I don't think she could've faked that just for our benefit."

Jeff continued playing devil's advocate. "But she did survive, and you said it yourself. The lightning was all *around* the bed. Did she stay in the center of the mattress?"

Virginia answered, "For the most part, until the sparks died down. Then she jumped into Emory's arms."

"Then she's still a suspect. Who's next?"

Emory retrieved the next picture from the printer. "Myles Godfrey." He taped it into the *Business* column.

Jeff readied his marker. "Motive?"

Virginia offered one. "Business rivals."

Emory asked, "But is that enough to commit murder?"

"If you believe the rumors, it was enough for him to sabotage The Monolith," replied Virginia. "Plus, he's now trying to buy her company – something I'm sure is easier for him with Blair dead."

Emory tsked. "I don't know. Is it enough? How much would you have to hate a business competitor to actually kill her?"

Jeff stared at the board. "Or have them killed. I'm on the fence. We'll keep him as a suspect but move him to the bottom of the column."

As Emory repositioned Godfrey's photo, Jeff grabbed the next printout and grinned when he saw it. "Ah yes. The professor, Dr. Barry Sharp."

Emory scoffed. "He's not a suspect."

Jeff taped his picture in the middle column. "Are you kidding me?"

"He has no motive."

"His field of study is lightning! Excuse me, *fulminology*. That's literally our murder weapon."

"Again, what's his motive?"

Virginia chimed in. "Why did Blair want to delay his grant money?"

Jeff punctuated the air. "Thank you! There's your motive."

Emory pulled Dr. Sharp's picture from the board. "That's not a motive. You saw his reaction when you asked about that. He was totally surprised."

"Or he's also practiced in the dramatic arts." Jeff snatched the picture from his hand. "Regardless, it doesn't change the fact that something was giving Blair second thoughts about him."

"You don't know that." Emory reclaimed the photo. "It could've been a completely unrelated financial decision. Even if it were something to do with Dr. Sharp, he wasn't aware of it, so again I come to the conclusion that we have no motive. Another thing, how stupid would he have to be to murder someone so elaborately with lightning? He'd be the obvious suspect. If anything, it's more likely someone's setting him up."

Jeff asked, "How big a crush do you have on this guy?"

Emory rolled his eyes. "Would you stop it with that! I'm just being logical."

Jeff looked to Virginia. "Miss Tiebreaker?"

"I'm sorry, Emory. That escrow delay is nagging at me. Until we have an explanation for it, I vote he's a suspect."

Emory taped his photo back on the board. "Then we need to find the explanation."

"Already on it," said Virginia. "I set up a video conference with Dr. Arthur Igataki for tomorrow. He's the consultant the EARTH Foundation contracts to review grant applications."

Jeff pointed the sharpie at her. "Good call. All right, who's next?"

Virginia replied, "Edgar Strand."

"Our friendly neighborhood axe-wielder. Virginia, you've had direct contact with him. Your thoughts?"

"He and Blair got off on the wrong foot. If you add up the lawsuits, gargoyles, Easter Island heads and now the end of his marriage, he had plenty of motive to kill her."

"Plus, he's next door." Emory taped his photo in the third column. "That puts him at just about the top of the list as far as opportunity goes."

Jeff wrote *Revenge* under Edgar's picture. "Next."

Virginia spoke as the printer started again. "Coming up is Rue Darcé, who replaced Blair at Geister Innovations & Engineering."

Emory took the page from the printer and taped it in the first column. "Is a promotion and a raise worth killing for?"

"Maybe it's more." Jeff wrote *Money?* under her picture. "We still don't know who's going to inherit ownership of the company."

"You're right." Emory returned to the printer. "The title to the company is either in the Pangram Box or part of the will's residuary clause."

"Speaking of the Pangram Box, what about Zyus Drake?"

Virginia kept her eyes on her laptop. "I'm trying, but I haven't been able to find a photo or anything on him. No social media accounts."

Jeff said, "He probably deleted them after what happened to him."

"I found something."

"What is it?" asked Emory.

"Juniper gave me a list of a few people Blair invited to every party because they were excellent conversationalists. I've been combing through their social media, hoping someone posted pictures from the party Zyus attended. I found one." Virginia turned her laptop around, allowing Emory and Jeff to see a picture of a beautiful forty-ish woman with a tall, handsome man in his late twenties.

"Whoa!" said Jeff.

"The woman is Clair Suffolk, a Nashville socialite."

Emory stepped closer to get a better look. "Are you sure *that's* Zyus?"

"She tagged the man to an account called Zyus.Drake, which is no longer active." She turned the computer around and read, "She captioned it, 'I met this stunning (and persuasive) trainer at Blair Geister's party. I start the gym next week!'"

Jeff crossed his arms. "I can't believe that's what he looked like before. Damn."

"I'm printing it now."

Emory retrieved the printout and taped it into the third column. "The obvious motive for him would be revenge because he blames her for what happened to him. We need to know more about their relationship."

Jeff stared at the image. "Yeah, that was weird when he said they didn't have that kind of relationship. I assumed they were lovers."

"Exactly. If they weren't lovers, what were they to each other?"

Virginia had a suggestion. "Maybe he was a paid escort. She was rich and focused on her work. Maybe she didn't take time to develop a personal relationship with a guy, so she paid for some companionship – like *Pretty Woman*."

Emory sat on the sofa next to Virginia and took another look at the post. "That could explain his comment."

Jeff wrote *Vengeance* under Zyus' picture. "She called him a trainer. Could you use that tidbit to find out more about him?"

"I'll try."

Jeff tapped the pen to the second column, with the lone photo of Dr. Barry Sharp. "The *Foundation* column is a bit sparse."

Emory rejoined Jeff at the board. "What about the coal mine her foundation is closing down. I know Juniper mentioned the miners don't know that yet, but I'm sure some must be suspicious."

Jeff tapped Emory's chest. "She did say there was a near riot when they found out she was buying it."

"I found an article on it." She scanned the article and read an excerpt aloud. "Coal mine supervisor Spike Dean led an employee revolt against the temporary shutdown, staging a sit-in that turned violent when sheriff's deputies were brought in to remove them." Virginia looked up from the laptop. "Obviously, this Spike Dean figured out the shutdown was never meant to be temporary."

"Agreed." Emory tilted his head toward the sharpie in Jeff's hand. "Sounds like a possible motive. Revenge for the loss of his and his friends' jobs."

Jeff looked to Virginia. "Picture?"

"There's one with the article, but you can't see his face too clearly. Printing now."

Emory pulled the black-and-white picture from the printer and examined it with Jeff. Spike Dean, hands cuffed behind his back, wore a miner hat that cast a shadow down the middle of his forehead as a deputy led him from the mine.

Jeff took it and taped it to the second column. "Yeah, can't make out much. It'll do for now, but we should try to find a better picture of him."

"What about house staff?" asked Virginia.

Emory watched for Jeff's reaction when he asked his next question. "Kenn Marty and the others?"

Jeff laughed. "I see what you're doing. They each got a quarter of million dollars in the will, but I doubt any of them knew that ahead of time."

Virginia said, "Everyone except the gardener, George Henry. He started working here after the will was filed."

Jeff held up his index finger. "Then he had no reason to kill her. Are we done?"

Emory identified an omission. "We're missing one very important suspect."

"Who?" asked Jeff. "Oh, you mean—"

"Our employer."

Virginia closed her laptop. "Juniper? No."

"I agree. Why would she hire us?"

Emory replied, "I don't know, but there are important details she's not telling us, particularly about Tommy Addison's death. Also, why was she convinced Blair Geister's ghost was coming after her? What did Juniper do that was so terrible, and why was she afraid her boss would find out?"

"You're right. Printing her picture now."

Without arguing, Jeff waited by the printer. "We have three categories and three PIs. What do you say we divide and conquer?"

"That's fine with me," replied Emory.

Virginia said, "Me too."

"Good." Jeff taped the picture of Juniper to the first column with the question *Cover-up?* written as the motive. "In the *Business* category, we have Myles Godfrey, Rue Darcé and Juniper Crane. In the *Foundation* category, we have Dr. Sharp and the miners. In the *Personal* category, we have Eden Geister, Zyus Drake and Edgar Strand. I'll take *Business*."

Emory snapped a picture of the board with his phone. "I'll take *Foundation*."

Jeff scoffed. "I don't think so. Virginia can be more objective about it."

Virginia put aside her laptop. "I think I should stick to the *Personal* category. I've already built relationships with two of those suspects."

"She's right." Emory tilted the top of the drafting table to where it was before, concealing the murder board. "And I should take the *Foundation* category because that's right in my wheelhouse."

"Is that what you call it? All right. I'll take *Business*." Jeff pulled his phone from his pocket for a quick glimpse. "How did it get so late?"

Virginia stood and stretched. "It's not late."

"It is for me. I didn't sleep well last night. I say we call it a day."

Emory checked the time on his phone. "It's a little early to stop working. I want to search for the Pangram Box. We only have sixty-two hours until the deadline."

"It's Friday. We've been working every waking hour. Let's take the rest of the afternoon off and take advantage of that awesome movie theatre downstairs."

Emory sighed. "Okay."

"Great!" Jeff turned to Virginia. "Can you figure out that projector?"

Virginia closed her laptop. "Probably."

"Excellent. Pick out a good movie." Jeff emptied the wine bottle into his glass on the desk. "Emory, you select a wine. I'll find some noshables, and we'll all meet in the theatre."

In the wine cellar, Emory perused the racks for an inexpensive red. When he came to the bottle of *Coyote Red* from La Fleur's Winery, his eyes turned to the painting on the wall. He stared at the haunting figure of Hugo Hickory searching for his lost heart while Waya'ha watched. Emory picked up the bottle of wine, and the painting swung away from the wall. He placed the bottle on the table and opened the safe to find nothing inside. *But there was something inside when we first opened it. I'm certain I saw something.*

He closed the safe and returned the bottle to the rack. When the painting swung back to the wall, he stared at it some more.

Emory gasped. "Is that…"

Jeff walked into the cellar, his arms laden with bags of veggie chips, left hand clutching the stems of three wine glasses between the fingers. "Are you having a problem deciding?"

Emory turned to his partner and announced, "I know what Blair Geister's up to."

CHAPTER 23

JEFF SMIRKED AT his partner. "I don't think Blair Geister's up to anything at the moment, unless... Are you seeing her ghost now too?"

"I'm talking about what she was up to with the hunt for the Pangram Box. She's acting out the ghost story."

"Hugo Hickory?"

"The Pangram Box is Zyus' lost heart. That's why it moved before we could get it. Now it's somewhere else in this house, and I bet you it'll move again when we get close to it."

"Are you saying the Pangram Box won't ever be found?"

Emory shook his head. "It has to end up somewhere. Whether that's an accessible place, I don't know. Did she put in that contingency about not damaging the house while searching to torment Zyus? Would she be that cruel?"

"I know some Easter Island heads and rooftop gargoyles who'd be giving you the side-eye if they heard you ask that."

"A feud with a neighbor is one thing. Hugo Hickory deserved his fate, but does Zyus Drake? No, she said in the will that this was a test of guilt — to see if she were truly responsible for what happened to him. What point would it serve to have a predetermined verdict? I have to believe there is an endgame. It's just a matter of figuring out how to get there."

"Okay. Where's the next hiding place for the Box?"

"I haven't figured that out yet."

"Well, think about it during the movie. Pick a bottle, and let's go."

Emory grabbed a random cab and followed Jeff down the hallway to the movie theatre, where they found Virginia in the projector room.

Jeff unloaded the chips and glasses onto a shelf. "Did you figure out how to get it running?"

"I think so. Blair has a huge video library. Any requests?"

Emory put down the wine. "I'm fine with anything."

"Action." Jeff pulled a corkscrew from his pocket and opened the wine. "And turn up the volume. I like to *feel* my movies." He filled each glass. "All right everyone, take a glass and a bag, and let's get this movie started."

Emory followed Jeff down the aisle but stopped at the third row from the front. "How about here?"

"We don't have to sit together." He proceeded to the middle seat in the front row. "I'm in seat C if you need me."

Emory took a seat two rows behind him. "I think I'll be okay."

The lights dimmed, and the screen lit up with a caravan of Humvees – and one Fun-vee – driving through the desert to the tune of AC/DC's *Back in Black*.

Jeff reclined his chair and locked his fingers behind his head. "I love this movie."

Virginia slid into the third row and sat a couple of seats from Emory. "I knew this would make him happy."

Meanwhile, Emory kept thinking about the Pangram Box. He stared at the picture of the Hugo Hickory painting on his phone. By the movie's midpoint, he'd finished his wine and half a bag of veggie chips. He stood and mouthed, "Bathroom," to Virginia before exiting the theatre. As he walked down the hall, he glanced at the open door to Juniper Crane's bedroom and the broken TV on the floor. "I wish I understood what happened in there."

He detoured to the bedroom and stood before the fallen TV. He touched the jagged edges of the broken aluminum mount on the wall, and pieces of it crumbled in his fingers. "What could've possibly done this?" He noticed a black spot behind the mount, half on the wall and half on the ceiling. "More water damage."

Emory took pictures of the stain, the mount and the back of the TV. He turned his phone to the door and snapped a picture of the spot where Tommy Addison had died, according to Juniper. He walked to the doorway and photographed that view of the TV, mount and stain.

A thought occurred to him, a strange memory from his childhood. "In the woods. Could that..."

He left the room and ascended the back stairs to the main floor. He proceeded to the den to re-examine the water damage stains on the floor and ceiling. He snapped pictures of both before heading upstairs to Blair Geister's bedroom. He stared for a moment at the homemade sign he had taped to the door, proclaiming the room a crime scene.

I won't disturb anything. He entered the room, turned on the light and scanned the hardwood floor for signs of a water stain. He stepped inside and glanced at the hole in the floor where the metal panel had been – a couple inches from the left leg of the headboard. He squinted, trying to estimate distances. "It would probably be near the head of the bed."

Dropping to his hands and knees, he looked beneath the bed but couldn't make out anything in its shadow. He turned on his phone's flashlight and held it before him. He crawled under the bed and found it – a dark spot similar to the others. He snapped a few pictures and crawled out.

"Is it even possible? I need to find out." His eyes wandered from the bed to the holes he had hammered into the wall. He shook his head and left the room, returning to the theatre in time for the movie's climax.

Once the credits rolled, Virginia was the first to pop up. "I'll get the lights."

Emory asked, "Was it everything you hoped for?"

Stretching, Jeff turned around to reveal a broad smile. "Yeah, I definitely want to see if we can convert the basement in our office to a home theatre now."

Emory met Jeff in the aisle. "How about I make us all some dinner?"

"I'm actually really tired. I think I'm just going to head to bed. You and Virginia go ahead."

Virginia came out of the projector room. "I'm going to crash too."

Emory held the theatre door open for his partners. "Okay, I'll lock up."

When the three PIs headed for the stairs, Virginia eyed Jeff. "Where are you going?"

Jeff grabbed the handrail. "Eden is staying in the guest room, right?"

Emory hesitated to answer. "Yes."

"And you moved the bed in Blair's room, so it's no longer dangerous."

"True, but—"

Jeff started up the stairs. "I'm not going to pass up a chance to sleep in a solid-gold bed."

In Blair Geister's bedroom, Jeff stripped down to his boxers and hung his clothes on the arms of a reading chair in the corner of the room. He started toward the bathroom but remembered, "My toothbrush is in my bag, downstairs." He licked his teeth. "I guess I can go one night without brushing. Sorry Mom."

He turned off the overhead light and slipped under the covers on the left side of the golden bed. He raised his right hand to touch the bars of the headboard. "Solid gold."

Within ten minutes, he was sound asleep, his hand still clutching the bar.

From one of the holes Emory had bored into the wall by Blair Geister's bed, something crawled out. It hesitated for several minutes, as if trying to find its bearing in this new world. It descended to the floor and toward the gold leg of the nearby headboard.

One of its eight legs tapped the metal like it was gauging the temperature of bath water. Satisfied, it ascended.

The brown spider with the black fiddle on its back continued to the lateral bar at the top of the headboard and waited.

When it sprung to life again, it attempted to descend one of the interior bars but lost its footing. The spider fell onto the underside of Jeff's forearm.

Once the shock of the fall abated, the spider crept onto the pillow, toward Jeff's face.

CHAPTER 24

EMORY ROLLED A suitcase down the hallway to the master bedroom. He opened the door but closed it again when he saw Jeff in bed. *Oh, he's already asleep.* He parked the bag next to the wall and headed toward the back stairs. Before taking the first step, though, he stopped himself. Something was bothering him. It was just a flash, but...

He backtracked and opened the door again. The moonlight diffusing through the window near the bed gave Jeff's skin a ghostly pallor, but he was the most beautiful ghost Emory could ever imagine. *What is that?* He thought he had seen something amiss with Jeff's face during his previous glimpse, but it didn't hit him at first. Now he was sure.

He stepped closer but still couldn't make it out. He took another step and froze. He could make out the distinctive markings of the brown recluse spider on Jeff's right cheek.

"No!" he gasped before covering his mouth.

Jeff didn't stir.

If I wake him, he could spook the spider into biting him. What do I do?!

Emory had an idea. He ran into the bathroom and returned

with a glass of water. He looked at the pillow and saw the spider hadn't moved.

He stood over Jeff. *I can do this.*

Emory positioned the glass two feet above the spider. He held his breath, his hand shaking. A drop of water splashed from the glass, hitting the pillow to the right of Jeff's face.

The brown recluse moved a half-inch closer to Jeff's eye.

Crap! Emory turned the glass over. The water washed down Jeff's cheek, delivering the spider to the pillow.

Jeff grunted awake and wiped his face with both hands. "Emory, what the hell are you doing?"

"Jeff, get out of the bed!"

"Why?"

Emory hurled the open end of the glass onto the pillow.

"What are you doing?" Jeff followed Emory's arm down to his hand and the glass with its imprisoned arachnid an inch from his face.

The spider lurched onto the side of the glass.

Jeff screamed and rolled himself off the bed, knocking Emory back as he fell to the floor.

Emory lost his grip on the glass. "Crap! It's loose!"

Still on the floor, Jeff scooted away from the bed on his hands and feet. "Get it!"

The spider scurried to the end of the pillow at the edge of the bed. Emory reached for the glass, which puffed the pillow, catapulting the spider to the floor. "Where'd it go?"

Jeff pointed. "Right there!"

The spider started scurrying toward Jeff. Emory spotted it and stomped on it.

"God almighty!" Jeff jumped to his feet. "Where the hell did that come from?"

"I'm guessing out of one of the holes in the wall."

Virginia appeared in the doorway. "Guys, what's with all the racket?"

Jeff tapped his foot by the smashed spider. "That damn spider tried to Zyus Drake me!" He shuddered.

She bent over for a look and backed away. "Is that a brown recluse?"

"Yes! Thank god, Emory showed up. Actually, why did you show up?"

"I was locking up when I saw your bag in the den." Emory rolled the suitcase into the room. "I didn't want you showing up for breakfast in the buff."

"I can't stay in here." Jeff grabbed his clothes and shoes from the chair. "I'll sleep in Juniper's room."

"Ooh, you might want to change the sheets first." Virginia feigned smoking with her index finger and thumb. "You'll wake up high."

Jeff sighed. "I'm tired. I don't feel like making a bed."

Emory grabbed the handle of the suitcase. "I'll sleep in Juniper's room and take care of the sheets. You can have Tommy's room."

Jeff followed him from the room. "I also don't want to sleep in a dead man's sheets."

"I already changed them."

Emory awoke in Juniper's windowless room with no idea of the time. He tapped his phone on the nightstand. *A little early. No one else will be up yet.* He turned over on his side with the intention of culling another hour of sleep. Seconds later he opened his eyes again. *Now I have to pee.*

He swept himself from the bed and took two steps when something pierced his big toe. Emory yelped, grabbed his foot and sat back on the bed. He switched on the bed lamp and inspected the injury. A black metal fragment from the TV mount protruded from the front of his toe. After pulling it out, he went down the hall to the bathroom to clean and bandage the small wound. On the way back to the bedroom, he snapped his fingers. "I forgot to pee."

He pulled an about-face just as the door to Tommy Addison's room opened. Jeff leaned against the jamb. "Good pre-morning."

"I'm sorry. Did I wake you?"

Jeff tilted his head from side to side. "No, it's just the most uncomfortable bed I've ever slept in."

Emory looked over Jeff's shoulder at the barren dresser top. "I just realized something. Tommy Addison had a son."

"Yeah, Juniper said that during the will reading. She wanted to make sure the son got the money bequeathed to Tommy."

"I know, but it didn't occur to me at the time. Tommy lived here. Alone."

Jeff finished Emory's train of thought. "Where's the son?"

"Exactly. Not only that, where are the pictures?"

Jeff looked around the room. "Yeah, you'd think he'd have at least one. But you know, not everyone prints pictures. You just look at your phone for them."

"We really should've made a point of going to his funeral too."

"The kid must live with his mother. I guess they were divorced."

Emory shook his head. "Those are assumptions. We should find out for sure."

"You're right. We haven't really focused on him. We know how Blair died, but his death is still a mystery."

"About that. I might've figured it out."

"Well, don't be coy. Tell me."

"Come here. I need to show you something." Emory led him into Juniper's room, to the stain in the corner of the roof. "You see that black spot behind where the TV was mounted?"

"Yeah. When the TV exploded, it must've burned it."

"You know what's directly above this room?"

Jeff shrugged. "The locutorium?"

"The den. And above that is Ms.Geister's bedroom. Remember the black spots we found on the ceiling and floor of the den? The water damage?"

"You think the water leaked into the TV and caused it to explode?"

Emory shook his head. "I don't think it was water."

"Then what?"

"What I'm thinking is crazy, so before I put myself in a position where I have to defend the idea, I want to know if it's even possible."

"Okay. How?"

"We need to go back to Oak Ridge."

CHAPTER 25

SITTING AT HIS desk, Sheriff Rome scribbled on a ledger pad until his hand started to cramp. When he dropped the pen to massage it, his office phone rang.

"Hello? Wayne, yes. I was just jotting down some notes, trying to make sure I don't forget anything important." The sheriff spent the next twenty-two minutes recounting events from eight years prior. Once he finished and had answered all Wayne's questions, he thanked him again for his help and ended the call.

He stood to stretch his legs and noticed his Gatlinburg mug was empty. "Coffee."

Leaving his office, he headed to the break room, passing the deputies' desks and the front door along the way. The door swung open behind him, and the sheriff turned around to greet a young man with a backpack. "Can I help you?"

"Someone just stole my bike."

"Oh, I'm sorry." Sheriff Rome nodded to the only occupied desk. "Deputy Harris over there can help you."

"Cool. Hey, do you have a bathroom I could use first?"

The sheriff continued in the direction he was heading. "Follow me. What's your name, son?"

The young man replied, "Phineas."

Phineas entered the single-toilet bathroom and locked the door. He let the backpack slide off his shoulders and pulled a cardboard box from inside. He opened box flaps and emptied a live rat onto the floor beside the sink.

Seconds later Phineas rushed from the bathroom and found the sheriff in the break room. Laboring his breaths, he pointed in mock panic. "Dude, there's a big rat in your bathroom!"

The sheriff lowered the coffee mug from his lips. "What? Are you kidding?"

"Seriously! I know what I saw. Rats creep me out."

The sheriff sighed. "It's okay. We'll get it."

Phineas followed the sheriff back into the main room. "Harris, bring your wastebasket. We have a rat in the bathroom."

Without questioning the find, the deputy removed the plastic lining from his metal wastebasket and joined the sheriff. As they headed to the bathroom, Phineas heard the sheriff say, "First birds and now rats. We're running a zoo."

Once they were out of sight, Phineas raced to Sheriff Rome's office. He pulled a listening device from his pocket and scanned the room for the best place to plant it. He opted for the framed Tennessee Medal of Honor hanging on the wall. After securing it, he darted for the front door and ran from the building.

CHAPTER 26

WITH JEFF AT his side, Emory drove his car toward the security station of Oak Ridge National Laboratory. "Get your ID ready." He tilted his body toward the door. "Would you mind getting mine?"

Jeff pulled Emory's wallet from his back pocket. "Is this place even open on Saturday?"

"Dr. Sharp said he works every day but Sunday."

"Did you get us on the list?"

"I hope so. I texted him this morning, but I haven't heard back." Emory could see in his periphery Jeff giving him his *Seriously?* face.

"We drove all this way on hope?"

"We do everything on hope." Emory put down his window and greeted the mustached security officer in the booth window, handing over their IDs. "Hello. We're here to see Dr. Barry Sharp. Emory Rome and Jeff Woodard."

The officer checked his computer and handed the IDs back. "Neither of you has been cleared."

"There has to be a mistake." Jeff lowered his head to smile at the officer. "He told us to come up today. Could you call him?"

"No," the officer replied without inflection. "If you're not—"

Emory noticed the edge of a red snake tattoo just above his wrist. "You're the officer who was here the other day when we came."

"I remember you."

"I don't know if Dr. Sharp told you, but he's helping us with a case – a double-homicide. It's vital we talk to him today. Would you mind calling him?"

The officer thought for a second before picking up his phone and dialing. "Dr. Sharp, I have two men here to see you – Emory Rome and… Okay, I'll let them in." He hung up but didn't say anything to the PIs. Instead, he typed on his computer before stepping away from the booth window.

Jeff strained to see. "What's he doing?"

"I have no idea."

The security officer appeared a moment later with two guest passes on lanyards. He handed them to Emory. "You know where the fulminology lab is?"

"I do."

The officer opened the gate and waved them forward. "Have a good day."

After parking, the PIs headed for the lab and knocked on the door. Dr. Sharp greeted them a moment later. "Emory, such a nice surprise. And uh… George?"

"Seriously? Do I look like a George? My name's Jeff."

Emory shook his hand. "Hi Dr. Sharp. Thank you for seeing us."

"You're lucky you caught me." Dr. Sharp led them through the laboratory.

Jeff cleared his throat and side-eyed his partner. "Emory said he texted you this morning."

Dr. Sharp opened the door to the control room. "I'm sorry, but I don't think I've even looked at my phone today."

Emory saw the room had changed, now in disarray and with a half-dozen open boxes. "What's going on here?"

"I was notified last evening that my lab is now officially closed. They moved the date up arbitrarily. I'll no longer have access to the facility come Monday, so I've been scrambling to pack up all my research and what little equipment I have that isn't owned by the government. Hopefully, they'll let me buy the rest once I get my grant." Dr. Sharp emitted a slight laugh. "Did you guys come to help me move?"

Emory wasn't sure if he were kidding or asking, but he avoided volunteering. "Actually, I have a fulminology question for you, if you don't mind."

"Then you're in the right place." Dr. Sharp motioned to the chairs and took one himself. "What can I answer for you?"

"As you know we were hired to investigate Blair Geister's death. Well, we've determined without a doubt she was murdered."

Dr. Sharp's head jerked back. "*Scheisse!* Sorry. I don't like to curse in English."

"Someone hooked her solid gold bed up to the lightning rod on her roof." Jeff dropped his elbows to his knees and stared at the professor. "Now, who would possibly think to kill someone with lightning?"

Emory spoke up before Dr. Sharp could respond to the accusatory question. "Which brings me to the reason we're here. When I was a teenager, I experienced something."

"Seriously?!" Jeff pushed back in his chair. "He gets your backstory before I do?"

"It's not my backstory. It's just a curious incident that I believe has some bearing on the case." Emory returned his attention to the professor. "I was in the woods, beside a pond, when something came toward me through the trees."

Dr. Sharp leaned forward. "What was it?"

"It was a sphere of blue light."

Jeff scoffed. "Are you saying you were abducted?"

"What? No."

"They just probed you?"

"No. Jeff, it wasn't a UFO. It was about the size of a cantaloupe, and it floated – more like drifting with the wind than self-propelled.

It blew up a few feet from me, throwing me back into a tree and knocking the wind out of me. I think it was—"

Dr. Sharp finished his thought. "Ball lightning."

Emory smiled at the confirmation. "Yes. Am I right?"

"I need a bit more information than that."

Jeff grimaced. "Ball lightning? Isn't that a myth?"

"No, not at all." Dr. Sharp popped out of his chair. "Ball lightning's been reported by witnesses all over the world, since at least ancient Greece."

Jeff said, "So have UFOs."

Dr. Sharp searched the open boxes. "Yes, but I can't create a UFO in my lab."

"You've created ball lightning?" asked Emory.

"Oh yes. Here it is." Dr. Sharp pulled an iPad from a box. "I can't take credit for it. I was just recreating Tesla's experiments. He was the first to do it." He tapped the iPad a few times before turning it around to show the PIs a video. Two Tesla coils of different sizes produced streaks of lightning between them. "Keep your eye on the smaller terminal." A ball of light floated up from the terminal and extinguished five seconds later. "Did you see it?"

Jeff sneered at the professor. "Yeah, but it didn't last very long."

"The life span and size of natural ball lightning varies. Going back to your account, Emory, was there a storm or at least a raincloud?"

"It had been raining. I remember I was soaking wet."

Jeff asked, "Why were you out in the rain? Were you camping?"

"Not exactly."

Dr. Sharp returned the iPad to the box. "There are wide-ranging theories on the causation of ball lightning in nature, but I believe it's an offshoot of standard lightning, ionizing the air around the strike point and creating a globular pocket of plasma."

Jeff stood as if ready to leave. "Fascinating. I mean, not really, but it felt like a good way to end the discussion."

"Jeff, I had a reason for bringing this up. Dr. Sharp, I hadn't thought of that incident in years, but it came to mind last night when I was examining the evidence in Tommy Addison's death."

"Who's Tommy Addison?"

Jeff sat back down. "He was Blair's handyman. He died that same night."

"Dr. Sharp, would you mind looking at this?" Emory took his phone from his pocket and scanned through the pictures.

"Only if you'll start calling me Barry." Dr. Sharp smiled at him before stepping behind his chair to look over his shoulder.

"Agreed."

Jeff scooted his chair closer to Emory's. "Thanks Barry."

Emory held the phone for both to see. "This is a picture of the floor beneath the headboard of Ms. Geister's bed. Notice the black spot?"

Dr. Sharp nodded. "That could be a burn from the lightning that struck the bed."

Emory scrolled to another picture. "This is a similar stain on the ceiling of the den, which is directly below the bedroom." He continued scrolling. "This is the floor of the den, and this is the ceiling of Juniper Crane's bedroom, below the den."

"What's that coming out of the wall?"

"It's a TV mount. The TV fell to the ground. Ms. Crane said Blair Geister's spirit came out of the TV, floated across the room and killed Tommy Addison in a violent rage before disappearing. She described the spirit as an orb of light."

Jeff asked his partner, "You think the lightning striking the bed created a ball of lightning that penetrated two floors before exploding?"

"Yes. Dr. Sharp… Barry, is that possible?"

Jeff asked, "Can it go through a solid floor?"

Dr. Sharp replied, "There's a report from England in the 1600s of ball lightning entering a church through the wall like a ghost and killing several people when it exploded. To answer your question, Emory, it is possible, but I would want more evidence before declaring it a fact."

"I think I have it." From his pocket, Emory pulled a baggie with a shard of black metal and handed it to the professor. "This is from the TV mount in the picture. Try to break it."

Dr. Sharp applied pressure, and the metal crumbled between his fingers. "*Scheisse*. This is likely an aluminum alloy, cast with silicon to make it lightweight, but that makes it highly susceptible to internal corrosion when heated. Contact with plasma could also speed galvanic corrosion, causing it to become brittle." The professor smiled at Emory. "I support your theory."

Driving back to Geisterhaus, Emory and Jeff called Virginia to fill her in on the presumed cause of death for Tommy Addison. Afterwards, Emory asked Jeff to make a video call to Cathy Shaw. The medical examiner answered with, "Hey handsomes!" and an energetic wave to the camera.

Jeff greeted her with a grin. "Hey Cathy. Do you have a few minutes to talk to us?"

"Is this about the Geister/Addison case?"

"Yes," answered Emory. "The sheriff is coming by the house this afternoon to examine some evidence we discovered, but we wanted to run it by you to make certain it aligns with your findings."

"What evidence?"

The PIs told her about the lightning rod rewiring and Emory's ball lightning theory.

Cathy took a moment. "When you asked me about lightning before, I dismissed it because both victims died indoors with no evidence of a lightning strike, but damn if you didn't find it."

Emory asked, "Would you say that contact with lightning is consistent with the anomalies you found – Blair Geister's ruptured eardrum and Tommy Addison's eye petechia?"

Cathy whistled air between her teeth and tilted her head. "Consistent isn't really a term you can use when it comes to lightning-related injuries. If I find visceral congestion and cyanosis along with petechia, I know the COD is asphyxia. If I see something as basic as saltwater in the lungs, I know it's drowning. But lightning's a trickster. Rarely do you have a mode of lethality with such a vast array of potential expressions – from walking away without a scratch to nearly complete incineration. Apart from the victims in this case, I've only examined two other lightning-strike victims. When I was an intern doing an ER rotation, we had a woman come in with everything beneath her right knee disintegrated from where the lightning exited her body. She didn't make it. Then when I was a resident, I had a male lightning victim who looked perfectly fine, but he was suffering from maddening tinnitus – ringing in the ear. What I'm trying to say is that lightning could explain it all – the myocardial infarction, petechia and ruptured eardrum."

Emory sighed in relief. "Thanks Cathy. That's exactly what we needed to know."

"Glad to help. Now when are you guys going to take me out on the town like you promised?"

Jeff asked, "How about next Friday?"

"I'm going to hold you to that, Bright Eyes."

"Bye Cathy." Jeff hung up the phone. "Lightning is the perfect murder weapon."

"I wouldn't say that," Emory replied. "The perfect murder weapon would be one that didn't leave a trace."

"It barely left one. She had the deaths ruled as heart attacks."

"But the killer couldn't have known that for certain. You heard Cathy. Lightning's impact on the body is unpredictable. Whoever killed Blair Geister had no idea what state her body would be in."

"Or that it would end up killing someone else. Okay, what would be the perfect murder?"

Emory shook his head. "There's no such thing. Murderers always forget something. Some minute detail that can be found if you just look."

"If you were going to murder someone, how would you do it?"

"I wouldn't."

"I'm not saying that you would. Just put yourself in the mindset of someone capable of murdering another person in cold blood. How would you go about it to give yourself the best chance of getting away with it?"

Emory sighed. "Hypothetically, the most successful murder would be one that was never identified as a murder."

"You'd want it to look like natural causes or an accident."

"Yes, but how you went about it would depend on the intended victim – their age, health, habits, et cetera. You could push a young skateboarder's head into a cement curb and have his skateboard nearby, and perhaps no one would question if it were ruled an accident, unless the victim was known to never skate without a helmet."

Jeff thought for a moment. "Say your victim is a forty-year-old male in perfect health with no unusual habits."

"I don't know. If I'm remembering correctly, the leading cause of death for that age group is unintentional injury, mostly from accidental poisoning like drug overdoses or interactions. An over-the-counter potassium-sparing diuretic mixed with a common salt substitute could cause a heart attack in an otherwise healthy individual. Viagra mixed with the nitrates from eating bacon can do the same thing."

"Seriously? I guess no post-sex BLTs."

"Right? Now the example you gave is of a man in perfect health, but people are usually in their forties when they start worrying about their cholesterol levels and might be on cholesterol-lowering medications. Grapefruit's interaction with these drugs is pretty common knowledge, but not a lot of people realize that other fruits, such as tangelos, have furanocoumarins, the chemical in grapefruit that causes the interaction. They could inadvertently eat that without knowing that it could cause a heart attack. You can get furanocoumarins from over-the-counter supplements. Dissolve a large dose in his drink, so it interacts with the medication he's taking and throw some tangelos in his fruit bowl. The effect from furanocoumarins can last for three days, well after it's gone through the stomach. The ME might not find any trace of the fruit in the stomach, but it wouldn't raise any flags."

Jeff gaped at his partner. "Damn, that's cold."

"You asked!"

"I wasn't expecting that much detail. Okay, what about if you didn't care that people knew the victim had been murdered, but you still wanted to get away with it?"

"That makes it more difficult." Emory inhaled as if a thought had struck him.

"What is it?"

"I just remembered something that happened when I was a kid. A couple of kids propped a scarecrow up on the train tracks, hoping to make a freight train throw on its brakes."

"What's the point of that?"

Emory shrugged. "Just a prank. Anyway, the train never even slowed down. It got me thinking what if that had been a person who looked like a scarecrow."

"You mean on Halloween."

"No. Someone drugged and dressed up like a scarecrow and tied to the posts. The train would've gone right through them."

"You do have a sick mind."

Emory laughed. "You can't catch a killer without thinking like one. Okay, what about you?"

"What about me?"

"Same question. How would you murder someone?"

Jeff touched his chest. "Me. That's easy. I wouldn't."

Emory repeated Jeff's hypothesis. "Put yourself in the mindset of someone capable of murder."

Jeff shook his head. "Yeah, I'm not feeling it. I can't even hypothetically think so deviously. It's just not who I am."

"You jerk. You made me do it."

"Oh look! We're home."

Emory turned onto the driveway to Geisterhaus and parked to the right of Jeff's car. When he exited the vehicle, he glanced inside the passenger-side window and saw clumps of dirt on the driver-side floor. *Huh. His car was spotless before we left Knoxville, and he didn't want to dirty it. That's why we took my car.* As the two approached the front door, Emory stopped.

"What is it?"

"Um…" Emory searched for words.

Jeff snapped his fingers. "I forgot. I brought some fresh cloths. I'll meet you inside."

As Jeff walked back to his car, Emory stepped inside the house and stood there. *What do I do? Wait! I have an idea.* He walked back outside and intercepted Jeff, who was now dragging a piece of luggage behind him.

"I told you I had it. It's just one bag."

Emory pointed behind him with his thumb. "Virginia's in there going nuts looking for her keys. She can't find them anywhere."

"Why is she stressing?" Jeff pulled out his keychain. "She knows I have a copy."

Emory's eyes widened, and he jabbed a finger into Jeff's chest, growling, "It was you!"

"What? What are you talking about?"

"When we first saw Zyus Drake at Blair Geister's will reading, I commented on his mask. Virginia explained they're used in the military, and she said that she had one. You heard her."

"So?"

"The night you stayed in Knoxville, I saw someone wearing the mask by that huge cedar tree, holding a shovel."

"You told me. Zyus Drake."

"I chased him out the front gate, and then I walked down the driveway back to the house. I was soaking wet from the rain when I got back to the house, and I saw Zyus about a minute later completely dry. There's no way he could've cleaned up that quickly, which means the guy I saw was someone else." Emory jabbed his finger into Jeff's chest. "You!"

CHAPTER 27

JEFF SHOT HIS partner an incredulous look. "What are you talking about?"

Emory again pressed his finger into Jeff's chest. "I saw the dried mud on the driver-side floor of your car."

Jeff lifted his open hands at his side. "You mean dirt?"

"You're fanatical about the cleanliness of your car, and I saw it before we came here to work on this case, when we were walking to my car. It was spotless inside and out. If you had truly gone from your home to the apartment where Bobbie is staying, back to your apartment to sleep and then down here, at no point would you have come into contact with muddy ground."

"I parked across the street from the cat-sitter's apartment, and there was mud in the median when I ran across the street."

"What street does she live on?"

"Morg…"

"Morgan Street? There aren't any medians on Morgan Street."

"I wasn't going to say Morgan Street. I was going to say Morgue Street."

"Morgue Street? There's no such place."

"Yes, there is. It's right by… the hospital."

"I don't believe you. And you were exhausted yesterday – not because you couldn't sleep the night before but because you were up all night, renting a truck for some reason, driving down here, doing whatever you did... What were you doing here?"

Jeff threw up his hands. "Nothing because I wasn't here. You're being ridiculous."

"Stop lying to me! You have the nerve to guilt me for not trusting you? Give me a reason I should trust you."

Jeff turned away from his partner. His shoulders dropped, and he faced him again. "All right. It was me."

"Explain yourself."

"Okay. I'll... I'll tell you." Jeff's eyes scrolled from the landscape on Emory's left to his right and back again.

"Stop stalling! You think I don't know you're concocting a lie?"

"I was not."

"Yes, you were. The truth doesn't need time to think. You just tell it."

Jeff raised a hand to his lips and sighed. "In my defense, you weren't supposed to find out."

"That's not a defense! What were you doing here in the middle of the night with a shovel?

"I was trying to surprise you. I was following a hunch, digging for the Pangram Box, but it was a dead end."

"Then why leave? Why not just say... You're lying."

"What? I'm not lying."

A thought popped into Emory's head. "Were you burying something?"

"No. Of course not."

"Then you should have no problem with my borrowing a shovel from the gardener." Emory turned from him to walk away.

Jeff grabbed Emory's arm. "Why?"

"I'm going to dig around that cedar tree until I find whatever you buried."

With a wry expression, Jeff called his bluff. "You wouldn't do that. That tree is protected by the state. There's no way you'll risk hurting it."

"It shouldn't be that difficult to find freshly disturbed dirt. That's all I'll touch."

"All right!" Jeff clenched his fists. "All right. I'll tell you the truth. But you can't repeat what I say to anyone. Not even Virginia."

Emory tried to imagine what Jeff wouldn't even tell his best friend. "Okay."

Jeff took him by the arm. "Let's walk."

"Why?"

"I need some air, and I don't want to risk anyone else hearing what I'm going to tell you."

"Fine." Emory followed Jeff around the house and toward the river.

Jeff stayed silent, waiting until they stepped onto the pier to the boathouse before speaking again. "We should skinny-dip later."

"I told you I can't swim."

"I could teach you." Jeff glanced at Emory, who didn't respond. He opened the door to the boathouse. "Let's talk in here."

Walled on all four sides, the wooden structure had two arched cutouts on both sides for docking boats, only two of which held a vessel. At the far end hummed a generator, powered by the water-wheel on the other side of the wall. A pipe carrying electricity to the house, Emory presumed, ran from the generator and disappeared beneath the floor.

As they walked across the wooden planks, the walls moaned. Jeff stopped in the middle of the boathouse and let out a tiny laugh. "I guess the boathouse is haunted too. Hey, we still haven't figured out what the light in the water was."

"You're stalling again."

Jeff looked everywhere but Emory's face as he blurted out, "I buried someone."

Emory gasped and froze. "What do you mean you buried someone? Who?"

"My old boyfriend."

Emory gasped again.

Jeff faced him to ask, "Would you stop doing that?"

Emory threw his arms up. "Then stop giving me things to gasp about!"

"Just hold your freak-out until I've had a chance to explain."

Emory gritted his teeth and growled, "Fine. Explain why I shouldn't be freaking out right now."

The boathouse wailed and swayed a bit with the river's current, prompting both men to adjust their footing. The two boats tapped the posts to which they were moored.

"That moaning." Jeff looked up at the ceiling beams.

"It does sound like a ghost. Is this place safe?"

"It should be. It's not that old."

Emory shook his head and aimed forward with his hand as if to recalibrate the conversation. "Okay. Stop stalling."

Jeff sighed. "I'll start from the beginning. I met him at a fraternity party when I was a freshman at UT. I don't remember which fraternity. I know it wasn't the one I eventually pledged. I guess that doesn't matter, but it was the first time I saw Trevor Park. He was this handsome, sexy nerd who looked so out of place – kind of like you anywhere outside a crime scene. I got him a beer and made a joke. I don't remember what the joke was either, but I've never in my life made someone laugh so hard. Of course, that endeared him to me right away. It ended up being one of the best nights of my life. I swear, for a bacteriology major, he was surprisingly good at beer bonging.

"Anyway, we became an item. He came home with me over the winter break, and my parents loved him. The next semester, we got an apartment together, and all was good. Wonderful really. He used to write me little poems and leave them on my pillow.

Not sappy love poems. More serious, even sad. One of my favorites later inspired the name for the agency." Jeff recited the poem from memory:

> *The mourning dove flies*
> *On the broken heart's wings.*
> *The mourning dove cries*
> *While the thoughtless bird sings.*
> *And the mourning dove dies*
> *In the fervor hate brings.*

"Then summer came. He headed back home to Idaho, determined to come out to his ultra-conservative parents and tell them about me. I tried my damnedest to talk him out of it. From everything he had told me about his parents, I knew they wouldn't take it well, but my thoughts undersold the fervor of their hate. He showed up at our apartment two days after he left, completely distraught. He had come out to his parents, and they were brutal in their response. They completely disowned him, gave him five minutes to pack his stuff and get out of their house. They cut him off financially, which wasn't as big a deal because he had scholarships and grants to get through school. He found out through a cousin that they gave all the belongings he left behind to Goodwill.

"Then he got sick. Who gets the flu in summer? Honestly, I thought at the time he was heartsick about his parents, and his body just shut down on him. He came down with pneumonia, and the next day, he was... gone." Jeff turned away to wipe his eyes.

Emory's demeanor evolved from mistrust to empathy. "I'm sorry. Did his parents regret their actions after he died?"

"They never came to Knoxville and never even claimed his body. I wanted to claim it and give him a proper funeral, but his parents refused. To make sure I didn't get him, they donated his body to your alma mater for med students to dissect."

"Damn."

"What kind of parents would do that to their kid? I couldn't stand the thought of it. I drove overnight to Nashville, broke into the Vanderbilt morgue and stole his body. I made a coffin for him and buried him."

"Where?"

"My parents own thirty acres outside Bristol that they've been planning to develop for their retirement, but they hadn't done anything with it. It's mainly used by hunters who completely disregard the *No Hunting* signs I posted all around the perimeter. Anyway, I'm getting sidetracked. I held a funeral for Trevor with just me, and I buried him there. After I opened the agency, my parents started talking again about building a house on the property, and that's when I moved his body to the basement at Mourning Dove."

Emory surmised the rest. "Once construction started on the office, you were afraid his body would be found."

"My parents still haven't done anything with the property, despite all their talk of retiring, so I temporarily put him back there. But I knew I needed to find a permanent place for him."

"You buried him in the protected zone around the red cedar?"

"What better place than a landmark that will remain untouched. And I figured I could come visit him every month or so, since this place is being converted to a museum."

Emory gave Jeff a lingering hug. "You did a good thing. Thank you for telling me."

The pier creaked and swayed again.

Emory stepped back to reclaim his footing. "I didn't realize these things moved this much."

"They don't usually. I hope Blair Geister's buildings are better constructed than her boathouses."

Emory laughed. "Now, I need to tell you something."

"What is it?"

Emory started to answer, but the boathouse moved again. The

powerful lunge to the side sent both men to the floor planks. They looked at each other, and both said, "Run!"

They sprang up and hurried toward the door, through which they could see the pier collapsing. The boathouse lurched to the side, separating from the pier. The walls twisted, planks flying loose.

The building screeched, and Emory's eyes shot up to the falling ceiling.

CHAPTER 28

THE WALL OF the boathouse that held the waterwheel broke away, taking the generator with it. Jeff dodged a support beam from the roof, and it impaled the wood-planked floor beside them. He looked out the open door of the now floating structure and saw houses along the riverbank whizzing by. "Jump!"

Emory backed away from him. "I can't swim!"

Gripping Emory's hand, Jeff pulled his partner through the door and forced him to jump from the crumbling boathouse into the fast-flowing river. Once Jeff's head again rose above the chilly water, he realized his hands were empty and Emory was nowhere to be seen.

"Emory!"

He dove under the water to search, but he couldn't spot anything through the silt. Coming up for air, he again called for his missing partner.

Emory's hands broke through the surface and slapped at the water as his head bobbed up for air.

Jeff sprang into action, torpedoing through the dozen feet separating them. He wrapped his arms around Emory's waist, pressing his partner's back to his chest, and steadied him so he could breathe.

Emory continued slapping at the water, prompting Jeff to try calming him. "Hey, I got you. I got you."

Emory calmed his frantic movements and relaxed into Jeff's embrace.

"I need you to turn around and hold on to my shoulders."

Emory hesitated but complied. Now facing each other, Jeff could see the panic in Emory's eyes. "I'm going to turn around, and you just keep ahold of my shoulders. I'll swim us to the bank. Okay?"

Once Emory nodded, Jeff turned his body around so that Emory's chest pressed against his shoulder blades. Jeff began swimming. A few minutes later, the men crawled onto the muddy ground at least ten houses down from Blair Geister's estate.

Emory rolled over and plopped his back onto the muddy ground, the river still lapping at the soles of his size fourteen black bike-toe dress shoes. Jeff followed suit and put his hand into Emory's. "Are you okay?"

"I'm good." Emory squeezed Jeff's hand. "Thank you."

Jeff smiled. "Consider that your first swimming lesson." He lifted his head to get a sense of their location. "We're quite a ways down river. I'll call Virginia to pick us up." He took out his phone and tried in vain to call. "Damn! The water killed it."

Emory tried with his phone. "Same here. Looks like we're walking."

Jeff worked his way to his feet and helped his partner to his. As the two walked along the bank, he put an arm around Emory's shoulders. "Are you sure you're okay?"

"I'm fine."

"I tell you what. I don't think I'll ever step foot into one of Blair Geister's buildings again."

From the river bank, Virginia inspected the visible remnants of Blair Geister's pier. The boathouse was destroyed, taking half the pier with it. She heard a noise and turned to see Jeff plodding toward her from the house, wearing only a bright-blue pair of shorts and holding something in his hands. "Did you shower already?"

Jeff walked past her. "No. Something's bothering me."

"What is it?"

Without answering, Jeff slipped on a pair of goggles. He ran the length of the remaining pier and lowered himself into the water.

For the next several minutes, she watched Jeff's head break the water's surface before disappearing again at least four times.

Sporting wet hair and fresh clothes, Emory appeared at her side. Virginia wrapped an arm around him. "Feel better after your shower?"

Emory adjusted his khakis. "Better, but I can still feel silt in places."

"At least you two weren't hurt."

"Thankfully. Where's Jeff?"

Virginia nodded toward the water, where Jeff's head had just popped above the surface.

Jeff swam toward them and slogged onto the bank. "Most of the pilings show signs of charring about a foot from the bottom – like someone took a welding torch to them. It was only a matter of time before the river's current snapped the wood."

"The lights in the water," Virginia muttered.

"I bet you're right," said Emory. "Sabotage."

Jeff removed his goggles. "No question. Who would do that?"

Virginia's eyes turned toward Edgar Strand's property. "I have an idea."

Jeff clenched his fists and stomped forward. "I'm going to kill him!"

Emory stepped in front of him. "You're not confronting him."

Jeff pointed at the ersatz boathouse. "He could've killed us!"

"Emory's right. You're too angry. I'll talk to him, so we don't end up with an assault charge. Why don't you two go into town and pick up some new phones."

"Great idea." Emory placed a hand on Jeff's back in an apparent effort to push him toward the house.

Jeff relaxed his hands. "Okay, but be angry at that asshole, and make sure he knows he could've easily been up on manslaughter charges. Twice now!"

Virginia smirked. "I'll put on my mean face."

Virginia knocked on Edgar Strand's door, and fifteen seconds later, she saw his pasty face grousing at her through the peephole window. "The gargoyles are still there!"

"I haven't been able to talk to Juniper. She's been out of town, but she's coming back today."

"I'll believe it when I see it."

"Anyway, I'm not here about that. I wanted to warn you that you need to get your boathouse inspected. The one next door just collapsed for no apparent reason."

Edgar scoffed. "I'll tell you the reason. She bypassed standard regulations in the design and probably did the same when she picked the construction materials. Proves my theory that she bribed the Army Corps of Engineers to approve the permit. Thank you for the concern, but my boathouse is fine."

Edgar started to shut the peephole, until Virginia blurted, "My partners were almost killed when it collapsed."

He opened it again, revealing a look of concern. "There were people on it? Was anyone hurt?"

"Emory, my partner, almost drowned." Virginia opted to embellish her answer with a lie. "He's in the hospital now."

Edgar dropped his eyes and paused a moment. "I have to go now."

"Wait. I need to ask you something about water towers."

"What do you want to know?"

"You know, it's a bit awkward carrying on a conversation through that little door in your door. Do you mind if we talk inside?"

Edgar hesitated but relented. "Come in."

Virginia followed Edgar to the living room. "What are water towers used for? Do they collect rainwater?"

"Some are used to store water – potable or unpotable. Most towers pressurize treated water so it can be pushed out into the community."

Virginia motioned toward the table, to the framed picture of Edgar with the Calhoun water tower over his shoulder. "Do you take care of this town's water tower?"

"Yes. I also built it."

"Impressive. Do you ever have to dive into them when they're full of water?"

"Oh yes." Edgar responded with a proud smile. "To inspect them and sometimes for repairs."

"Then you're experienced at underwater welding?"

Edgar seemed to realize where Virginia's questions were leading, and he didn't look pleased. "I believe your time is up."

CHAPTER 29

RETURNING FROM PHONE shopping, Emory and Jeff were almost back at Geisterhaus when a patrol car drove up behind them.

Jeff glanced over his shoulder. "I told you you're driving too slow."

"I am not." Emory turned onto the driveway to the house, and the patrol car followed. "It's got to be Sheriff Flynn. He said he'd be here this afternoon."

After parking, the PIs greeted the sheriff and Deputy Nunley.

Sheriff Flynn put on his hat and tipped it to them. "You wanna show me what you found?"

"Absolutely." Emory led them to the front door.

Jeff followed them inside the house but stopped short of the stairs. "Emory, you don't need me for this. I'm going to find Virginia."

Jeff walked down the hallway to see if he could find Virginia in the kitchen. Along the way, he heard sounds coming from the library. He cracked open the door to see Eden Geister and the gardener going through the books, pulling them out and looking at the shelves before returning them without even glancing at the covers. He opened the door the rest of the way to make his presence known. "You know, there are better exercises for your lats. There's actually a gym upstairs."

Eden's shoulders jumped, and she dropped a book. "Jeff! You startled me."

George Henry jumped away from the shelf like a teenage shoplifter caught in the act. "We were looking for some gardening books."

"That's right." Eden picked the book off the floor. "Blair had some nice volumes on Southeast floriculture and indigenous flora, and I thought they might as well go to Mr. Henry instead of sitting here on these dusty shelves."

Jeff crossed his arms. "Oh, I'm sorry. I wasn't aware Juniper gave you permission to start liquidating your cousin's assets."

"I don't need her permission to give away a couple of books!" She shoved the book back onto the shelf.

George made his way to the door. "Eden, it's okay. Forget about the books. I don't want to cause any trouble for you." He grunted for Jeff to scoot from the doorway and coughed as he left.

Eden glared at the PI. "Isn't it about time you all packed your bags and got the hell out of here?"

"Oh absolutely. Right after we identify your cousin's murderer." Jeff grinned. "Any ideas on who she might be."

"Get out of my way!" Eden stormed through the door and disappeared down the hall.

Jeff laughed to himself and continued his search for Virginia. He found her a couple of minutes later on her laptop at Blair Geister's desk. "Did you at least punch the neighbor?"

Virginia kept her attention on the computer. "No, but he definitely sabotaged the boathouse."

"You didn't kick him in the nuts? Nothing?"

"The guy's an ass, but I kind of feel sorry for him."

Jeff sat on the edge of the desk. "Regardless, I imagine Juniper will press charges when she finds out."

"I'm going to plead his case. I just feel bad for him. Anyway, I'm glad you're back. I was just setting up the video call to Dr. Igataki for Emory. Where is he?"

"He's taking the sheriff through the crime scene, so you might have to interview him yourself."

"That's fine. Oh!" Virginia slapped him on the leg. "You're not going to believe what I found out. Two things actually. One cool and one huge."

"Start with the cool."

"I know why Blair Geister gave Zyus Drake 114 hours to find the Pangram Box."

Virginia ended her statement with a long pause, prompting Jeff to throw open his hands and ask, "Why?"

"I checked out her Wiki page again. I was looking at the list of buildings she owns that are more than twenty stories. The Monolith, forty-four floors. The Somerset, twenty-six floors."

"The floors add up to 114?"

Virginia smiled. "Exactly!"

"Good job. Now what's the huge news?"

"It's about Zyus—" Virginia began before she was interrupted. Juniper Crane entered the office with Miss Luann at her side.

"Welcome back!" Virginia got up to greet Juniper with a hug.

Juniper waved to her companion. "You both remember Miss Luann."

"Of course." Jeff sidled his partner and grinned at the clairvoyant. "I had a feeling you were coming."

Virginia elbowed him.

"Thank you for your texts," said Juniper. "I can't believe Ms. Geister was murdered. Who would do such a thing?"

Virginia replied, "We're working on that."

Juniper smiled at them both. "I appreciate everything you three have been doing. Miss Luann is here just to verify Ms. Geister's spirit is now at rest."

"About that, we now have an explanation for your *ghost*." Jeff enclosed the last word with air quotes and told Miss Luann. "No offense."

"Jeff, I'll fill them in on everything. Can you take the video meeting? The laptop's all set up. All you have to do is join the call…" Virginia glanced at her watch. "…in one minute."

"I'll take care of it." After the others left the office, Jeff hopped behind the desk and opened the video meeting to find a bespectacled, middle-aged man in a white dress shirt and striped bowtie. "Dr. Igataki?"

The man adjusted the angle of his camera. "It's Saturday. You can call me Arthur. You must be Emory Rome."

"Actually, Emory is assisting the local sheriff at the moment. I'm his partner, Jeff Woodard."

"Very well. You wanted to discuss my work with the EARTH Foundation?"

"Yes. I want to ask you about two grant applications. Let's start with Eden Geister."

"I assume you would like to know why her grant was declined."

"Please."

Dr. Igataki scooted closer to the camera, resting his forearms on his desk. "I found some… errors in her work that… overstated her results."

"Were they intentional errors?"

"I'm a scientist, Mr. Woodard. I deal in facts. I cannot answer that question without speculation."

"Understood." Jeff thought of another way to ask the question. "In your opinion, could those errors could have been unintentional?"

"I'm not comfortable—"

"I'm just asking for your opinion. I understand you don't have the necessary data to judge with absolute certainty, and I'm not asking you to swear to it. I'm just asking for your professional opinion."

Dr. Igataki sighed. "In my opinion, a scientist would have to be exceedingly sloppy or just plain inept to have made those errors unintentionally. In any of these scenarios, funding for the researcher would not have been justifiable."

"Thank you, Doctor. I appreciate your candor. Just out of curiosity, does the foundation support your research?"

Dr. Igataki shook his head. "Oh no. The EARTH Foundation supports scientific endeavors related to environmental matters. I'm a stem cell biologist. My research is focused on tissue regeneration."

"That sounds very interesting, Dr. Igataki. Do you review all the grant applications for the EARTH Foundation?"

"I don't know that I'm the exclusive reviewer."

"Did you review the grant application for Dr. Barry Sharp?"

"I did."

"What were your findings?"

"I found his research to be sound and promising. His grant was approved."

"Then why would Blair want to delay the payment?"

Dr. Igataki pushed back into his chair. "I can't say."

"What is it, Doctor?"

"I hesitate to bring this up. Rumors are not facts, so I would've never mentioned it to Blair if not for the morality clause attached to each of her grants."

"Doctor, it could be important."

After some hesitation, Dr. Igataki acquiesced. "Scientific communities, regionally, are very much like small towns where everyone knows everyone's business. I heard from the director at Oak Ridge of possible sexual misconduct involving a former lab assistant. Ms. Geister likely wanted time to ensure proper investigation of the allegation."

Jeff fought back a smile. "Thank you, Doctor. I won't take up any more of your time."

"You're welcome." The doctor waved and signed off.

"I knew there was something off about him!" Jeff closed the laptop and jumped back at what came into view when he did. A woman in a purple polyester skirt suit was sitting on the sofa staring at him. "Miss Luann. You startled me."

"I'm sorry." Miss Luann rose to her feet. "I didn't want to interrupt your meeting. I have to talk to you."

"What about?"

She sauntered toward him. "You need to get Emory away from this place. He won't heed my warning to stay out of the woods, and this place is surrounded by woods."

"I do appreciate your concern, Nostradama, but you should know your prophesies are zero for two. Emory almost fell off the roof, but he survived."

Miss Luann continued toward him with an unblinking gaze. "Emory's danger won't be found on a rooftop."

"You also predicted there would be three deaths here. Well, if Eden Geister really were in mortal danger the other night, Emory pulled her out of it. Like I said, zero for two."

"I never said there would be a third death. I said there would be a third spirit, and I never said that spirit would be Eden's." The clairvoyant rested her palms on the desk across from Jeff. "And I was right. There is a third spirit here now."

Jeff could feel the hair on his arms rising. *There's no way. She can't know about Trevor.*

"Miss Luann," Juniper called as she entered the room with Virginia at her side. "We've finished our conversation. Do you want to start on the house now?"

"I already have." Miss Luann reversed direction, toward the door.

Virginia grinned at Jeff. "Juniper's agreed to remove the gargoyles and move the Easter Island heads to the woods on the other side of the property."

Juniper added, "But I'm going to leave Edgar Strand's fate

concerning the boathouse up to you and Emory, since you're the ones he almost killed with his antics. The sheriff is already here if you want me to report him."

"At the very least, he should be charged with vandalism and reckless endangerment." Jeff's words caught a disapproving look from his partner, causing him to pivot. "But Virginia seems to think he's suffered enough. I'm sure Emory will agree with her. He usually does. Let him go."

"Very well." Juniper turned her attention back to Virginia. "No matter what, he will have to pay to rebuild it, but I'll consider making the new one unobtrusive."

Emory entered the office behind them. "Everyone's here. Ms. Crane, Sheriff Flynn is taking the evidence, including some of the floorboards in Blair Geister's bedroom. I just don't want you to think the damage was done in search of the Pangram Box."

"Thank you for letting me know."

"Also, now that her death is officially a murder, he wants to interview everyone again, starting with you."

Juniper put a hand to her chest. "Oh."

"He's in the locutorium."

"Very well. I'll go talk to him." Juniper's hand moved up to her lips as she headed out the door.

"Jeff, how did the meeting go?"

Although Virginia asked the question, his eyes were on Emory as he answered. "Highly informative. Eden didn't get the grant because she made some presumably intentional errors to pretty up the results of her research."

Emory closed the office door. "Did she honestly think no one would notice?"

Virginia slipped into one of the chairs in front of the desk. "Maybe she thought her application would just be rubber-stamped since she's family."

"Oh, but that's not all." Jeff's green eyes gleamed above a

growing grin. "Dr. Barry Sharp is apparently being investigated for sexual misconduct with an intern."

Emory was about to take the chair next to Virginia, but he froze when he heard the news. "I can't believe he would do that. He's too... respectful of people."

"Well, it's true. Dr. Igataki told me and that the EARTH Foundation grants come with a morality clause."

Virginia finished his thought. "That's why Blair wanted to delay his payment."

"Exactly!" Jeff swiveled back and forth in his chair. "Hey, what was your other big news? You were going to tell me something before Juniper showed up."

"You're not going to believe this." Virginia paused for a moment, looking at each of her partners. "I know the nature of Zyus and Blair's relationship, and guys... it's disturbing."

CHAPTER 30

CONFUSED, EMORY EASED himself into the chair. "I don't understand. What's a cash master? Is it like an accountant?"

Jeff laughed. "Not even close."

"Don't laugh at him," said Virginia. "I had to look up what it was."

Jeff locked his fingers in front of him and his eyes on Emory. "Cash masters are part of a sexual subculture. It's someone who dominates other people in exchange for tributes – cash or gifts."

Emory asked Virginia, "How do you know they had this type of relationship?"

"I hacked into her Twitter account and read through her DMs. She had a long chain that started about a year ago with a MasterZD, an account that has since been disabled. She initiated it, saying how much she liked his pictures. He replied that if she liked them so much, she should get him something off his Amazon wish list. From there, it turned into the whole cash master thing. He would talk… dirty to her, and she would send him money or buy him expensive gifts."

"Zyus was a male prostitute?"

"Not exactly," replied Jeff. "Prostitutes exchange sex for money.

In most cash master/slave relationships, they never even meet. It's all online."

"Then I don't understand what you're paying for."

"It's financial domination, or findom for short. The slave is basically paying for the master to treat him or her a certain way. A degrading way. A female findom slave is rare, but it looks like Blair Geister was a trailblazer in that arena too."

"How do you know so much about this?"

"I had a college roommate one semester who moonlighted as a cash master," Jeff replied, receiving a frown from Emory. "Don't look at me like that. I had no control over his activities."

Virginia continued relating what she found. "Anyway, Blair and Zyus would DM each other up to twenty times a day – most of the time chatting like online pen pals, peppered with some S&M talk. She started sharing everything with him, from problems she was having at work to movies that made her cry. And he'd do the same, telling her all about his family and dreams for the future."

"That sounds like they were dating," said Emory.

"Except that they never met – at least not until the night of the party."

Jeff asked, "Why then?"

"Zyus had been pushing to meet in person, but Blair resisted. She mentioned the party in one of her messages, and he said it would be the perfect opportunity to meet. He could play the part of her new personal trainer, and he would leave after the party. He said he just wanted to meet her finally. She relented, and we know what happened after that. The last DM between them was her giving him her phone number and directions to her house."

Emory shook his head. "Unbelievable."

"I know. The whole time I was reading, I kept thinking, it doesn't make sense. She was such a success. Why would she degrade herself like that?"

Jeff swiveled in his chair. "Maybe it does make sense, in a weird way. She was carrying around guilt about her brother."

Emory wasn't sold. "Eden told us she went to therapy to get over it."

"Maybe she just buried it. She achieved monumental success, but part of her – the part that held onto that guilt – felt she didn't deserve it. Or maybe Blair was just much more colorful than we realized. Another reason we should find rich clients to be on retainer for. They're freaky and have lots of secrets to protect."

Emory walked to the drafting table and flipped it up to see the murder board. "I bet that's the reason for the cone of silence around Zyus' lawsuit against Blair. The nature of their relationship must've come up during the depositions."

Jeff joined him at the board. "Which means Juniper probably knew about it. I want to talk to her."

Emory told him, "Even though we know the truth about this situation now, I doubt she'll dishonor the NDA."

"That's okay. I have other questions for her."

Virginia joined her partners and touched the news photo of the mine foreman's arrest. "And I want to delve into another nagging loose end."

Jeff looked to Emory. "What about you?"

"I'm going to follow Hugo Hickory. Let's hope my heart's not too dark."

Jeff descended the front stairs, and after passing two deputies, carrying Blair Geister's mattress between them, he spotted Juniper and Sheriff Flynn talking in the locutorium. He loitered on the bottom step until the sheriff left her and exited the front door.

"Juniper, could I have a few minutes of your time?"

"It would be a pleasure. I'm sick of answering questions. What is it you need?"

"I need to ask you some questions."

Juniper's shoulders slumped. "Very well."

"One thing I've been curious about. Why didn't you tell us what happened to Zyus Drake instead of referring to him as the *man with the disappearing face?*"

"Because it's just so… gruesome. What was I supposed to say? That the skin on his face corroded and fell off?" Juniper shuddered. "I'm really not comfortable talking about this."

"All right." Jeff brushed the topic aside. "You mentioned that Tommy Addison had a son. Why didn't he live with him?"

"Rue got full custody in the divorce."

"Rue. Why does that name sound familiar?"

"You met her at The Monolith opening. She's the interim CEO."

"Seriously? Rue Darcé is Tommy Addison's ex-wife?"

"She went back to her maiden name after the divorce."

"Blair Geister's handyman and her heir apparent used to be married?"

Juniper frowned at him. "He wasn't a handyman. He was the facilities manager. He had a degree in engineering."

"Why didn't you tell us about the marriage?"

"I didn't think it was relevant."

"We're going to need to talk to Rue Darcé again. Could you give me her number?"

"Yes, but she's actually coming to Geisterhaus tomorrow morning to pick up Tommy's things. I'll be back here before she arrives."

"Great. We'll talk to her then." Jeff held up his index finger. "Just one more question. Why were you convinced that Blair's ghost wanted to kill you? What did you do that would've caused her to seek vengeance?"

"I told you I can't talk about it. I signed a non-disclosure—"

"I remember, but NDAs cover the words and actions owned

by a particular entity – in this case, Blair Geister. I'm guessing she wasn't even privy to the information you're keeping secret, so she didn't technically own it. You did. There's nothing to keep you from telling me what you did."

Juniper locked her face in a grim stoicism and looked past Jeff on both sides in an apparent move to make sure they were alone. She told him in a soft voice, "I hired you, which I assume means you have a fiduciary obligation to hold any information I share with you in confidence. Is that correct?"

"As long as it doesn't put anyone's life in danger."

"Very well." Juniper placed her fingertips on her lips. "I've wanted to share this with someone for so long, but I didn't dare. The night of the party, Zyus Drake didn't end up in the unfinished guest room of his own accord."

Jeff gasped. "You took him there."

"I didn't want some stranger sleeping in my bed! On top of that, he was so drunk, I was afraid he was going to throw up. I gave him a pillow and blanket from the linen closet and fashioned a makeshift bed on the floor. He didn't object." Tears dripped from her reddened cheeks. "The opposite in fact. He kept thanking me for taking care of him. He passed out almost as soon as he laid down." She wiped her eyes and threw out her hands. "It's my fault. What happened to Zyus Drake is my fault!"

Emory stepped into the wine cellar and flipped the light switch. He walked to the center of the room and rested his arms on the back of one of the chairs surrounding the chestnut table so he could stare at the painting on the far wall.

Hugo Hickory's desiccated face. The heart clenched in the

snarling mouth of Waya'ha's coyote spirit. The answer to the Pangram Box was here. He just knew it.

Emory took a picture of the painting with his new phone. "I need to think like Blair Geister. She was an architect. Architects are creative, which is the impetus for this puzzle. She designed beautiful buildings. No matter how beautiful, a building must be functional. The form serves the function. She put the painting over the first location for a reason. It has to mark the way forward. She wouldn't have created a random path."

Emory rubbed his face. "I don't know." He did a slow spin, trying to detect anything that would trigger his mind.

"Don't know what?" asked a voice from behind.

Emory jumped and swung around to see a familiar mask. "Mr. Drake, you've got to stop popping up like that!"

"Blair gave me free reign to look around the house – at least for another thirty-seven hours."

"Yes, but can't you at least announce yourself when entering a room?"

"Sorry for scaring you." Zyus pulled his mask from his pocket and slipped it over his head.

"No, I'm sorry. You just startled me."

Zyus faced the painting. "You keep coming back to this room. Is the Pangram Box in here?"

"I can honestly tell you I don't believe it is."

"Have you narrowed down where it could be? Made any progress?"

"I might have a furious compulsion to decode riddles, but I'm not going to help *you* find it."

Zyus crossed his arms. "Man, I read you wrong. I thought you were someone who liked to help other people."

"And I didn't see you as someone who would extort money from someone."

"What are you talking about?"

"I know about your former profession, Mr. Drake, and your relationship to Blair Geister."

Zyus took a chair and rested his pythonic forearms on the table. "Sit down. Please."

Emory hesitated but decided to hear him out.

Zyus inhaled a deep and whistling breath and compressed it from his lungs. "I've had a lot of time to myself these past few months. Time to think about my life now and my life before. I'm not proud of my life before, but that doesn't mean I feel any guilt about it either. I didn't start out as a cash master. There was no plan for it. I posted some workout shots on Twitter, and all these people started responding. Guys mostly. They offered to buy me things, send me money, serve me. It didn't take me long to realize I could get all my bills paid for without lifting a finger. It was a game. Roleplay. I'd post pictures of myself and insult my followers, and they'd send me money for the privilege of serving me. I justified it because I wasn't having sex with any of them, and if they weren't serving me, they'd find one of the thousands of other cash masters to send their money to. It might as well be me."

"You took advantage of their feelings of inadequacy."

"I guess, but they got something out of it too. I filled a need for them. No one forced them to send me money. I wasn't there holding a gun to their heads. When Blair reached out to me, there was something different about her. She wasn't my first female follower, but we clicked. It started out as the same old game, but then I realized I was sharing things with her I wasn't sharing with the others. And she told me everything. We'd never met, but I'd never felt more connected to anybody. I was falling for her."

Emory noticed Zyus' bloodshot, watery eyes and figured the man must be crying, but his tears remained hidden beneath his olive vinyl mask.

"I was excited to finally meet her. She didn't disappoint. She was just as beautiful in person, and there was this energy about her that you couldn't help but be drawn to. We met about an hour before the party. I hugged her and wanted to kiss her, but then she reminded me of her ground rules for the party. I was supposed to pretend to be her new trainer, and I promised I would never break her confidence about our relationship. That was between me and her. I made the mistake of telling her how I was feeling about her. Man, it was like someone flipped a switch, and all that energy just turned off. She got all serious and told me *we* could never happen, not like that. Then she went off to prepare for the party. They were setting up the bar, so I went over and had a couple of shots. By the time the party actually started, I was buzzing pretty good. Well, you know the rest."

"Did you... love her?"

"I think I did. Then after this happened." Zyus pointed to his own face. "I begged her to help me."

"Help you how?"

"Surgery. I needed plastic surgery to fix my face. I couldn't afford it myself, so I asked her to help. She didn't want anything to do with me anymore. That's when I sued her to get the money."

"And during the deposition, you revealed the true nature of your relationship."

"I had to. My lawyer made me use that secret as leverage. She agreed to a million-dollar settlement if I'd signed an agreement not to say anything about the incident or our relationship to anyone. It didn't matter. It was too late. The doctors I went to afterwards said there wasn't much they could do. If I'd gotten to them sooner, when the wounds were fresh, they could've helped repair a significant amount of the damage. But that window was closed and all hopes dashed. Of course, there were other treatments that even a million dollars couldn't pay for, but Blair refused to give me another dime."

"Who else was there when you gave your deposition?"

"Me and Blair, our lawyers, the arbitrator and Blair's assistant, Juniper."

CHAPTER 31

WAYNE BUCKWALD PULLED into the TBI parking lot after sunset. He'd come on a Saturday to avoid another confrontation with his boss about unapproved investigations. "I know I'm going to regret this."

He entered the building to find it empty except for a couple of other agents seated in the expansive office space. Without exchanging words, he settled in at his desk. As the computer booted up, he pulled the notebook from his shirt pocket and turned it to the notes he had taken during his last conversation with Sheriff Rome.

Wayne spent the next hour researching a TBI case involving Emory's biological father. He read about Carl Grant and the twisting path that led him to Sheriff Rome's attention. "This is unbelievable. Why didn't Emory ever tell me?"

Wayne read about Carl's affiliations and a plot that mentioned the former Crescent Lake, Crown-of-Thorns Mountain and a name he didn't know how to pronounce.

Wayne was so engrossed in his research, he didn't notice someone coming up behind him.

"What's Deignus?" asked Steve Linders, reading over his shoulder.

Wayne jumped and yelled at his partner, "Damn it, Steve! You scared the bejeezus out of me!"

Steve laughed and took a seat next to him. "Sorry."

"What are you doing here?"

"Closing up the suicide case. I got the ME report a little while ago, and it confirms everything we already knew. The question is, what are *you* doing here? You never work weekends."

Wayne squirmed a bit. "Just doing some research on an old case."

"You're doing that favor for the sheriff who came to see you, aren't you? The father of your last partner."

"I'm working on an old case."

Steve kicked back in his chair. "I thought you didn't like him."

"I don't, but the sheriff shouldn't bear the iniquity of his son."

"Okay, so what is Deignus?"

"None of your business."

"I'm your partner."

Wayne chopped the air with his right hand. "Not on this, you're not."

"That's okay." Steve rose from his chair. "I need to get home anyway. See you Monday."

Once his partner had left, Wayne continued his research. "Here we go. The evidence log." He scrolled through the list. "Damn, it's long. This is going to take forever. I'll do a search."

He typed the words as he spoke. "Picture." No results appeared. "Photo." One result appeared: *Photograph of a boy.*

"That doesn't tell me anything. I'll have to see it. The crypt is closed on weekends."

Wayne turned off his computer. "I'll have to come back early Monday morning." He got up and scooted his chair toward his desk. "Before Bachman gets in."

CHAPTER 32

OVER A DINNER they had prepared together, the PIs discussed the case. Emory recounted his conversation with Zyus, and Jeff filled them in on Tommy and Rue's defunct marriage. Virginia updated them on her investigation into Spike Dean following his arrest during the mine closure. "I haven't found anything online about him, other than a few news articles with the same info as the first. I forwarded the article to a friend of mine at Knoxville PD to see if she can find more information on him."

Jeff asked, "What is up with these people who don't have at least one social media account?"

Emory said, "I'm not on social media."

"That's because you refuse to share anything personal."

"It's because I was in law enforcement. You don't want criminals learning anything about your personal life. They could use it against you."

Looking at her phone, Virginia groaned. "Oh no."

"What is it?" asked Jeff.

"It looks like the sheriff released the information about Blair and Tommy being killed by lightning. She read an excerpt aloud for them. "Construction tycoon's death now blamed on lightning. In a bizarre twist, the deaths of Blair Geister and her handyman, formerly ruled natural heart attacks, are now being considered induced by lightning, the result of a mis-wired lightning rod."

Emory sighed. "I wish he'd kept that quiet. Now the killer knows we're looking for him."

"If he or she didn't already." Jeff clinked his fork against his plate a couple of times. "I think I'm ready for bed. It's been a long day."

"I agree." Emory joined his partners in scooting back from the table. "That swim today wore me out."

Virginia snickered, but Jeff did not. "That's not funny."

"The one time I make a joke, and you can't even give me a courtesy laugh."

"Too soon. I was ready to kill that neighbor."

Virginia headed upstairs, while the guys went down.

When they stepped into the hallway on the lower level, Emory was about to open the door to Juniper's room when Jeff stopped him. "Emory, I'm worried about you."

"Me? Why?"

"Well, after a near-drowning experience, people are in danger of dry-drowning up to twenty-four hours later."

Emory let his hand drop from the doorknob. "What?"

"It's when water gets in the lungs and irritates them, causing them to fill with fluid—"

"No, I know what it is, but I'm fine. I'm not coughing or having any problems breathing."

"Still, I'd feel better if I could keep an eye on you until that twenty-four-hour window has passed." Jeff opened the door to Tommy's room and nodded toward the bed.

Emory smiled and walked through the door.

Sweating, Jeff rolled over in the bed and exhaled a great breath at the ceiling. "You, Emory Rome, are a hell-fire sermon."

"What do you mean?" Emory asked between his own pants of air.

"Because you make my soul shudder."

"Is that a good thing?"

Jeff tousled Emory's hair. "It's a great thing."

Emory smiled at him. "I feel the same way."

"You do? You should tell me that sometime. Hey, I just thought of something. Right before we took our river cruise—"

"Now it's okay to joke about it?"

Jeff tilted his head to the side. "Enough time has passed. You were going to tell me something."

Emory's mind went to his last encounter with Anderson Alexander. The director of the Tennessee Bureau of Investigation had warned him against working with Jeff and handed him a file on his partner. When Jeff shared the story of his college boyfriend, Emory realized it related to the information contained in that file, but now he was having second thoughts about revealing everything. After a mini-debate in his head, he opted to go with his first instinct. "I found out why you're on the government's no-fly list."

Jeff gasped with excitement and turned onto his side to face him. "Seriously? Why?"

"The reason you're on the no-fly list is because you're listed by the TBI, and thereby the FBI, as a potential terrorist for illegally transporting a biologic agent."

"What?!" Jeff sprang up to a seated position. "That's ridiculous! I'm not a terrorist, and I've never transported any agent – biologic or otherwise!"

Emory sat up too. "Actually, you might have."

"What are you talking about?"

"You took Trevor Park's body."

"Is a body considered a biologic agent?"

"I wouldn't have even thought of it until you told me your story. I guess it is, technically."

"No. This doesn't make sense. No one even knows for sure I took it, except you. I was questioned a couple of times but never arrested."

"Well, the TBI must've suspected you strongly enough to put it in your file, even if they didn't have enough to arrest you."

"How do you know it's in my file? And what file?"

Emory hesitated. "The file the TBI has on you."

"I don't understand. When you were still with the TBI, you said you looked it up and the reason I was on the list was redacted."

"I recently came across an unredacted copy." Emory left out the part about receiving it from the head of the TBI.

Jeff squinted at him. "When did this unexpected meeting between man and document occur?"

"I found out the day we closed the Crick Witch case."

"And you waited all this time to tell me? Why?" When Emory didn't answer, Jeff jumped off the bed and filled in the blanks. "Were you looking for evidence? Were you *investigating* me?"

"No, I was just waiting for the right time to tell you."

"Right time? I would've told you right away, as soon as I found out."

"All right! I didn't believe you were guilty of anything, but you do have a tendency to take the path less legal."

Jeff opened his mouth as if he were going to object but exhaled instead.

Emory continued his explanation. "If I'm being honest, I have to admit I had an uneasy *what if* feeling way, way in the back of my mind. But then when you told me about taking the body, it dawned on me that might be what the file was referring to, although…"

"What?"

"It doesn't seem like enough, and it doesn't explain why the computer record was redacted. Was there anything unusual about how Trevor died?"

"Other than the fact that he was twenty-one and died of the flu, no."

"Did Trevor have a job?"

"Look, it's been a long day, and talking about Trevor just brings up painful memories. Can we drop this for now?"

"Of course."

Jeff slipped back under the covers. "Thanks."

"I'm sorry I didn't tell you sooner."

"Yeah. You're at waist deep in apology debt."

"How about I pay off a little of that debt right now."

Jeff perked up his eyebrows. "I'm listening."

Emory took a deep breath before speaking. "Before I was adopted, my name was Beck."

"Beck Rome?"

"Emory Beck."

"That's... unexpected. Why are you telling me this?"

"I know you've checked on my past using Emory Rome and found nothing before college. This should tell you what you want to know."

Jeff was silent for a second before telling him, "Come here." He lifted his right arm, inviting Emory to rest his head on his chest.

Emory awoke to voices in the hallway outside the bedroom door, but he couldn't discern who they belonged to. He glanced to the left at an uncovered and nude Jeff, who was sound asleep on his stomach, hugging the pillow under his face. Not wanting to wake him, Emory did a controlled fall to the floor and picked himself up to soft-step around the bed. He was about to plant his ear against the door, but it swung open. Emory jumped back and covered the front of his boxers.

Jeff pushed up from the bed. "What? Emory?" He rolled onto his back and rubbed his eyes.

"Uh, Jeff." Emory pulled the sheet over his partner's nakedness. "We have company."

Jeff eyed the blonde intruder in a midnight-blue jumpsuit. "Aren't you…"

"Rue Darcé," she replied, still clutching the doorknob in her left hand and papers in her right. "I'm sorry. Eden led me to the room but didn't tell me it was occupied."

Jeff propped himself up on his elbows. "An important detail to omit."

Emory found his pants on the floor. "Ms. Darcé, would you give us ten minutes to make ourselves more appropriate?"

"Certainly." Rue retreated into the hallway, closing the door.

Emory slipped on his pants. "Well, that was awkward."

Jeff tilted his head. "It was?"

"Get up. We need to dress, and you have to pack all your things so she doesn't mistake them for Tommy Addison's."

A few minutes later, the PIs exited the bedroom. They found Rue sitting on the back stairs, drumming her leg with the rolled-up papers. Emory said, "The room's all yours, Ms. Darcé."

"Thank you, gentlemen."

Jeff parked his suitcase in the hallway. "Will you be here for a while? We need to ask you a few questions about Tommy."

She shook her head as she passed them. "I plan to be out of here in ten minutes."

"Then could we talk while you pack?"

Rue agreed, and the PIs followed her back into the bedroom. She threw the papers on the bed and looked around the space. "I hope Tommy had a suitcase here. I didn't bring any boxes."

Jeff picked up the papers. "What is this?" He showed Emory the first page, drawing attention to Eden Geister's name at the top.

Rue opened the closet door and glanced over at Jeff. "Eden Geister's CV. Curriculum vitae. She asked me to consider her for my previous position, VP of Innovations. Yes!" She pulled out a camouflage suitcase and opened it on the bed. "Juniper tells me you guys think Tommy was killed by lightning?"

"Ball lightning actually," replied Emory.

Rue grunted. "It figures the most interesting thing about Tommy would be how he died."

Jeff dropped Eden's CV back on the bed. "Why do you say that?"

"Tommy just wasn't the most exciting person you'd ever meet. He was handsome, sure, and charming when he made the effort, but if the conversation didn't revolve around sports, construction or politics, he wasn't so much for words."

Emory asked, "If you felt that way about him, why did you marry him?"

Rue grabbed some hanging clothes from the closet and threw them into the suitcase. "You don't know how many times I've asked myself that. I'd just started at Geister. I was visiting a site, and he was there in his hardhat. Opposites attract I guess, but that engine slogs down a finite course of growing indifference until you run out of life to share. Then he went back to school to get his degree, taking an interest in a field I've lived and breathed for twenty years. I suppose it was sweet of him to make the effort, but you can't force passion. It's either there or it's not. After he graduated, Blair gave him a shot at the corporate life – put him in charge of a small team working on The Monolith. He was… managing, propped up by those around him, but even those crutches broke after our divorce. Blair was going to fire him, but I pleaded with her not to. I knew she was looking for someone to oversee some work at her house, and I asked her to transfer him. The job came with a place to stay, so I didn't feel as guilty about taking the house."

Emory asked, "Was Mr. Addison close to his son?"

Rue shot him a puzzled look. "Why are you asking about Liam?"

"We were just wondering why he didn't have any photos of him."

Rue emitted a tiny laugh. "I don't think it would've occurred to him to print and frame a photo. He has plenty on his phone, I'm sure. I've texted some to him."

"Does Liam text him?" asked Jeff.

Finished with the closet, Rue started emptying the dresser drawers. "He's eleven. I know I'm in the minority, but I don't believe children should have their own phone. I've told him I'll get him one when he enters high school." Rue examined a scroll of papers from one of the bottom drawers before tossing it on the bed. "Don't need that."

Jeff grabbed the scroll. "How often did they see each other?"

"I have full custody."

While she cleaned out the last drawer, Jeff unrolled the scroll. "Are these blueprints?"

"Architectural drawings. The section of The Monolith Tommy was working on before he moved down here." She struggled to close the suitcase.

Emory jumped to her aid. "We'll get that for you."

"Thank you." Rue stepped aside to let the PIs work on closing the suitcase. "I'm usually a much neater packer, but I'm just drop-ping this off at a donation bin."

Once the suitcase was closed, Jeff lowered it from the bed and rolled it toward Rue. She grabbed the architectural drawings and the suitcase. "I do hope you find out who killed Blair and Tommy."

Emory picked up the other papers on the bed. "You forgot Eden's CV."

Rue pursed the left side of her lips. "You can just toss that."

She left the room with the guys trailing her. "If you need to ask me anything else, I start working from the new offices in The Monolith tomorrow. You can reach me there."

"We'll help you to your car." Emory took possession of the suitcase.

"Thank you."

The PIs followed Rue to her luxury SUV, and she opened the back. "Would you let Juniper know I can't get Tommy's truck today? Actually, it'd be great if she could just donate it for me so I don't have to deal with it."

"What truck?" asked Jeff.

"I think she said it's in the garage."

Emory loaded the suitcase into the car. "Oh, I didn't realize that was his truck."

Jeff nodded toward an oncoming orange sportscar. "Who is this in the Lotus?"

The car zoomed past them and came to a screeching halt. Myles Godfrey exited the driver side. "Good morning, gentlemen. Rue."

Without acknowledging him, Rue got into her car and drove away.

Jeff bent down to look inside Myles' car. "Emory, you're not going to believe who's with him."

Emory's jaw dropped when he saw a masked Zyus Drake step out of the passenger side. "Holy crap."

"Hi guys. Myles, this is Emory and Jeff. They're private investigators who are figuring out what happened with Blair."

Emory asked, "You're working with Mr. Godfrey now?"

Zyus nodded. "No one knows Blair's work better than him."

Myles sized up the PIs. "As I understand it, Blair's will did not specify an inheritor for any of her properties, except for this estate. They're either part of this Pangram Box or the residuary clause that's being read tomorrow."

Jeff stared down at Myles. "What's in it for you?"

Zyus answered for him. "I promised Mr. Godfrey if he helps me find the Pangram Box and the deed to The Monolith is in it, I'd sell it to him for a quarter of its value."

Emory asked, "Why would you do that?"

"Twenty-five percent of millions is better than zero percent, which is all I'll have if I don't find it in the next twenty-three hours."

"Speaking of which…" Myles placed a hand on Zyus' back. "Times a wasting."

While Myles and Zyus walked away, Jeff clenched the left side of his face. "What do you want to do?"

"I want to find that Box before they do so Zyus won't owe Myles Godfrey a thing."

"Works for me." Jeff pulled his keys from his pocket. "And I want to key this car."

Emory grabbed his wrist. "No!"

Jeff grinned. "Come on. I've never damaged anything this expensive before."

Emory pulled him away from the car. "Somehow, I don't believe that's true."

CHAPTER 33

AFTER SHOWERING AND dressing in the upstairs gym, Jeff and Emory found Virginia and Juniper whipping up eggs and hash browns in the kitchen.

Juniper greeted them with a raised flute of orange juice. "Boys! Glad to see you up. Mimosa?"

"I'll take one." Jeff hurried to the mimosa station set up on one corner of the island. "Emory?"

"Sure. Do you all need any help?"

Juniper took a sip and returned her attention to the eggs. "You could set the kitchen table."

Jeff handed Emory a full flute and clinked glasses. "Juniper, I think this is the happiest I've seen you."

Juniper laughed. "I am happy... or on my way there. You three have helped me realize that Ms. Geister isn't after me, and Miss Luann told me last night that her spirit is definitely at rest now. I know you all don't believe in that, but I feel better knowing all my bases are covered. On top of that, the residuary clause will be read tomorrow, and this will all be over. I can kick Eden out of here. Oh, and you all must be happy."

Virginia flipped the hash browns in the frying pan. "Why's that?"

"You'll be able to go home."

Right arm laden with a stack of four plates, Emory shut the cabinet door. "Go home?"

Jeff finished his thought. "We haven't figured out who killed Blair or Tommy yet."

Juniper waved off their concern. "You all have done enough. You did what I hired you to do. Actually, I guess you could go home today, but I'm hoping you'll stay. The thought of being alone in this house with that woman…"

Virginia pulled a serving dish from a cabinet. "You're staying here tonight?"

"Yes. The reading is at 7:20 in the morning, and I have to set up for it. Is anyone in my room?"

Emory stopped in front of Juniper. "I'll get my stuff out of there, but there's still a murderer on the loose. We need to find out who it is."

"Let the sheriff take it from here. Oh, five settings. Rue Darcé should be here soon, and I'm going to ask her to join us."

Jeff broke the news to her. "Rue has already come and gone. She asked if you could get rid of Tommy's truck for her."

"Oh. I suppose. I wasn't expecting her so early."

"Zyus Drake arrived as she was leaving," said Jeff, as if sharing a juicy piece of gossip. "And he brought a friend. Myles Godfrey."

Juniper dropped her spatula. "What on Earth is that man doing in this house?"

After a sip of orange juice, Jeff answered, "Helping Zyus search for the Pangram Box." He licked the pulp from his upper lip.

"He can't do that! Ms. Geister didn't say he could have any help."

Placing plates on the table, Emory replied, "She didn't say he couldn't."

Juniper huffed. "There goes my mood."

After breakfast, Juniper went on a grocery run, leaving the PIs alone for clean-up. Knowing they had less than a day before Juniper would end their involvement in the case, they headed upstairs to the murder board to narrow their list of suspects. Before reaching the office door, they heard an argument down the hall. Myles Godfrey was standing in front of the guest bedroom door, arguing through a three-inch crack at Eden Geister on the other side. Meanwhile, Zyus Drake lurked a few feet away.

"It's not in here!" Eden growled. "I would've seen it."

"Blair granted him total access to the house!" Myles replied.

Virginia opened the office door and whispered, "Guys, we have work to do."

Jeff took a step inside the office, but Emory stayed still. "Aren't you coming?"

"In a minute. I want to talk to Zyus." Emory left his partners and approached the masked man. "What's going on?"

Zyus nodded toward Myles. "I think the Pangram Box is in that room, and he needs to get in there to look for it."

"What makes you think it's in there?"

"It's the only room I haven't searched, and it's where... it happened."

Emory thought for a second about his time in the guest room and wondered where it could be in there.

"Have you reconsidered helping me? I could use all hands on deck."

Eden slammed the door shut, and Myles yelled, "You have to leave sometime!" He rejoined Zyus and tilted his head toward the guest room. "I see the family resemblance. Let's check out the rest of the house. We'll come back once her highness deigns to leave the royal bedroom. What's going on here?"

Zyus placed a hand on Emory's shoulder. "If I'm reading Emory's face right, he was just thinking about helping us."

Myles crossed his arms. "Zyus told me you already looked for this Box. You had your chance to find it and failed miserably."

"I haven't even tried… full-force."

Myles laughed at him. "How old are you? That's the excuse of a defeated, blubbering child. *I wasn't even trying.*

Emory hardened his face. "Mr. Drake, I will find the Pangram Box for you."

"Oh good," said Myles. "Go ahead and try. I thrive on competition."

"You hear that?" Emory pointed to the air above him. "It's Blair Geister's spirit laughing at you."

"She never beat me!!" Myles screamed.

After checking in with his partners at the murder board, Emory began his search in earnest. Riding a renewed inspirational vigor, he returned to the wine cellar, determined to decipher the riddle behind the Pangram Box.

He walked around the room, staring at the Hugo Hickory painting from every possible angle. He repeated something Jeff had said to explain some of the decisions the puzzle's creator had made in her personal life. "Maybe Blair was just much more colorful than we realized."

Emory's eyes focused on the white stone tile behind the wine racks. He glanced at the stone-tile beneath his feet before returning his gaze to the painting, to the blanket on the ground beside the coyote. He scanned the walls around the room and looked up at the white batten ceiling. "This room is white." He inhaled and held his breath for a couple of seconds. "I think I know!"

He raced up the stairs and into the office, where his partners were removing photos from the murder board. "Guys!"

Jeff held up a picture from the board, cutting him off. "Rue Darcé. Still a suspect?"

"No. After talking to her this morning, I just don't think the motive was strong enough to drive her to murder."

"We all agree then." Virginia took the photo from Jeff and tossed it in the wastebasket beside the desk.

Emory waved his arms in front of him. "Guys, can we take a break from the murder board for thirty seconds?"

Virginia plopped onto the sofa. "Sure. What is it?"

Emory's eyes darted from Virginia to Jeff, who took a seat behind the desk. "I know where the Pangram Box is."

Virginia jumped up. "Seriously?"

"That's great!" said Jeff.

Emory held up his hands to temper their excitement. "Well, sort of. I know the path it's taking."

Virginia sat back down, disappointed. "Okay. That's good too, I guess."

Jeff asked, "Emory, what the hell are you trying to say?"

"I know the stops, but I don't know the order. The sacred colors. Remember Waya'ha's blanket was woven in the Cherokee's sacred colors – black, blue, red and white. Those colors correspond to certain rooms in this house. The wine cellar is white—"

"The library is red," said Virginia.

Jeff said, "The guest room is blue."

Virginia shook her head. "But there's no black room here. I think we'd notice that."

"Yes, there is," said Jeff. "The theatre!"

Emory grinned. "The only problem is I don't know the order the Box will travel."

Jeff put an arm around him. "But still, we just need to find the hiding place in each of those rooms, and then we can figure out the order."

Emory added, "And hope that the final room really does allow us access to the Box."

Emory walked past the closed guest room door and heard movement on the other side. *She's still there. I'll try the library first.* He heard another noise and realized it didn't come from the guest room. He proceeded down the hall and opened the master bedroom door to find Myles Godfrey with his fingers in the crater Emory had hammered into the wall. "I wouldn't do that if I were you."

Myles jumped and turned around. "Do what?"

"Brown recluses."

"I'm not scared of spiders." Myles' finger followed an imaginary line from the hole in the wall to the one in the floor. "This is how it happened? Someone wired the bed to electrocute her. Serves her right for having a solid gold bed." He eyed the bathroom door. "Is the royal throne gold too? Pretentious bitch. Killed in the way she feared the most. Poetic justice."

"What did you have against her?"

"Have you ever had a tormenter?"

Emory thought of his former partner, Wayne Buckwald, and answered to himself.

Myles gripped the nearest bedpost. "Someone who's given everything that you're owed? The business. The respect. The accolades. The adoration. I was in this business for fifteen years before she became a thing, and then everyone acted like she invented the I-beam."

"You give her no credit for her talent?"

Myles scoffed. "It wasn't her talent that got her noticed. It was her sex. She was doing nothing any different from me, but everyone made such a big deal out of the fact that she was *a woman in a business dominated by men.*"

"Even if – and I don't believe it is – but *if* that's what got her noticed, she didn't build an empire based on novelty. She had to put in the work to create a billion-dollar company from nothing."

"No more work than me!" Myles spoke down to the floor as if Blair Geister were in hell. "Well, I'm not number two anymore, Blair. Watch me thrive in the absence of you."

"You did it, didn't you?"

"I never lifted a finger against her."

Emory shook his head. "The acts of sabotage at The Monolith."

Myles held his hands up, exposing his manicure. "My days of getting my hands dirty are well behind me. Now whether people in her employ were eager for some extra cash in exchange for a little tinkering is another story. It's not like Blair inspired loyalty among her staff."

"Was their tinkering exclusive to The Monolith?"

Myles waved a finger at him as he walked past him. "You're trying to stall me. I have a treasure box to find."

CHAPTER 34

ALONE IN THE library, Emory glanced at the large wall clock for the time. *Fourteen hours left. I'll never find all four at this rate. I've searched everywhere in here, and I cannot find the safe. Am I wrong about the colors? Maybe I should see if the guest room is free yet or go to the theatre. If I could just find a safe in one of these rooms, I'd feel confident that I'm actually on the right track. I need to relax. Clear my head.*

Emory closed his eyes, took several deep breaths and held them for ten seconds. *Blair definitely appreciated the culture of Indigenous Peoples, which explains the location of the first safe.* He opened his eyes and looked around the library, pointing to items as he mentioned them. "There are two paintings and one tapestry in this room, but I've checked them all. They're not permanently attached to the wall or any kind of mechanism. That means the key to this room is something else. The clock. The chime is off by two minutes. Could that mean something, or is it just defective? No, Juniper said she insisted everything be fixed right away."

Emory approached the clock and moved the minute hand from the nine to the twelve. The clock chimed five times. "Has it been fixed?" He moved the hand two minutes into the future. The clock was silent. He moved the time ahead to six o'clock, and the clock chimed as it should. He moved it up to seven o'clock with the same result. He moved it forward to eight o'clock, and the clock did not chime. "That's it! No chime." He moved it two minutes forward, and the clock chimed eight times. "8:02. What's significant about that? Eight two. August 2nd? That's familiar. Something someone said. Eden! The Gatlinburg story. That's Blair Geister's brother's birthday!"

He again looked around the room. Nothing had moved. Emory released a defeated breath. "Of course not. The clock hits that time twice a day. If that were the trigger, someone would've seen the safe by now. I have to do something to expose it. But what?" The clock moved ahead to 8:03. A thought occurred to him. "Could it be that simple?" He pushed the minute hand back and again heard the chimes. This time he pushed the 8 and 2 on the clock at the same time before the chimes ended. The face of the clock within the inner silver circle slid open, disappearing into the wall and revealing another lockless safe. "That's it!"

"I have to be ready this time." He grabbed the handle with his left hand and held his right hand by the door to try snatching the contents before they could leave the safe. He opened the door and threw his hand inside, but there was nothing to grasp.

Emory's shoulders slumped. "I'm out of sequence. At least I'm pretty certain now that the colors are the key. It's either in the guest room or theatre." He closed the safe door. The clock moved ahead to 8:03, and the face returned from the wall to conceal the safe.

"That's the wrong time," a voice said from behind him.

Emory turned around to see a smiling face in the library doorway. "Dr. Sharp."

The professor walked toward him. "That clock is off a few hours."

"I saw that too. I was just fixing it." Emory checked his phone and set the clock to the correct time. "What are you doing here?"

"Juniper invited me and asked me to wait in here." Dr. Sharp shook Emory's hand.

"I'm glad you're here." Emory motioned to a couple of chairs. "Could we talk for a minute?"

"Of course." Dr. Sharp joined him in sitting.

"We found out why Ms. Geister wanted to extend your grant escrow."

"You did? What was it?"

"She suspected you were in breach of the grant's morality clause."

"What?!" Dr. Sharp pushed back in his chair with such force, he had to grab the arms to keep it from tipping over. "I know you don't know me well, but I assure from the depths of my being I'm about as vanilla an individual as you're likely to encounter. I've had one speeding ticket my entire life. I've never been in a fight. I've never been intoxicated. I've had two serious relationships in my life, and both concluded amicably. I had never experienced a demeritorious action in my work environment until this current administration, as you know, and I informed Blair Geister of that when I applied for the grant. What in the world could've made her question my morality?"

"She heard of possible sexual misconduct with a former lab assistant."

"What? Who?" Dr. Sharp chopped the air. "It doesn't matter. I've had eight lab assistants in my career. Interview each one! Where would she get such an idea?"

"Apparently another scientist reported hearing it from the laboratory director at Oak Ridge."

Dr. Sharp's shoulders slumped, and he shook his head. "It wasn't enough to fire me. They had to assault my character."

"Who?"

"The new director and those who put him in charge."

"To what end?"

"If they want you out but have no justification for releasing you, they create one."

Emory wanted to believe him, but he just wasn't sure.

Jeff stared at the murder board in the office, while Virginia sat on the sofa with her eyes glued to her laptop. "We've been at this for hours, and we've only narrowed our suspect list to seven people. I wish your friend would get back to you about the mine supervisor, we could possibly take one of these off. The problem is everyone had means, motive and opportunity. How do you narrow down the suspects when no one has an alibi that covers the entire window of opportunity?"

Virginia stood and stretched. "Admit it. We need Emory."

Jeff crossed his arms. "I'm just as capable... *We're* just as capable of zeroing in on the killer as he is." He snapped his fingers. "How about this – Zyus Drake strikes me as a man of action and not really a planner. Would you agree?"

"From what you and Emory have told me, sure."

"Then if he were going to kill Blair, I don't believe he would be methodical about it. I feel like he would use his hands."

"I'm with you on that."

"Good!" Jeff pulled his photo from the board and crumpled it. "See? Now we're down to six."

Juniper rapped on the door but didn't wait for an answer before opening it. "I just wanted to let you all know Kenn Marty is preparing dinner for us tonight."

Jeff attempted to conceal the murder board, but he was too late.

"What's that?" Juniper asked. "Why's my picture on there?"

Jeff smiled at her. "It's just a murder board. Or crime board. It's where we post photos of... everyone involved in a case to provide visual cues for discussion. You're on here because you're the client."

She read the writing under her picture. "But it has *Cover-up?* written on it.

Virginia popped up from the sofa. "Juniper, the truth is these are suspects in Blair's murder."

Juniper covered her chest with both hands. "You think I killed her?"

Virginia explained, "We have to be completely impartial in our investigations, no matter how much we like the people involved. Anyone with motive, means and opportunity is a potential suspect. Anyone."

Jeff added, "Unfortunately, that does include you."

"What motive would I have?"

He answered, "The fact that you were afraid Blair's ghost was after you for something you did means you might've had a motive to kill her – to conceal whatever it was from her."

"But I've already explained that to you. I'm the reason Zyus Drake fell asleep in the unfinished guest room."

"Which is why we were going to remove you." Virginia pulled Juniper's picture from the board. "We just hadn't gotten around to it yet."

Juniper took a moment to respond. "I guess I understand. You don't know me truly well enough to realize that I could never kill anyone. I can't be upset that you're thorough. That is your job. It was just shocking to see myself up there." She headed for the door. "Dinner in thirty."

Once she left, Jeff hurried to shut the door. "I thought you locked the door."

Virginia's phone atop the file cabinet chimed. "You went to the bathroom last."

"Are you sure?"

Virginia rolled her eyes as she checked her phone. "Oh my god!"

"What is it?"

"A text from my friend at Knoxville PD."

"She found some information on the mine supervisor? What's his name?"

"Spike Dean. She forwarded me his mugshot." Virginia turned the phone around to let Jeff see the picture.

Jeff took a step closer. "That's the gardener."

CHAPTER 35

WITH VIRGINIA AT his side, Jeff pounded on the guest room door.

"I told you, I'm not leaving this room at all today!" Eden yelled from the other side.

"Eden, it's Jeff and Virginia. We need to talk to you."

"Go away!"

"Sure. Okay. Maybe the sheriff can get you to answer why you conspired with George Henry, or rather *Spike Dean*, to kill your cousin."

A few seconds later, the lock clicked and the door open. Eden waved them inside. "Come on in. Excuse the mess."

The room was indeed a mess. Every painting that hung from the indigo walls was now on the floor leaned against them. The furniture was in disarray, and even the bed had been pulled several inches from the wall.

As Eden led them down the two steps to the sunken seating area, Jeff told her, "I don't think you'll be getting your security deposit back."

Eden sat at one end of the couch and Virginia at the other, while Jeff pulled up the chair from the writing table. "First off, I didn't conspire with anyone."

Jeff scoffed. "You knew George Henry was actually the supervisor of the coal mine that Blair bought to close down and that he held a major grudge for taking away his livelihood. Then you gave him a fake name, and you talked her into hiring him here under the pretext that he was this amazing gardener at the college where you work. That access allowed him to execute her in a brutal manner. If you didn't orchestrate her murder, you had to reasonably assume that consequence, and in all likelihood, you desperately hoped for it, believing her death would result in this huge inheritance for yourself. Excuse me, Eden, but conspiracies don't come more clear-cut than that."

"You only have a splinter of truth in that clumsy club of accusations. His real name is George Henry Dean. People call him Spike because of his widow's peak."

Jeff smirked at Virginia. "Three first names. The parents just set him up to be a serial killer."

Eden rolled her eyes. "I met him in the course of my research on coal slurry before Blair ever thought of buying that mine. When I heard she'd bought it, I let George know there was no way she did it with the intention of keeping it open. Telling him was a mistake, because it infuriated him and led to the riot that got him arrested. Fortunately, Blair dropped the charges."

Virginia asked a question to which she already knew the answer. "Were you in a relationship with him?"

"Yes. After the arrest, George discussed forming a co-op with a group of his mining colleagues so they could make an offer to buy the mine back from Blair. I told him they would never be able to offer enough money because she was closing the mine on principle, not for profit."

"Why did you talk your cousin into hiring him here as the gardener?" asked Virginia. "You had to know he wished her harm."

Eden's face froze for a second before dropping. "Yes, but not enough to actually kill her. Blair had just turned down my grant. I was angry at her. George grilled me for dirt on her, but I didn't have anything – at least nothing so egregious he could use it for leverage to force her to sell the mine to him. He was going to hire a private investigator, but then I heard that her gardener had died. George thought if he could get close to her, he could find the dirt himself, and then we could both get what we wanted. He'd get the mine, and I'd get my grant."

Jeff thought back to when Juniper told them the mine was immediately signed over to the EARTH Foundation, but that transfer had not yet been announced to the public. He glanced at Virginia and could tell she was thinking the same. "And after Blair was murdered?"

"I really thought she'd had a heart attack. George and I were hoping she left everything to me, but we know how that went. Then we pinned our hopes on finding that stupid Box."

Jeff waved at the room. "Which, I assume, is the reason for the spruce down."

"Myles Godfrey and that freak seem to be convinced it's in here."

Virginia asked, "Assuming you found the Box, and it had the deed to the mine or any of the buildings, what then? It's not like you could've made a claim to the property. People would know the deed was stolen."

"We could bargain with Zeke or whatever the hell his name is to split the contents three ways or we'd hold it until the deadline past, and he'd get nothing."

Jeff suggested, "Or, you could forge your cousin's signature on the deed to the mine, and George Henry could say she sold it to him before she died."

Eden scowled at him. "You have a devious mind, Mr. Woodard."

Virginia patted the cushion between them. "Eden, getting back to George Henry, you do realize he almost killed you."

"What are you talking about? George has never raised a hand to me."

Jeff said, "He let you sleep in Blair's bed, knowing it was rigged to kill."

"That just proves he didn't do it. He would've never let me sleep there if he knew."

"What makes you sure?" asked Jeff.

"I see you're receiving guests now." said Myles Godfrey, who had entered the guest room unseen.

Eden popped to her feet. "I told you to stay out."

"The door was open, and as I understand it, you have no claim to this property whatsoever. Don't let me interrupt you. I've just got a Box to find."

Eden waved him off. "Oh, help yourself. I told you already it's not in here."

Jeff looked past Myles and saw Zyus standing in the hallway, leaning against the opposite wall. Myles asked him, "Zyus, are you sure you don't want to help me look?"

Zyus waved *no* with his hands. "I'm not going in there."

Eden joined Myles in searching the room. "I'm not going to let you find it without me!"

Virginia whispered to Jeff, "What should we do?"

Jeff replied, "One of us needs to warn Juniper about George Henry."

"And the other?"

"Watch what happens here."

"Have fun then." Virginia left the room.

Within a few minutes, Myles had discovered his first clue. He stood in the bathroom, swinging the door back and forth. "This door clicks."

"I know," said Eden. "There's something wrong with it. The door to this room does it too."

"Does anything else in this room click?"

"Not that I've noticed."

"It's a combination lock!" Myles declared. He stepped out of the bathroom and closed the door. He inched it open again, counting each click he heard until the door could open no further. "Twenty-five clicks."

Eden darted to the bedroom door and did the same. "Twenty-five clicks here too!"

"Great!" said Myles. "Now we just need to figure out a two-number combination – no higher than 25 each – that would mean something to Blair. Any ideas? Her birthday?"

"May 31st," replied Eden. "That won't work. Her brother's birthday was August 2nd."

"Let's try that," said Myles. "Move your door eight clicks, and I'll move mine two."

Jeff watched as they clicked their doors, but nothing happened.

Eden said, "You try eight, and I'll do two."

The result was the same. After several more attempts at guessing the combination, Myles muttered, "Think like Blair." He mocked her voice as he continued, "I'm Blair Geister. I get everything I want. I'm god's gift to construction and the environment and…"

"Earth Day!" Zyus yelled from the hall.

Myles widened his eyes. "Earth Day."

"Maybe." Eden looked to Zyus. "When is that?"

"April 22nd."

"I'll do four." Eden closed her door and opened it four clicks.

Myles closed his door and counted as he clicked, "…Twenty, twenty-one, twenty-two."

The two steps leading from the bed area to the sunken seating area slid to the right, revealing a lockless safe like the one found behind the Hugo Hickory painting in the wine cellar.

Jeff bolted out of his chair and opened it before the others could see. Just like the other safe, something was inside, but it disappeared.

Myles and Eden crowded behind him to look in the safe. "There's nothing in it," said Jeff. "It's just an empty box."

"What is it?" asked Zyus from the hall.

Myles replied, "It looks like a safe, but it's empty!"

While Eden and Myles cursed Blair, Jeff headed for the door.

Zyus asked Jeff, "Is it like the one you found in the wine cellar? Is it a decoy?"

Jeff cringed, hoping Eden and Myles didn't hear the question, but he didn't look over his shoulder to see. "It's just an empty box, Zyus. I'm sorry." Jeff hurried away to tell Emory the good news.

Dr. Barry Sharp had just finished explaining the reason behind the rumor when Juniper entered the library carrying a box. "Emory, I'm glad you're here. Would you mind taking pictures for us?"

"Not at all. What's going on?"

Juniper placed the box on a chair and pulled two items from it. "Ms. Geister would always hold a little ceremony with grant recipients at the close of escrow to present them with a framed statement of the grant and an Earth sculpture made from blue quartz. I apologize for the lack of a public ceremony in this case, but coming on the heels of Ms. Geister's death, I didn't think it appropriate. Maybe in a couple of months we can have a more formal engagement."

Dr. Sharp glanced at Emory before responding to Juniper. "I understand, but I think we should wait because it's what Blair Geister wanted. Emory has informed me she was going to place a hold on the grant until she could investigate an unfounded rumor of inappropriateness with an unnamed intern. The allegation is utterly false, but you will need time to investigate it."

Juniper placed the frame and crystal sculpture on the chair beside the box. "I appreciate your straightforwardness. I knew about the potential delay, but I wasn't aware of the reason." She paused for a moment. "Here's what we're going to do. Emory, can you investigate the allegation on behalf of the foundation?"

"Of course."

"Very well. Dr. Sharp, until evidence proves otherwise, you're innocent and we'll not change course on the basis of a rumor. We'll proceed as planned with the first installment. If the allegation is confirmed, we'll cease funding and recoup the money spent. Do you agree?" Juniper extended her hand to him.

"Absolutely." Dr. Sharp shook her hand. "Thank you!"

Juniper grinned at them both. "All right then. Let's do this."

Emory heard a faint clunk behind him. He turned around and looked to the direction of the sound, at the wall clock. *Is that what I think it is?*

Juniper regained his attention. "Emory."

He faced them again and saw she was holding the frame and sculpture in a presentation pose. Emory pulled out his phone and snapped several pictures.

Once the ceremony ended, Juniper and Dr. Sharp left Emory alone in the library. He returned to the clock, changed the time to 8:02 and pushed the eight and two. The face slid open, revealing the safe. Emory turned the handle with his left hand and positioned his right hand to grab its contents. As soon as he opened the safe door, the Box disappeared out the bottom.

It was a longshot. At least now, if I'm right, it's in the final location – either the theatre or the guest room. But which?

Jeff barged through the library door. "Emory! Myles Godfrey just found a safe in the guest room, and I saw something in it for a split-second."

Emory clenched a fist in excitement. "That's excellent! I found the one in here behind the wall clock, and just now it had something in it that disappeared too. That means there's one location left."

They both said, "The theatre!"

CHAPTER 36

EMORY AND JEFF entered the theatre and hit the light switch on the wall, exposing the black-quilted walls and recessed lighting over the four rows of reclining seating, facing a nine-by-sixteen-foot screen.

"Where do we start?" Jeff asked. "The projector room or the seating area?"

"Seating area." Emory descended the steps and proceeded all the way to the screen before turning to face the chairs.

After at least thirty seconds of silence, Jeff fell into one of the chairs. "Anything striking you?"

Emory motioned to each item as he mentioned it. "The walls and ceiling are padded – black vinyl – for soundproofing. No apparent breaks except for the lights. Eight steps from the entryway to the aisle. Projector room on the same level as the entrance."

"The door!" Jeff jumped out of his seat. "In the guest room, the doors clicked like a combination lock. That's how Myles found the safe."

Emory shook his head. "So far, Blair's not repeated a puzzle. I don't think she'd start now."

"It's worth a shot." Jeff bounded up the steps. He tried the door to the projector room. "Nothing." He tried the door to the hallway.

"No clicks here…" Jeff stopped short of closing the door when he saw someone on the other side.

"There you are," said George Henry. "Eden tells me you're looking for the Box."

Jeff smiled to cover his concern. "It's already been found. It was empty."

"She's under the impression you think that was a decoy, and you're looking for the real one."

Damn! She heard me and Zyus!

George stepped into the entryway and locked the door behind him. "Let's look together."

Jeff's eyes followed George's right arm to the pocket of his camouflage jacket, where something was pointing his direction. "Am I supposed to believe that's a gun?"

George responded by removing the pistol from his pocket.

"Well, you've made a believer out of me. What do you want?"

Emory, who was too far away to see the gun, approached. "What's going on?"

"We have company." Jeff descended the steps, followed by the gardener.

"Mr. Henry, we're a bit busy right now." Emory's eyes dipped to the man's hands. "Why do you have a gun?"

Jeff waved a hand toward the gun-wielder. "Allow me to introduce you to Spike Dean."

"The coal mine supervisor?"

Jeff tilted his head toward the gun. "AKA our killer."

George Henry frowned at the description. "I'm not going to kill you. I just need your help."

"To do what?" asked Emory.

Jeff answered for him. "He thinks we can find the Pangram Box."

"All I want is the deed to the coal mine. I don't care about anything else in there."

"But the mine's not…" Emory began before Jeff shook his

head, signaling him not to mention that the mine wasn't even in Blair Geister's possession at the time of her death. "…is not guaranteed to be in the Box even if we can find it."

George coughed. "I know that, but unless by some miracle, Blair Geister named Eden the beneficiary in that residual clause or whatever you call it, it's my only chance at getting the mine back."

"And if we refuse to help you?" asked Emory.

George held the gun to the back of Jeff's head as he talked to Emory. "Then I'd have to go back on my word not to kill at least one of you. Between the two of you, I'm guessing you're my best bet at finding it, which makes him expendable, if you need any encouragement."

Emory held up his hands. "No encouragement needed. I'll find it."

George asked, "You think it's in this room?"

"Yes."

"You, sit down." George motioned Jeff to a seat in the front row before taking one in the second row, gun fixed on the back of the PI's head. He glanced at his watch and told Emory, "The deadline is in seven hours. You have that long to save your life, but you only have three hours to save your partner's. You should probably get to it."

Emory took a deep breath and returned to scanning the room. "I wonder about the arrangement of the chairs. There are five in the front row, and each subsequent row has an additional chair from the row in front of it."

"What does that mean?" asked Jeff.

"I have no idea."

George Henry entered a coughing fit that lasted half a minute.

Jeff turned around in his chair. "That's a nasty cough you have there. Black lung?"

"The beginnings of it, but I can still run you under the table."

"Okay, I'm not sure what that even means. The mine made you sick. Why would want to go back to it?"

"It's all I know. Besides, if I was one of the owners, I wouldn't have to go back under. I could just run the mine the way it should be."

Emory pointed at each row. "Five, six, seven, eight."

Jeff said, "Schlemiel. Schlimazel."

Emory shook his head. "No, it's the number of seats in each row. It adds up to twenty-six." He focused on the chairs in the front row and snapped his fingers. "Each chair has a letter on the front of the left arm. I can see *A* through *E* right here in the front row. If the letters don't repeat in each row... Mr. Dean, what does your seat say?"

George leaned forward to look at his letter. "Mine is *J*."

Jeff looked at the letter in front of the left arm of his chair. It was a black *C* on an oval button with muted back lighting. He touched the letter. "My letter clicks when I push it."

George said, "Mine too."

"That's it." Emory grinned at his partner. "The Pangram Box. The final key to unlocking it is a pangram!"

George turned the gun toward Emory. "What *is* a pangram?"

"A sentence that uses all the letters," replied Jeff before turning his attention to his partner. "Which pangram?"

"The most common one is *The quick brown fox jumps over a lazy dog.*"

"I'll get the *T*." Jeff headed down the aisle.

"Wait a second." George stood, aiming his gun at Jeff. "Where do you think you're going?"

Emory answered for him. "This will go much faster with two of us hitting the letters. Plus, I don't know how much time Ms. Geister allotted to go from one letter to the next without the puzzle resetting."

"Okay." George walked to the front of the theatre, gun brandished before him. "I'm watching both of you. Don't spook me."

The PIs ran around the theatre, calling each letter in the pangram as they clicked it. When they were done, nothing happened.

Jeff looked around for any movement. "Maybe we need to put a space between each word."

Emory asked, "What would serve as the space button?"

"I don't know."

Emory sighed and rested his hands on his hips. "Maybe we just have the wrong pangram. There are others that are pretty well known."

"Do you remember them all?" asked Jeff.

Emory shook his head. "Can you look it up on your phone?"

Jeff pulled out his phone to try. "I have no service."

Emory checked his phone. "Me either." He thought for a moment. "The presentation. Each recipient of an EARTH Foundation grant receives a sculpture of the Earth made of quartz. *Jackdaws love my big sphinx of quartz.*"

"I don't know. That's a pretty thin connection."

"Just try it."

The PIs went through the letters until Jeff yelled from the back of the room, "Z!"

All three men looked around the room, and Jeff walked back toward the screen. "I don't see anything."

Emory tilted his head. "I hear something. Humming."

Jeff approached his partner. "I hear it too."

"Me too," said George.

Jeff pointed. "It's coming from the screen."

The PIs hopped onto the narrow stage below the screen and followed their ears to the source of the hum at the left edge. "It's coming from here," said Emory.

Jeff gave the screen a solid thwap with the side of his fist, the entire screen moved to the right, exposing a doorway to an unlit space on the left. The humming stopped. "Must've been the stuck door."

Emory looked at the new opening and smiled at his partner. "We found it!"

Emory was about to step into the dark space behind the screen when George growled, "Back away from the door." As the PIs complied, George craned his neck to look inside. "I can't see anything. What do you see?"

"Well, nothing from here," answered Jeff, now a couple of feet from the secret space.

George aimed the gun at Jeff. "You, get down here with me."

Jeff jumped off the small stage to stand by George, who planted the barrel at the base of the PI's neck.

George told Emory, "You go inside and bring out the Box. If you do anything stupid, your partner's going to have some bit parts on the silver screen."

Emory pulled out his phone and turned on the flashlight before walking through the doorway. As soon as he stepped inside, an overhead light triggered on, exposing a five-by-five room painted black from ceiling to floor.

George yelled, "Is it in there?"

A moment later, Emory exited the space empty-handed, triggering the light inside to go out. He jumped off the stage. "I found the Pangram Box, but it's built into the floor behind a column."

George waved the gun, signaling for him to go back. "Well, bring it out."

"I can't. The Box has a clear lid so I can see that it's filled with documents and gold bars. I think the documents are deeds to everything Blair Geister owned."

Jeff asked, "Can't you open it?"

Emory shook his head. "The lid is some sort of tempered glass. I tried to stomp on it, but we're going to need something harder than my rubber soles to break through." Emory pointed at George's shoes. "Are those steel-toed boots?"

George looked down. "Yeah."

"Take off one of your boots, and I'll use it to break the lid."

"I don't take my boots off for any man." He crawled onto the stage and aimed the gun at the PIs as he stepped closer to the dark entryway. "Both of you stay right where I can see you."

Emory inched closer to the front row of chairs. "We're not moving."

George stepped a foot inside, triggering the overhead light, and he looked back at Jeff and Emory.

When George turned his eyes to the space again, Emory stepped in front of the middle seat in the front row. George took another step inside and turned back to the PIs. "Where is it?"

"Behind that black pedestal in the middle of the room."

George took three more steps to look behind the column.

Emory pushed the *C* on the middle chair. The screen slid back to the left, closing the door to the secret space. He could hear a gunshot from behind the screen and stuffing pop out of the back of seat *A*. "Run!"

Jeff grabbed Emory's arm and stopped him from running up the aisle. "That's the direction the bullets are heading. Let's go this way." He nodded toward the emergency exit to the right of the screen.

"We don't know where it goes!"

Another shot hit seat *B*.

"Does it matter?" Jeff ran to the door and held it open for Emory.

The exit led to a dusky, narrow stairwell that ran in one direction up two stories. Emory darted up the stairs with Jeff hot on his heels.

Jeff asked, "How did you know pushing the letter *C* would close the room?"

"I didn't for sure, but the safe in the library automatically closed when the hands moved away from 8:02. I figured any letter out of sequence would close the screen."

"Good thinking! Hey, what's that hump down the back of your shirt?"

Emory replied, "The Pangram Box!"

CHAPTER 37

EMORY SPOTTED A red-glowing sign at the top of the emergency exit stairs. "Almost there."

Puffing behind him, his partner patted his butt. "Keep up the pace. Was there really a box in the floor?"

"No, just the one in my shirt. It was on top of the pedestal. I made up the rest."

"Nice! Although the gold bars part was a bit over the top."

"I was afraid it might be. I was just really trying to entice him to go inside the room himself."

A gunshot crackled through the air, and the bullet chiseled through the wall beside them.

Jeff pushed Emory's back. "Hurry!"

Emory threw all his momentum onto the push bar, and the exit door flung open. He hurried to the other side of the door and held it until Jeff came through. Emory looked around to gain his bearings. Although close to midnight, the surroundings were revealed through the silver blue filter of the full moon's radiance. "We're beside the garage. Let's get to the house."

"No. We don't want to put the others in danger. We'll take cover in the woods."

Emory ran across the clearing to the edge of the woods. He hid behind a tree as his partner ran a few steps past him.

Jeff motioned for him to keep running. "What are you doing?"

"How's he going to know we ran into the woods if he doesn't see us?"

"Good point." Jeff crouched with his back against the tree. "Can you see the door?"

"I'm watching it."

"Okay. I'm texting Virginia." A few seconds later, Jeff tapped Emory's arm. "Uh, I think we have a problem."

"What is it?" Emory followed his partner's gaze and looked behind him to see lantern lights moving through the trees. "Oh no. The full moon."

The cloaked and hooded witches emerged from the darkness of the woods into the clearing with arms open to the moon. They spun and danced, gathering in celebration of the night.

Emory saw George Henry plod out from behind the door, gun held before him. "There he is!"

"The witches are entering the line of fire! We have to warn them."

"Wait. He's seen them, and he's pocketed the gun, but he's heading for the house."

Jeff stood in plain sight to call attention to their location. "Emory, come on! We have to hide!"

It worked. George heard him and was now running toward them.

The PIs darted into the woods. Before long, Emory could see the vertical posts of the boundary fence ahead of him. He also felt movement in the back of his shirt, followed by a clunking sound. "The Box!" Emory turned around to retrieve it and was about to start running again when splinters of bark erupted from the thin tree next to him.

"Next one's in you!" George Henry yelled as he closed in on his position.

Emory saw that he was in the small clearing around the historic cedar tree. He had nowhere to seek cover.

"You too!" George aimed the gun at a target behind Emory.

Jeff joined his partner, hands up.

George attempted a smile through a minor coughing fit. "Just so you know, Jeff, this is what I meant by running you under the table." He nodded at the object in Emory's hand – a metallic cylindrical container, eighteen inches between its two capped ends. "That the Box?"

Before Emory could answer, a cloaked witch entered the clearing.

George crossed his arms to conceal the gun and nodded toward the house. "Your coven's that way, lady."

The witch continued on her way, walking behind him.

George again brandished the gun. "You've had your fun. Now give me the Box, or I'll shoot you both and take it."

Emory looked at Jeff for any sign of ideas. Seeing none, he tossed the Box to George's feet.

Instead of picking it up, George kept the gun fixed on the PIs. "Now face the fence."

Jeff said, "You have what you want. Just take it and go." Under his breath, he told Emory, "Split up and run."

Emory was about to carry out Jeff's plan, when he saw the wayward witch reappear from behind George. She held a large stick over her head and swung it down, thwapping George Henry's arm.

The gun dropped from his hands, as he screamed and cradled his arm to his body.

The witch grabbed the gun and aimed it at the miner. "Down on the ground! Now!"

George Henry complied.

The witch pulled her hood back, revealing her face.

Jeff grinned at his partner. "Virginia."

"I'm so happy to see you," said Emory.

"How did you…"

"I got your text and called the sheriff, but I was afraid he wouldn't get here soon enough. That's when I saw the witches from the window and you three running into the woods. I ran outside, told the coven my friends were in danger, and one of them let me borrow her robe."

Jeff hugged his friend from behind. "Thank you."

In the driveway twenty minutes later, Emory, Jeff and Virginia gave their statements to Sheriff Flynn as Deputy Nunley arrested George Henry and stuffed him into the backseat of her patrol car. The three PIs hung out beside Emory's car as the interviews moved to others at the estate.

Once he and Zyus had given their statements, Myles Godfrey asked the sheriff, "Are we free to go now?"

The sheriff gave Zyus a leery look. "You can both go."

"Come on, Zyus. We have about four hours to find the real Box."

As Myles and Zyus headed toward the house, Jeff called out to the masked man. "Zyus, could we have a word with you?"

"I'll meet you in there," Zyus told Myles before approaching the PIs. "Have you changed your mind about helping me?"

"We have," answered Emory.

"Great! Come on then." Zyus waved them toward the house. "We don't have much time."

"No," said Jeff. "He means that we have already helped you."

Emory opened the back door of his car and retrieved the Box. He smiled as he handed it to Zyus. "I believe this belongs to you."

Zyus inspected the item. "Is this—"

He was interrupted by Sheriff Flynn. "Investigators, I wanted to thank you personally for all your help." He shook each PI's hand. "If you ever need anything, you just call my office."

"You're very kind," said Emory. "Thank you."

As the sheriff walked away, Virginia tugged at her cloak. "I'm going to return this now." She left for the witches, one of whom was missing a cloak.

From the backseat of the nearby patrol car, George Henry yelled in the direction of the approaching sheriff, "I never killed anyone! I wasn't going to kill them!"

CHAPTER 38

WHEN SHERIFF ROME approached the door to the sheriff's station, he checked behind himself and overhead to ensure no low-flying birds followed him inside. Seeing clear skies, he proceeded through the doorway.

Deputy Loggins, a short man about the same age as his boss, stretched and yawned from behind his desk. "Good morning, Sheriff."

"Did I wake you?"

The deputy laughed. "It's just been a quiet night. Nothing to report."

"Glad to hear. Go on home."

"Thanks Sheriff." He jumped from his chair and headed for the door. "Oh, there's fresh coffee brewing."

Once the deputy had left, Sheriff Rome settled into his office. He stared at the phone for a minute before picking it up and calling his son.

Emory was alone, packing his suitcase, when his cell phone rang. He saw the name pop up on the screen and answered, "Hi Dad."

"Emory, how are you?"

"Uh, good. Just finishing up a case."

"What kind of case?"

Emory closed the suitcase. "Murder."

"Did you find the killer?"

The PI smiled. "We did."

"Good job!" The sheriff paused for a few seconds, perhaps waiting for Emory to respond. "I'm proud of you."

"Thank you, Dad." Emory sat on the bed. "I really appreciate that."

"I mean… Even if you hadn't found him." Sheriff Rome fell silent again. "You understand?"

Emory pinched his lips. "I understand."

"Well, that's all I called to say. I'll let you go now."

"Bye, Dad."

Wayne Buckwald arrived at the evidence crypt ten minutes before seven in the morning. He had placed a cup of coffee and a breakfast sandwich at his desk beforehand so his boss would see he was already there when she passed by on the way to her office.

The crypt, on the lower level of the TBI's Knoxville Consolidated Facility, was a large warehouse of evidence collected over the years. Wayne didn't know how old evidence had to be before it was destroyed or even if it ever were, but he hoped evidence from eight years ago would still be there.

Although there was an emergency exit at the back of the room, the only way into the crypt was through a single metal door guarded by the cage – a small room behind thick, bullet-proof glass. A thin older man with black hair appeared behind the glass and sat down with a mug of coffee in his hand.

Wayne tapped on the glass. "Excuse me. Could you help me?"

The man pointed at the clock. "Ten minutes."

"I know, but I'm in a hurry."

"Ten minutes."

"Really? Thanks crypt keeper." Wayne crossed his arms. "While we wait, answer me something. What's the expiration date on evidence?"

"Expiration date? There's no expiration date."

"You never toss anything?"

"Not in the eighteen years I've been here."

"Good to know. Listen, since you're already basically working, could you just let me in?"

The crypt keeper looked at the clock. "Nine minutes."

Wayne sighed and began to pace. He asked again at the five- and two-minute marks but continued to be denied.

At 7 a.m. sharp, the crypt keeper walked over to the computer by the window and typed. "Thank you for your patience."

"Like I had a choice."

The man picked up a handheld scanner and aimed it at Wayne's badge until it beeped. He returned his attention to the computer. "Catalog number, and how long do you expect to have the items?"

Wayne read him the number he had jotted down in his notebook. "I'm not going to check the evidence out. I just need to see if something's in there."

"Everything's listed online in the evidence log—"

"The description was too general. I need to physically see it."

"Okay." The crypt keeper gave him the shelf number and directions, and he buzzed him through the door.

Once inside the warehouse, Wayne wandered past shelf after shelf cluttered with boxes. "Raiders of the Lost Ark," he muttered. He made his way to the appropriate shelf and found twenty-three boxes with the catalog number he sought. "That's a lot of boxes to go through." He debated whether to even try. After a few seconds he reached for the nearest one. "Maybe I'll get lucky."

"It's light." He tipped open the lid. "It's empty." He tried the box beside it and found it empty too. He continued until he confirmed every box with the catalog number from the eight-year-old case was indeed empty. "What's going on here?"

He pulled out his cell phone and called Sheriff Rome.

From his office, the sheriff answered. "Hello?"

"Sheriff, this is Wayne Buckwald."

"Hi there. Good to hear from you."

"Listen, I've been looking into the case, and I found a photo listed in the evidence log."

"Is it the picture from the postcard?"

"That's just it. There wasn't a detailed description in the log, so I came down to the evidence room to see it, but all the evidence boxes—"

Wayne was interrupted by a violent strike to the back of the head.

CHAPTER 39

IN PREPARATION FOR the reading of the residuary clause to Blair Geister's will, Juniper Crane set up a makeshift desk in the locutorium for the attorney, but she forewent the audience seating this time, as the assemblage for this reading would be minimal. Besides Juniper and Esq. Jennifer Boone, attendees included Eden Geister, Zyus Drake and the three PIs.

Sitting behind the table, the attorney withdrew papers from her briefcase and checked her watch. She waited in silence for two minutes until 7:20 a.m. on the dot. "Let's begin. I understand Mr. Zyus Drake did find the Pangram Box. I'd like to invite him up to reveal its contents."

"Not so fast!" Eden approached the table. "The will stipulated that the house could not be damaged in the process of looking for the Pangram Box. The Box was found in a secret room behind the movie theatre screen." She held up her phone to show a picture of the gunshot-riddled screen in the theatre. "I believe this qualifies as damage."

Emory looked at the phone. "But he didn't do that!"

Jeff joined his partner. "And it was done after the Box was found."

Virginia added, "By your boyfriend, who happens to be Blair Geister's suspected killer."

Eden scrolled to a picture of the holes in the wall and floor of the master bedroom. "George didn't do this."

Emory said, "I did that, and it wasn't while looking for the Pangram Box. It was to determine how your cousin was murdered."

The attorney took the phone from Eden and inspected the pictures. She locked her eyes on Juniper. "The decision of whether to grant Mr. Drake the contents of the Pangram Box rests with the executor. What say you?"

Juniper grimaced, eyes going from the attorney to the floor, with a brief glance at Zyus. "The Box is his."

"Yes!" Emory clenched his right fist and smiled at his partners.

Esq. Boone summoned him. "Mr. Drake, please come forward and present the Box." Zyus approached the desk and handed it to her. The attorney held it up and pointed to the signed paper seal covering each cap. "I'll note that the seals do appear to be intact. I'll now open it to reveal the contents." Esq. Boone opened the metal Box and emptied three documents onto the table. She inspected all three before handing one back to Zyus. "The Pangram Box contained a deed, a notarized agreement and a letter, which I'll ask Mr. Drake to now read."

Zyus cleared his throat and read from the letter. "If I'm reading this letter, it's because I found the Pangram Box within the allotted time and parameters, which means that Blair Geister does accept at least partial blame for the incident that led to my… disfigurement. As recompense, Blair is bestowing on me two gifts. The first is the deed to the penthouse condominium at the Somerset in Knoxville – with all lifetime HOAs waived. The second is a promise. As it doesn't relate to the core mission of the EARTH Foundation, Blair Geister's estate will endow a private grant of twenty million dollars to Dr. Arthur Igataki to fund his research into skin regeneration, with the stipulation that I… will be his first patient once the research is ready for human trials."

Zyus buried his face in his hand and wept. Juniper went to him and placed a hand on his shoulder.

Jeff was about to turn his teary eyes away from his partners when he saw wet cheeks on both.

Once Zyus had regained his composure, he took the documents and left the locutorium.

Esq. Boone took a moment to sip from her water glass. "I will now read the residuary clause of Blair Geister's last will and testament." The attorney held a document before her. "I hereby bequeath all my assets not mentioned herein or part of the Pangram Box, should it be properly claimed, to a single beneficiary – the nonprofit organization I established, the EARTH Foundation."

Eden stormed out of the room. "Ridiculous!"

The attorney continued. "The assets now owned by the EARTH Foundation include all commercial property and businesses. I established this structure so the EARTH Foundation can ensure any and all business conducted by Geister Innovations & Engineering is done in an environmentally conscious way and, in turn, so Geister Innovations & Engineering can fund the work of the EARTH Foundation well into the future. My genuine hope is that my life's work will provide an everlasting legacy of environmental stewardship and help build a better world for many generations to come." Esq. Boone put the document down. "That concludes the reading of the will. Thank you."

Jeff raised his hand. "I have a question. Blair's company now belongs to her foundation? How does that work?"

Esq. Boone replied, "Assuming the foundation chooses to keep the status quo, the company would continue to run as it has been, with a board and CEO, et cetera, and the profits would go to the foundation in continuance of its mission."

Virginia gasped. "Oh my god! Juniper, do you realize what this means?"

Emory said, "As president and CEO of the EARTH Foundation, you now run everything."

Juniper looked like the reality of the situation was just coming into view. "I don't know what to say."

"Well, I do." Virginia hugged her. "Congratulations."

Jeff said, "We should have a drink. Celebrate."

Esq. Boone interrupted them. "Actually, I need Ms. Crane to stick around. We have a pile of papers to go over."

Juniper nodded to the attorney before returning her attention to the PIs. "We'll have a drink in Knoxville the next time I'm up there. My treat."

Jeff grinned at the last statement. "I should hope so."

As the PIs left the locutorium, they found Eden sitting on the front stairs with her head in her hands.

Virginia placed a hand on her shoulder. "Eden, are you going to be okay?"

Eden lifted her head. "The thing is, my actual research might've been good enough. I just didn't have confidence in it, so I padded the numbers. It's funny that one little mistake, something that entered your head for just a few seconds and you acted on it, could devastate your whole life. She would've given me everything, but she didn't trust me after that."

Juniper walked out with the PIs as they carried their luggage to Emory's car. "I really can't thank you all enough. On top of all your work, I feel like you've given me my sanity back."

Jeff told her, "You could make us the official investigation firm for the EARTH Foundation and all its subsidiaries – i.e., Geister

Innovations & Engineering. You've already asked Emory to look into the accusation against Dr. Sharp, which we'll get on right away. We could run background checks for all grant candidates and potential employees, investigate suspected corporate espionage, uncover—"

Juniper smiled and patted him on the back. "Let me get a handle on everything before I make any promises."

"Guys." Virginia turned their attention toward Zyus Drake, who was pacing in the driveway.

Emory asked, "Mr. Drake, is everything all right?"

"Just waiting on my Uber. Myles left me here."

"Here." Jeff pulled his car fob from his pocket and tossed it to Zyus. "Cancel the car and just take mine."

Zyus caught the fob in his massive hand. "Are you serious?"

"Absolutely." Jeff pointed with his thumb to Emory and Virginia. "I don't get to spend enough time with these guys."

"Thanks. I'll get it back to you this afternoon."

"I'm not worried. I know where you live now."

As Zyus drove off, Virginia gave Juniper a hug. "I'm going to miss you."

"You too. Take care of yourself."

Jeff embraced her. "Thanks Juniper."

"I want to come by and meet that bobcat of yours."

"You're always welcome."

Emory extended his hand to her, and Juniper brushed it aside. "You're giving me a hug, too."

Emory complied. "Thank you for everything."

"Okay, now." Juniper backed away, waved and returned to the house.

Jeff opened the trunk to start loading the luggage but stopped before doing any actual work. "Hey guys, could you give me a few minutes? I just want to have one last look around." He stared into Emory's eyes to convey his meaning.

"Go ahead," said Emory. "We've got this."

Jeff left them and walked to the giant cedar tree in the woods. He grasped the little chain fence surrounding it and gazed down at the spot where he had buried Trevor Park. "I apologize for all the moving around. This time should do it." Jeff looked up at the sky through the canopy. "You know I love you. I don't have to tell you that. You were... a sweet, sweet man. You deserved more than this world gave you. I know I didn't deserve you. I don't know that I deserve Emory either. Maybe I do. He's damn exasperating. In some ways, he's a lot like you." Jeff laughed as tears cascaded down his face. "Actually, he's nothing like you. He's a pain in the ass. Both cheeks. Secretive. Serious. Rigid. Passionate, but afraid of it. Super smart, but stupid in areas most people take for granted." He wiped his eyes. "Okay, he's like you in that way.

"Please know that I haven't given up. I will find who did this to you."

Jeff inhaled a deep breath and pushed it from his lungs. "Anyway, I hope you like it here okay." He looked around at the birds flying from tree to tree, blue morning glories clinging to the border fence and the sparkling river in the distance. "It's a peaceful place, and you have a great view of the river." He looked down. "I don't know how this works. I don't know if your... spirit can see above ground. Or if it's even here. Or exists."

He glanced at the engraved marker embedded in the stone block a few feet away, and he remembered the words Emory read from it about how cedar trees were sacred to the Cherokee and how they believed the trees housed the souls of the dead. He returned his focus to the ground where Trevor was buried, and his eyes followed the nearby exposed root up to the massive trunk. He looked at the river and then back at the tree trunk. He heard sorrowful cooing overhead and tilted his head to see a mourning dove perched on the lowest branch. "I hope they're right."

CHAPTER 40

EMORY EXITED THE interstate in Knoxville. "I wonder if that's why Blair Geister revised her will a couple of months ago. She was feeling guilty about what happened to Zyus but torn about whether she actually had anything to feel guilty about."

From the backseat, Virginia added, "The puzzle served as a non-biased judge. If Zyus figured it out, he received retribution to make things right. If he didn't, Blair could have peace of mind, knowing she was not responsible and finally free herself from the guilt. Of course, we did stack the deck in his favor by finding the Box for him."

In the passenger seat, Jeff shook his head. "There's just one problem. She'd be dead when Zyus was presented with the puzzle, so she wouldn't know the outcome."

"Maybe she believed she would."

Emory had another suggestion. "Or maybe she was planning to give Zyus the opportunity before she died but put it in the will in case she didn't get around to it."

Jeff asked, "But why?"

"Maybe she was waiting until she knew she'd be out of the house long enough to give him the opportunity to look for it. She could stay at the apartment in The Monolith until time to solve the puzzle expired."

Virginia rested her forearms on the front seats. "Guys, this is all speculation. The truth is Blair Geister was a very complicated woman. We'll never know for certain the reasons behind a lot of her decisions, and I'm okay with that. She was still a remarkable person who did more good than bad."

"Agreed," said Emory. "I do feel bad for her, though. She spent half her life racked with guilt about the death of her brother. She came to terms with that, and then this thing with Zyus happens. And ultimately, no matter the game's outcome, she really didn't have any fault when it came to Zyus. It was an accident."

"You don't have to be at fault to feel guilty," said Virginia.

Jeff patted the center console. "I just had a weird thought. What if Blair rigged the bed herself?"

Virginia asked, "Why would she do that?"

"Self-inflicted karmic retribution for her brother's death."

"That's not karma," said Virginia. "Karma would be if Tommy Addison killed her because he then died in the process."

The guys looked at each other, but Jeff was the first to speak. "If Tommy did kill Blair, I know someone else he hated just as much."

His mind buzzing, Emory said, "The open pool umbrella. The oversized sheets. The architectural drawings he had in his room. I saw the CEO office in them."

Virginia grabbed their shoulders. "Guys, they're opening the new headquarters today."

Emory spun the car around and raced toward The Monolith.

Jeff asked, "Virginia, can you try calling Rue Darcé and tell her not to go into her office?"

"I'm already on it." Virginia placed her phone to her ear. "I'm in the queue."

Jeff pulled out his phone. "I'll call Juniper and see if she has Rue's cell number."

The three PIs bounded off the elevator on the fortieth floor of The Monolith and ran up to the receptionist desk. "Where's Rue Darcé's office?" asked Jeff.

"Do you have an appointment?"

Jeff lied. "Yes, and we're late."

The receptionist pointed to her right. "Take the second hall you come to on the right all the way to the window, and hers is the last office on the left."

They raced to Rue's office and found a young man placing items into boxes on the desk. Emory greeted him. "Hi. We're looking for Rue Darcé."

Jeff asked, "Why are you packing up her office?"

"I'm her assistant. The board appointed Ms. Darcé the permanent CEO this morning. No longer temporary. We're moving her to the CEO office. Can I help you with anything?"

"That's okay," replied Virginia. "We know where it is."

When they arrived at Blair Geister's would-be office, they found Rue speaking to her computer monitor. "No, everything's going well here. We're getting it up and running. The solar array windows are now online and should be at full power by this afternoon. Blair's dream is coming to life." She smiled at the PIs when she spotted them. "Oh, your investigators are here now."

Rue turned her monitor around, allowing the PIs to see Juniper's face on the screen. Juniper smiled at them. "I was just filling Rue in on everything that's transpired, and I told her you were trying to contact her, although I didn't know why exactly."

"Sorry about that. I always silence my phone in the boardroom, and my office number hasn't been transferred to this office yet. It's been a whirlwind morning. For you all too, I understand. Thank you for catching Blair and Tommy's killer."

Emory grimaced at the misplaced gratitude. "We're actually not sure we did."

"What?" asked Juniper.

Jeff looked at Rue. "We think the killer is your ex-husband."

"Tommy?"

Juniper said, "That's ridiculous. I saw him die. He had nothing to do with it."

Rue laughed and waved off the notion. "There's no way Tommy was suicidal."

"He died by accident," said Virginia.

Emory's eyes ping-ponged between Rue and the monitor. "He didn't plan his own death, but he did plan Blair Geister's."

Rue looked to the monitor. "I thought that miner… What's his name?"

"George Henry." Juniper turned her attention to the PIs. "He almost killed you last night. What proof do you have that exonerates him in Ms. Geister's murder?"

"That's just it," said Jeff. "We don't have anything to prove his innocence yet."

Emory held his palms parallel to the floor. "But if we're right, there's proof here of another murder plot, which would then prove George Henry's innocence because he would've never had access to this building during construction."

Rue looked around with disbelieving eyes. "What proof is here?"

Virginia replied, "We don't know."

Rue turned to the monitor. "These are the investigators you want to put on retainer?"

Jeff perked up at the last word, muttering to his partners, "The dream scenario."

Juniper called the PIs to attention. "Look, I know Tommy – to put it bluntly – despised Ms. Geister, although he was good at hiding that from her."

"What? I know that Tommy hated me after the divorce and the

custody battle, but what did he have against Blair? She gave him a job and a chance to prove himself, and when that didn't work out, she gave him another job with less responsibility and a place to live."

Juniper hesitated before answering. "He thought she was the wedge that split you two up."

"Then why move into her house?"

"I asked him that too. He said he just needed time to figure out what to do with his life. The job was easy, and it was a free place to live."

"All right, so he held some grudges. Who doesn't? What makes you think my ex-husband killed my boss?"

"Three clues." Emory counted on his fingers as he listed them. "The wayward pool umbrella, the king-sized bedding he had in his closet and a parking stub."

Juniper frowned at him. "You're going to have to tie that together for me."

Jeff started the explanation. "He rigged Blair's bed to the lightning rod so she would, in essence, be struck by lightning during the next storm."

Emory explained, "No doubt, he had heard the story of how her brother died and, to paraphrase Myles Godfrey, saw some kind of poetic justice in killing her that way. But we don't believe he intended for her to be found in her bed because he had no way of knowing what state her body would be in from the lightning strike. Lightning victims can show barely any signs of a strike, or they can be burned to a crisp. Regardless, he planned to move her body outside. That's where the umbrella came in."

Virginia turned her attention to Juniper. "When Emory spotted the open umbrella on the lawn, you told us that Blair insisted on the umbrellas being closed when not in use and that she would've gone out herself to close it if she'd seen it open. We think Tommy, knowing Blair was coming home and a thunderstorm was in the forecast, opened the umbrella to give a reason for her to be found outside.

You would've probably filled in the blanks when she was found by the pool next to the open umbrella, giving the sheriff a reason to explain why she would've gone outside in spite of the storm."

Jeff said, "After moving her body outside, he would need to clean up the actual scene of her death. That's where the bedding in his closet came in. He figured at the very least, the sheets on her bed would need changing, and maybe he'd have to flip the mattress. If the damage were extensive, he could swap the mattress with the same-sized one down the hall in the guest room. Once the body was taken away and the coast was clear, he would repair the wiring in Blair's bedroom, and then no one would ever know."

Rue crossed her arms and scowled at them. "Again I ask, where is your proof? You have all the proof in the world against this miner, but you seem to be twisting every coincidence to fit this damning accusation you've concocted against Tommy."

"There's something else." Emory nodded at Rue. "You saw that he had the architectural drawings to this floor."

"He did work here."

"Not for months. Why hold onto them?

"I'm sorry, but the fact that he hadn't tossed the drawings isn't enough to convince me. Do you have any proof to support your claims?"

Emory pointed to the monitor. "We don't, but Ms. Crane does. If you go to Mr. Addison's truck in the garage, you'll find a parking stub for Leland Cinema, about a block away from here. You'll see from the time and date stamp he was near here two days before the storm. He knew the inner workings of this building. It would've been easy for him to sneak in."

Rue asked, "Are you saying you think Tommy was responsible for the acts of sabotage we were experiencing here."

"Actually, no," replied Jeff. "But he planned to use them to explain your death."

Rue threw a hand to her chest. "My death?!"

Virginia said, "We think he rigged something here to kill you, just like he did with Blair. He'd make it look like it was an accidental result of sabotage to the building."

"Then go check my office. If you're sure Tommy wanted me dead, show me how he planned to kill me."

Jeff shook his head. "That's just it. Everyone knew you were next in line to replace Blair. We think he rigged *this* office."

Rue laughed. "All right then. Where is the instrument of my death?"

Jeff turned to his partner. "Emory, this is your purview."

Emory looked around the office for several minutes, while the others watched.

Perhaps to break the silence, Juniper spoke up. "Rue, since I have you on the line, I wanted to ask if you'd like to take over Blair's apartment in that building."

"You want me to move into the apartment she built for herself?"

"I was thinking we could treat it like a rectory. Have it as perk for you and each subsequent CEO."

"Can I think about it? Honestly, I'm just not sure I want to live where I work."

"I understand. If you don't want it, perhaps we can figure out another use for it. Maybe as guest quarters for visitors."

While Virginia scanned the office from the center of the room, Jeff stepped closer to Emory, who was creeping along the walls, inspecting every inch.

Emory turned around to speak to Rue. "When we came in you mentioned the solar panels were brought online this morning."

"That's right."

"In your speech the other day, you said that power goes to an inverter. Where is that in relation to this office?"

Rue pointed to the left. "It's a small room outside this office."

Jeff nodded toward a door in the office near the window. "Is that a closet?"

"It's a bathroom."

Virginia stopped what she was doing. "A bathroom. Would you mind if I use it?"

"I don't know if it's stocked yet, but you can see."

Virginia tried the handle. "It won't open."

"Oh, I have to open it for you." Rue got up from her desk. "Blair had hand panels installed at every door instead of keys, even the bathrooms. Actually, I don't know if I have access to it yet."

Jeff watched the direction Emory's eyes were going and followed the path to the bathroom.

Rue reached her hand up and placed her palm on the panel.

"Virginia!" screamed Emory and Jeff.

Virginia glanced at her partners and saw them running toward her. She looked at Rue and saw a green light in the hand panel.

Rue stiffened, her hand glued to the panel.

Virginia tackled her and knocked her to the ground.

Sparks jetted from the panel. Small flames spit from the top of the panel blackening several inches of the wall.

"What's happening?!" screamed Juniper from the computer monitor.

Jeff reached Virginia and Rue first. "Are you okay?"

"I think so." Virginia pushed herself up and turned her attention to Rue, lying on the floor underneath her. "Rue?"

The new CEO groaned and grabbed her right wrist. "My hand!"

Emory knelt beside her to inspect her injury, and he saw blisters already forming on her palm.

Rue's assistant entered with a box in his hands. "What's going on here?"

Emory yelled, "Call 9-1-1, and get us some ice."

Juniper pleaded, "Someone please tell me what's happening!"

Jeff went to the desk to respond. "Tommy rigged the solar power from the inverter to the bathroom hand panel. Rue's been electrocuted."

CHAPTER 41

ON THE WAY to Mourning Dove Investigations, Virginia spoke on the phone as Emory drove and Jeff sat in the backseat. When she hung up, she let them know, "Juniper said Rue's going to be okay."

Jeff patted her on the shoulder. "Thanks to you."

"Yes," replied Emory. "We're lucky the panels hadn't fully charged."

Jeff caressed their shoulders. "And most importantly, we have our very first retainer client!"

Virginia shook her head. "All about business."

"Hey, don't knock the business. Without the business, Rue Darcé would be lying on a morgue table right now instead of a hospital bed."

Emory glanced in the rearview mirror. "He is right."

"Thank you," said Jeff.

"Ooh!" Virginia faced Emory with a grin. "Speaking of business, are you excited about seeing your new office?"

"I hadn't even had a chance to think about it with all that's been going on. I am looking forward to having my own space, not that squatting with you guys hasn't been fun."

Jeff told him, "Don't be surprised if it doesn't look exactly the way you imagined."

"What do you mean? I did the design myself. I picked out everything – the flooring, curtains, desk, lighting."

Jeff replied, "Well, construction is all about interpretation."

"No, it's not. I wanted simple, sleek and modern."

"You mean boring, stark and barfy," said Jeff.

"What did you guys do?"

"Just some minor reconfigurations of your design suggestions."

Emory shook his head and looked at his two partners. "They weren't suggestions. You guys told me I could choose the look of my own office."

Virginia inhaled through her teeth. "That was before we saw the look. The plans needed some cosmetic surgery."

"A little nip and tuck." Jeff pointed at the windshield. "Keep your eyes on the road."

Virginia placed a hand on Emory's forearm. "It was for the best. You'll see."

Emory was unsuccessful in getting more information from his partners during the remaining two minutes of the drive. He parked across the street and headed for the front door with Jeff and Virginia at his side.

Virginia opened the door. "I hope they didn't leave a big mess for us to clean up. Oh good, they did clean up after themselves."

Jeff rubbed a finger on the nearest bookshelf. "Not enough."

Everything looked the same in the reception area, with the exception of a new high-back sofa bench on the left wall. The blue-gray antique was the width of a love seat, but the button-quilted back rose almost seven feet up the wall.

Virginia nodded toward the bench. "There it is."

"It's a door?" asked Emory.

Jeff walked over and ran his hand up the bench's back. "You know we don't do standard doors in this office."

"How do you open it?"

Virginia replied, "Third button across in the third row from the top."

Jeff waved toward the bench. "After you."

Emory glanced at the bench's legs and saw they didn't touch to floor but were about a quarter-inch above it. He joined Jeff beside it and counted to the button Virginia described in the padded back. The bench moved to the side revealing the entrance to Emory's new office.

Emory walked in and stood in the middle of the room, spinning around to take it all in. The wall opposite the door was concealed behind several full bookshelves. The office side of the door was a tall landscape painting of the Smoky Mountains, while the wall to the left of the door held a large, detailed map of the state of Tennessee. A seating area in front of the window included four eclectic chairs and a mahogany table. In front of the opposite wall stood a walnut antique desk with a matching swivel chair. "By cosmetic surgery, you really meant a different medical procedure all together."

"What do you mean?" asked Jeff.

"Cloning. It's a clone of your office."

"It's not a clone." Jeff ran his hand over one of the bookshelves. "You have completely different books. Yours are mostly reference books, including the entire collection of the ever-riveting Tennessee Legislature volumes so you can look up even the most obscure law in the state. Instead of a mural of the globe on the floor, you have this nice mosaic of a mourning dove in flight. And look at this." Jeff pushed a button next to the Tennessee map, and it dropped down inside the wall to reveal a massive monitor with a slideshow screensaver of Bobbie. "Your murder board is digital. There's an app on your laptop to populate it, so no more printing."

Virginia grinned at him. "What do you think?"

"It's not what I wanted, but I have to admit, it is pretty spectacular."

She hugged him. "I'm glad you're happy."

"It is funny, though. With all the furniture, the space looks smaller than I remember."

"There's a good reason for that." Virginia broke from Emory and searched the bookshelf nearest his desk. "Here it is." She pulled on a book, and a wall panel behind Emory's desk opened up.

"It's a panic room!" announced Jeff. "Once inside, you can lock it so it can't be opened from the outside."

"Why would I need a panic room?"

"It's not just for you," replied Virginia. "It's for all of us."

Jeff explained, "Now that we're dealing more with murder cases, we thought it would be a good idea to have some added protection so we're not sitting ducks here."

Virginia headed inside the panic room and waved them in. "Come on. Let's check it out."

Emory walked by the shelf to see which book was pulled. "*The Interpretation of Dreams* by Sigmund Freud?"

Jeff pushed him forward. "We can change that."

Emory walked through the secret door and saw a twenty-by-ten-foot room with a long couch, bunk beds, shelves stocked with food and water, a small desk with a computer and landline, a television mounted on the wall and a stocked gun cabinet. "Are you sure this isn't a bomb shelter?"

Virginia took stock of the shelves. "We wanted to be prepared for anything."

Jeff plopped down on the couch. "It's comfortable. I'm guessing this is a couch and not a sofa."

Emory laughed. "I'd say so."

Virginia headed for the door. "All right. I'm going to get settled in." She left the guys alone in the panic room.

Jeff patted the cushion next to him. "I looked up your name – your original name. I did find some interesting information about your past, but that story has a lot of blanks. Care to fill them in?"

"Like what?"

"You need to tell me what exactly happened when you were a kid and why your dad wanted to kill you."

"You're right." Emory sat on the couch and turned his body to face him. "Here's what happened."

CHAPTER 42

SITTING ON THE edge of his bed, Sheriff Rome hung up his cell phone and placed it on the nightstand. "Wayne's still not answering."

Lula Mae slipped under the covers. "You should've left a voicemail."

Sheriff Rome scooted Sophie from his side to the center of the bed. "I've left him two already. I'm not stalking..." He stopped when he heard voices from outside.

Lula Mae popped up from her pillow and clutched the now-barking dog. "What was that?"

"I don't know." The sheriff grabbed his gun from the nightstand. "Stay here."

Lula Mae shut Sophie in the bedroom and followed her husband into the living room. She watched him open the front door. As soon as he walked out onto the porch, someone hit his forearm with a staff, knocking the gun from his hand.

"Nick!" Lula Mae screamed before another man rushed inside to grab her. He was wearing a white ski mask with red-circle eyes and a jagged, thread-thin smile from ear to ear – had any ears been visible.

The two were dragged into the front yard and forced to their knees.

While a couple of people stood behind the Romes, several others were visible a few yards in front of them, all of their faces covered by the same terrifying ski masks.

The man with the Moses-like staff centered himself in front of the group facing the Romes.

Sheriff Rome took his wife's hand.

As Lula Mae turned to see her husband's face, she knew what was in his mind. The two men behind them were to be their executioners. They only awaited a signal from the man who appeared to be the leader.

The leader raised his staff, and those behind him stood at attention.

Lula Mae tightened her grip on her husband's hand, and she closed her eyes. Several seconds passed.

The man behind her placed his hands on either side of her head, eliciting a gasping cry from her lips. She opened her eyes to see each member of the group pointing up and to the left.

The man forced her to face that direction, and she saw her husband being subjected to the same treatment.

They faced the moonlit woods beyond their house. A moment later the moon was no longer the brightest light within their scope of vision. A fire erupted near the top of Crown-of-Thorns Mountain, and it snaked its way around as if all the dead trees just below the barren peak were catching fire in a chain reaction. Soon, a ring of fire encircled the mountain's apex like a crown of flames.

The men behind the Romes walked around them to join the others. The crowd parted, allowing the man with the staff to depart through the gauntlet. One-by-one, the others followed, leaving the Romes alone in the burning darkness.

EPILOGUE

Curled up on his couch with Bobbie nestled beside him, Jeff finished typing his case report into his laptop. When he was done, he
closed the file and looked at the name of the document, which as
usual, he left as a sequential case number until it was finished. He
right-clicked on the file and changed the name to "Case of A Light
to Kill By" before moving it to the folder named...

Case Closed